Better Off Dead

Tess James-Mackey

ROCK THE BOAT

This book contains material that some readers may find distressing, including graphic portrayals of violence, injury and murder, and discussions of sexual harassment and suicide.

A Rock the Boat Book

First published in Great Britain, the Republic of Ireland and Australia by Rock the Boat, an imprint of Oneworld Publications Ltd, 2026

Text copyright © Tess James-Mackey, 2026
Cover art copyright © Marta Barrales, 2026

The moral right of Tess James-Mackey to be identified as the Author of this work has been asserted by her in accordance with the Copyright, Designs and Patents Act 1988

All rights reserved
Copyright under Berne Convention
A CIP record for this title is available from the British Library

ISBN 978-1-83643-091-9
eISBN 978-1-83643-092-6

Typeset by Geethik Technologies
Printed and bound in Great Britain by Clays Ltd, Elcograf S.p.A.

This book is a work of fiction. Names, characters, businesses, organisations, places and events are either the product of the Author's imagination or are used fictitiously. Any resemblance to actual persons, living or dead, events or locales is entirely coincidental.

No part of this publication may be reproduced, stored in a retrieval system, or transmitted, in any form or by any means, electronic, mechanical, photocopying, recording of otherwise, or used in any manner for the purpose of training artificial intelligence technologies or systems, without the prior permission of the publishers.

The authorised representative in the EEA is eucomply OÜ,
Pärnu mnt 139b–14, 11317 Tallinn, Estonia
(email: hello@eucompliancepartner.com / phone: +33757690241)

Oneworld Publications Ltd
10 Bloomsbury Street, London WC1B 3SR, England

Stay up to date with the latest books, special offers, and exclusive content from Rock the Boat with our newsletter

Sign up on our website
rocktheboatbooks.com

Praise for *Better Off Dead*

'Both gripping and tense, with a complex main character whose journey to unravel an unsettling web of eerie events keeps you turning the pages. This is YA chiller thriller at its best.'

Ravena Guron, bestselling author of *Mondays are Murder*

'*Better off Dead* kept me up far past my bedtime! A heart-pounding thriller with a rich atmospheric setting, unpredictable twists, and a heroine you can't help but love.'

Anika Hussain, author of *Heartbreaker*

'A thrilling labyrinth of plot twists and red herrings. Tess James-Mackey brilliantly disorientates us so we question everyone and trust no-one.'

Scarlett Dunmore, author of *How to Survive a Horror Movie*

'Tess James-Mackey is the official queen of creepy YA and *Better Off Dead* is another riveting read! ... This book has atmosphere in spades and a pacy plotline that will make you want to sleep with the light on, long after you have finished reading it!'

Jan Dunning, award-winning author of
The Last Thing You'll Hear

'Pacy, atmospheric and brilliantly creepy with twists and turns which keep you guessing right up to the very last page.'

Sue Cunningham, author of *Cloud Nine*

'Unpredictable and chilling – a haunting mystery that kept me guessing until the very end.'

Jenny Pearson, author of
The Super Miraculous Journey of Freddie Yates

For my sister, Zoe

DECEMBER

'Who hurt you?' Winter's voice was soft but dangerous.

Lacy swiped the tears off her cheeks as she snapped her head up to look at her sister. As always, Winter was dressed head to toe in black – black jeans, black shirt, black eyeshadow, black hair. And judging by the tight muscle in her jaw and the scowl that creased her pale forehead, her mood was just as dark.

'Nothing,' Lacy murmured.

Winter raised an eyebrow and leaned against the doorframe. It should have been a casual movement but made her look even more menacing.

'I mean, no one,' Lacy stuttered. 'I'm fine.'

She bowed her head and a rogue tear dropped onto her duvet, narrowly missing the camera nestled between her legs. She scrubbed at her eyes, furious with herself for being so pathetic.

'Hey,' Winter said from above her. She had somehow crossed the space between the door and the bed in the time it had taken Lacy to sniff noisily. Winter was like a shadow, but her presence was so strong that Lacy felt like the invisible one.

Winter wrapped a hand around her wrist, and Lacy tried not to pull away from the cold bite of her sister's pale skin and the thick metal rings on her long fingers. 'Stop crying,' Winter said firmly.

Lacy sniffed again and nodded, wishing she'd managed to keep the tears hidden. Winter hated crying.

Once Lacy had finally got control of her emotions, Winter released her arm.

'Tell me what happened,' she demanded, still standing, her arms folded in front of her chest. Lacy wished her sister would lower herself onto the bed beside her and give her a hug. But that wasn't Winter. Winter didn't *cuddle*.

Lacy sighed and picked at the strap of her camera. Saying it out loud would make it seem even more pathetic. 'It was Ali and the others…'

'Your friends?' Winter asked sharply.

Lacy nodded. Though, to be honest, she wasn't sure they were her friends, not in any true sense. They had been a group since primary school. And despite the growing feeling that she wasn't really one of them, Lacy had stuck with them all through secondary school and into their second year of sixth form. But lately it was becoming impossible to ignore the fact that her friends didn't actually *like* her.

'What did they do?' Winter pressed.

Lacy glanced up from the camera and instantly wished she hadn't. Winter was staring at her with an intensity that made her stomach churn with dread.

'Nothing…' Lacy said reluctantly. 'Just the usual stuff. Messing around.' She shrugged and let out what was supposed to be a flippant laugh but sounded like it had been choked out of her.

Ali and the rest of her 'friends' kept her around as a plaything, a clown, someone to be the butt of the joke. They delighted in her embarrassment, the way her pale skin flamed red when they pushed her in front of an attractive boy, when they grilled her about the sex life they knew she didn't have.

She was used to it and accepted her role in the group. What choice did she have? It was them…or no one.

But today's game had gone too far, and Lacy could still feel the heat of her humiliation on her skin.

They'd been walking home in high spirits, Lacy trying to laugh along with the inside jokes she wasn't a part of. The Christmas holidays weren't far away, and the girls simmered with excitement. A group of lads in their year were draped over a picnic bench as though they owned it, as though they owned the world.

When Ali spotted them, she smiled in a way that made her perfect teeth look pointy and sharp.

'Cal,' she called, her voice sweet and sing-songy as she swung her glossy blonde ponytail from side to side.

Bile rushed to Lacy's mouth. She knew what was coming. She should never have told her friends that she thought Cal was the best-looking boy in their school, but they'd pressed her relentlessly for an answer.

Ali slid her arm around Lacy's shoulders, pinning her to her side. 'Lacy's never been kissed,' she said, sticking out her bottom lip in a sad pout. 'Don't you think that's awful?'

Lacy's cheeks burned as Cal's friends sniggered into their hands. The giggles from behind her made it clear that her own friends were enjoying this just as much.

'Would you be a gentleman and help her out?' Ali's hair somehow whipped across Lacy's cheek as she spoke. The silky ponytail was like an extra limb to Ali, and Lacy suspected it was the source of her power. She was often torn between wanting to run her fingers through it and wanting to rip it out of Ali's scalp.

Lacy braced herself for the cruel rejection that would come her way. She prepared her mouth to morph into a grin, a charade that she was in on the joke.

Cal stood, took a step towards her and cocked his head to the side, a thoughtful expression on his chiselled face as his eyes roamed her body. Lacy withered beneath his gaze and wondered what he saw when he looked at her. Grey, dull, forgettable?

Finally, he shrugged, as though the prospect of touching her wasn't *that* hideous.

Ali thrust her forwards, her fingers jabbing Lacy painfully in the side. Cal tugged her towards him and clamped his lips over hers before she had even registered what was happening.

Lacy shuddered at the memory and threaded the camera strap through her fingers, comforted by the smooth material.

'They're not your friends,' Winter said, sitting suddenly on the end of Lacy's bed, a low growl in her voice.

Lacy nodded.

'And you don't need them.'

Lacy couldn't nod at that. Winter didn't understand – she was a free spirit, so independent that the idea of her being lonely was laughable.

But Lacy… Lacy was a drab little nobody. Yes, her friendship group wasn't exactly supportive or even friendly, but at least she could say she was part of something. Without Ali and the others, she'd simply cease to exist.

'Lacy,' Winter said, her tone demanding eye contact. The heavy make-up outlining her eyes made her irises so dark they looked black. 'You need to be stronger. You can't keep being this pathetic.'

Lacy flinched but couldn't argue. She *was* pathetic.

'You're better than them,' Winter hissed, digging her jagged fingernails into Lacy's wrist. 'You don't *need* them.'

Lacy tried not to wince and focused on Winter's words. She wished it was that simple.

'All you need is this' – Winter tapped a black talon on Lacy's beloved camera – 'and this.' She took Lacy's trembling hand and placed it on her own chest. The chunky pendants that hung around Winter's neck were cold to the touch.

Winter released Lacy's hand and held up her own wrist, which jangled with an assortment of bracelets. Winter was a collector, a magpie. Her body was adorned with the various things she'd taken a shine to, and Lacy had once found her treasure stash under her bed – expensive-looking trinkets that probably hadn't been purchased – and other items Winter must have found intriguing enough to hoard: smooth pebbles, shards of broken glass, a tiny white skull.

Winter gently removed a silver bracelet from her wrist and fastened it around Lacy's.

Lacy thought she might cry again.

'September,' Winter breathed, the word heavy with meaning.

September. Just ten more months and they'd be gone. Away from this town, this country. They were moving to Paris.

'So forget them. Forget them *now*. You don't need anyone, especially not the filth that go to your school.'

Lacy cringed at the venom in Winter's voice. She wished she could hate them as much as her sister did, instead of longing for them to accept her.

'It's you and me – forever. I'm all you need, OK?'

Lacy took a steadying breath. Winter was right. She had looked after her all her life. Winter was the one she could depend on.

It was Lacy and Winter.

No one else mattered.

Lacy looked into the dark depths of her sister's eyes and nodded.

The next day, Winter had gone.

Their parents were worried – Winter had gone AWOL before, but this time felt different. In the past, it had always been spontaneous, never planned, never thought through.

She'd never packed a bag before.

Lacy tried to convince herself that it was normal. Winter came and went as she pleased. She'd be back. She tried to ignore the creeping feeling of terror that Winter had left for Paris already, too impatient to wait for Lacy to finish college in the summer.

Winter wouldn't do that. Winter would always look out for her.

The Christmas gift she had left for Lacy was testament to that. Tied with an ornate bow, a silky blonde ponytail lay across the foot of her bed. And with it, a note scribbled in looping black handwriting on the back of a card advertising holiday temp work:

See you in Paris.

CHAPTER 1

JULY

Lacy stepped off the train and her shoe vanished into the murky depths of a puddle. She gasped as a frigid spray of water splattered across her pale ankle, chilling her to the bone. As she bent to check if her tailored cream trousers had been ruined, an urgent beeping demanded her attention.

Behind her, the train doors were repeatedly closing on her suitcase, squashing the handstitched leather over and over.

'Wait!' she screeched, wincing at the grating harshness of her voice. She'd been working so hard to suppress her Black Country accent, but here it was, in all its embarrassing glory, being bellowed across the Welsh countryside.

Not that there was anyone around to hear it.

She tugged the bag free and it crashed into her shins before landing in the puddle to join her sodden feet. The train groaned as it pulled away from the tiny station. Lacy watched it leave and wondered if she'd made a terrible mistake.

This place was everything she wasn't, or at least everything she was trying not to be. If her sister could see her now…

Her camera bumped against her breastbone, offering a sharp reminder of why she was there. She rested her fingers on the bulky black case, the comforting weight of it making her shoulders ache as it hung heavily on her neck, where it belonged.

She inhaled, stretched her neck upwards, then tilted her chin downwards. Whatever she would face here, she would do it with poise.

But the sudden deluge of rain made elegance somewhat challenging. Lacy threw her blazer over her head, dreading the effect the moisture would have on her poker-straight, jaw-length bob. Looking like she'd stuck her finger into a plug socket was not how she wanted to arrive at her new job.

She wanted people to see her as she was supposed to be – fashionable, chic, elegant. She didn't want them to see the frizzy-haired working-class girl she had hoped to leave behind.

From beneath her makeshift canopy, she surveyed the station, if it could really be called that. The platform was a short strip of raised concrete, standing obscurely in what seemed to be an empty field. It was so short, in fact, that the conductor had instructed passengers to move to the first carriage if they wished to disembark. Lacy wondered if he had known she was the only passenger on the two-carriage train, and had been for at least the last hour of her journey.

Bae Peryg. The station sign was greening with lichen, and the Welsh name looked clunky to Lacy. Inelegant. Not like French. French was a language of art and sophistication, and in two months' time, she'd be surrounded by it. French people, French fashion, French *everything*. She and Winter had fantasised about moving abroad for years, but if she was going to make her Parisian dreams a reality, she needed cash.

She heard a raucous shriek overhead and saw with disgust how close she'd come to being shat on by a seagull. *No, Lacy, not shat on,* she corrected herself. *Defecated on.* The bird had left a wet splatter across the sign. It didn't feel like a good omen.

She shivered and warily cast her eyes up the platform. It was July but felt like a bleak February afternoon. The sun was close to disappearing entirely behind the mountains that surrounded her on all sides except one, where the grey ocean lay flat and uninviting.

Bae Peryg was a holiday park…so where were all the holidaymakers? Lacy had been expecting to share the train with noisy tourists bustling oversized bags and overloud children onto the carriage, excited for their week in 'North Wales's premier caravan site'. There was nobody.

Creeping dread inched up the back of her neck like overfamiliar fingers. She spun round but saw nothing behind her except more grass, more grey, more rain. She could smell a fetid dampness in the air. Something cold and rotten.

A sheep bleated forlornly in the distance, and Lacy flicked the feeling of wrongness off her shoulders with a scatter of rainwater. She jutted her jaw once again and strode forwards, away from the tiny station.

Poise, Lacy. Poise.

A narrow footpath snaked away from the train platform, through a scrubby field and towards a wooden kissing gate. Her ankle wobbled painfully over a rock and the suitcase bashed into her kitten heel. She bit back the furious curses that formed on her lips – words that would reveal what Winter had called their 'classless upbringing'. She was so close to being the person she needed to be before moving to Paris at the end of summer, but sometimes glimmers of her past burst through the cracks. She would have to work harder to suppress them.

The rain was starting to seep through the light material of her blazer, and Lacy's cheeks flamed with indignation. Someone should have come to meet her. This was no way for a company to treat its employees.

Beggars can't be choosers, a sly voice hissed inside her head, her sister's voice. Lacy pressed on, hating the truth of the words. She wouldn't be here if she had a choice. She would be working in a boutique, a museum, an art gallery… But her hometown was seriously lacking such venues. In fact, the only thing it wasn't lacking was bookies, pubs and greasy takeaways. Oh, and unemployment – there was an abundance of that.

So here she was, taking the only job she could get. After weeks of being unable to find work, she'd remembered the note Winter had left on the back of the card for the temping company. She'd called the number, and they'd immediately assigned her a job at the holiday park. She wasn't even sure what she was expected to do here, but at least it had the perk of getting her far away from home.

Although, she thought as a fat droplet of rain rolled down the centre of her forehead and off the tip of her nose, she was starting to wonder if this place was going to be an improvement on the shabby little town she'd left behind.

She hesitated, suddenly longing for her cramped living room, the uncomfortable springs of the lumpy sofa and the shiny faces of her mother's porcelain dogs staring down at her from the mantlepiece.

What if she'd got it wrong? What if that really was where she belonged? What if…?

A rush of wind shoved her in the small of the back and she stumbled forwards.

Stop it, Lacy. Don't forget the plan. Don't forget Paris.

She kept going.

Finally, as the path reached the brow of a rolling hill, civilisation came into view – if it could be called that. Rows and rows of beige-coloured static caravans stood in orderly lines across the fields. Lacy blinked at the sheer size of the park. There must have been hundreds of the things, queuing up to the edge of the coastal cliff as though waiting for their turn to plunge into the sea.

Lacy didn't understand why anyone would pay to travel to what felt like the end of the world, only to bunch so close together with a load of other people. They could have just stayed home and be spared the biting coastal wind that hurtled towards her now, throwing rain horizontally into her face.

Bae Peryg. Peril Bay. *Bleak* Bay would be more fitting.

Her suitcase travelled smoothly now that she'd reached the caravans and the concrete they sat on. It seemed the entire park had been tarmacked, with the odd patch of sad-looking grass sitting in thin strips between each pitch. It was like a huge, depressing car park – endless identical caravans interspersed with ugly family cars, all standing lifelessly, as though abandoned.

She bowed her head and scurried deeper into the belly of the park. The caravans offered little protection from the elements, despite the way they crowded about her, making her feel trapped and disorientated. How did anyone find their way around here? Everything looked the same, and the one sign she passed was nothing more than a broken stump and a pile of splinters. She eyed it warily, wondering if it had been battered to the ground by the weather, by a car reversing over it or a gang of holidaymakers desperate for entertainment.

But where were these yobbish tourists that had stomped the innocent sign to death? It was 7 p.m. There should have been families cooking dinner and putting their children to bed, but the windows of the caravans Lacy walked past were empty, black holes.

She swallowed, suddenly unsettled by the thought of missing some kind of apocalypse while she'd been trying not to touch anything on the painfully slow, smelly little train. Had everyone…*gone*?

She turned a corner, and her breath caught in her chest as she realised that, no, she was not the last person left on earth.

In the middle of the empty road, stood…

A person dressed as a bear.

Lacy blinked rapidly, willing her eyes to catch her brain up on what they were seeing so she could process the bizarre sight.

Saggy brown fur hung in folds that drooped over their limbs. The giant head was slightly twisted, giving them a broken, pained appearance. They seemed to be staring at Lacy, though it was impossible to be sure – the eyeholes were huge and dark.

She stayed still, waiting for the bear to make the first move. She couldn't decide if it was tacky and embarrassing, or horribly creepy.

The bear cocked its oversized head to the side and slowly raised a tattered paw into the air.

Creepy, Lacy decided. Most definitely creepy.

CHAPTER 2

'Um, hello?' Lacy said, blood colouring her pale cheeks. This is what her life had come to – she was making conversation with a giant possessed teddy bear.

The bear didn't move, but Lacy could hear a low, angry rumble bubbling up from its shaggy brown chest. Was it *growling* at her?

She glanced behind her, wondering if she could simply retreat and pretend she'd never come across this utter weirdo. When she turned back round, the bear had removed its head.

He was tall, with impossibly high cheekbones and heavy eyelids that made him look seriously fed up. To be fair, Lacy would have been fed up too if she'd had to traipse around an empty holiday park dressed as a soft toy.

A terrifying thought hit her. Her job description had simply read, **Holiday Park General Staff**. What if…?

'Are you Lacy Stevens?' the boy asked in a high-pitched Liverpudlian accent. The bizarre growling she'd heard earlier must have been his muffled attempt to ask her name.

'Oh, um,' Lacy stuttered, shaking herself out of her morbid imaginings of life inside a bear suit. 'Yes.'

He scrutinised her curiously, eyes lingering on her outfit. She'd rescued her clothes from a charity shop and knew that they wore her, rather than the other way around. Since Winter had left, just before Christmas, Lacy had doubled her efforts to become the person she wanted to be, the person she *needed* to be. But as she felt the familiar flush of embarrassment creep up her neck, she wondered if she'd ever be able to leave the mousey, awkward girl behind.

'How come you didn't come at the start of the season with the rest of us?' the boy asked, tilting his head to one side.

'Because this place was a last resort,' Lacy blurted. She winced, realising she'd just insulted the park, the job and probably the bear himself, judging by the unimpressed look on his tanned face.

Her fingers found the dainty silver bracelet that encircled her wrist, the one Winter had given her just before she'd left. Lacy felt the bumps of the cold chain and tried to imagine what her sister would say if she were here.

You shouldn't care what this nobody thinks of you, Lacy.

Lacy shoved her need to be liked deep into her stomach and jutted her chin upwards into the ceaseless rain. 'Are you here to greet me?' she asked, her voice clipped and carefully masking her Midlands accent. 'My train arrived fifteen minutes ago.'

The boy's eyes narrowed, and Lacy fought to return his gaze. She suspected she'd managed to make an enemy within ten minutes of arriving at Peril Bay.

'Apologies, m'lady.' He bowed theatrically before straightening and flipping his sweaty fringe away from his forehead. 'May I escort you to your lodgings?'

'Yes, thank you,' Lacy responded curtly, swallowing the need to apologise. Winter wouldn't have, so neither should she.

The boy sauntered slightly in front of her, his hips sashaying beneath the suit and making the bear's fluffy white tail shimmy from side to side. Lacy pulled her suitcase behind her, still holding her blazer awkwardly above her rapidly frizzing hair.

As they walked, the quiet of the apocalypse park gradually faded. Lacy couldn't place specific sounds – it was a jumbled blur of noises, with the occasional frantic chiming of a bell that made her twitch with alarm every time it sounded. A mob of seagulls screamed as they ripped a bin bag apart with their huge, sharp beaks.

She wondered what her accommodation would be like. She wasn't expecting anything fancy – she wasn't deluded. But a warm, dry room with somewhere to plug her straighteners in would be welcome right now. Somewhere quiet, where she could focus on her first university assignment.

Movement – that's all the brief she'd been given. She needed a photograph prepared, ready for her first term in September. It had to be something good, something that made people pause, made them think and reflect on…well, *something*. It had to be worthy of her place at the Paris School of Fine Art.

As usual, the thought of moving to Paris made her stomach clench in terrified protest. She hadn't even been able to share the news of her acceptance at the prestigious university with Winter, who had been unreachable for nearly seven months now.

Lacy returned her focus to the bear's wiggling arse and tried to convince herself that her pounding heart was due to excitement, and nothing at all to do with the certainty that she was destined to fail spectacularly.

The buzzing hum of white noise was building. The bear disappeared around the corner of yet another identical caravan, and Lacy wondered how he managed to navigate this place. She readjusted her blazer – not that it was offering much protection against the incessant drizzle – and followed.

She suddenly understood where all the people had been hiding. It was like she'd stepped through a portal into another world, a world filled with screaming children hanging off playpark equipment while their parents clustered around the perimeter, glugging pints in the pouring rain.

Thumping music from nearby arcade games clashed with the people-noise, and a Tannoy churned out endless messages – a lost child, a car alarm going off, two-for-one deals on pitchers of woo woo.

'Welcome to paradise,' the bear sighed, looking as repulsed by the sight of it as Lacy felt. He warily replaced his bear head, and Lacy could just about make out his explanation. 'We're not supposed to let them see us in our natural forms.'

Lacy yelped as a small boy whacked the back of her knees with a plastic sword before swearing furiously at her for getting in his way. His exhausted-looking mother caught up with him, clipped him around the ear and told him off for swearing, using the same colourful language he'd used.

Lacy swallowed as she slowly took in each garish detail of the scene. She longed to retreat around the corner of the caravan, which had somehow blocked most of the noise as well as the unpleasant view.

But she'd signed her name on the dotted line. She was here to work for two months. And then, she told herself, willing the words to bring her strength, *then*…Paris.

And, more importantly, her sister.

The bear had been accosted by a cluster of soggy children with sticky ice-lolly chins and wild sugar-fuelled eyes. He was waving and swaying playfully, but Lacy doubted the boy inside the bear was feeling quite so jolly. The kids circled him, reaching out to touch his shaggy coat. A feral-looking girl aimed a kick at his shin, and he roared, sending them all scattering back to their parents.

The bear-boy ducked into a room marked **STAFF ONLY**. A paw beckoned Lacy to follow.

He had removed his head again, and the bear grinned manically up at Lacy from where he'd dumped it on the floor. Cardboard boxes and ring binders haphazardly lined the shelves, which looked ready to collapse. The boy was bent double, rummaging through black bin bags strewn across the floor of the gloomy storeroom. He thrust his hand towards Lacy without looking up. 'This should do you.'

She stared disbelievingly at the two feather-light scraps of clothing she'd been handed.

'Shorts?' she breathed.

The boy shrugged as he stood. 'I think they want us to look peppy. And what says fun more than a pair of anaemic-looking thighs?'

He nodded pointedly at Lacy's well-concealed legs. He was right in assuming they never saw the light of day – she suspected she would blind the guests with their dazzling whiteness. Bear-boy, however, had a face so tanned that he looked like he'd spent his winter lounging on a tropical beach.

'And…' Lacy murmured, holding up the other garment he'd handed her. 'Green?'

Green was an understatement. Olive, she could cope with. Maybe even jade, for a bold accessory. But the polo-neck shirt was *lime*.

The boy couldn't contain his snort of laughter. 'Welcome to the team.'

She numbly waited for him to give her the rest of her uniform, hoping for a less horrific cover-up. Hell, she'd even wear a hoodie if it meant she could cover the acidic monstrosity. But the boy was no longer rifling through the bags.

'Is that…?' Lacy breathed. 'Is that it?'

'Yep,' he said brightly. 'We're only allowed one set each. Management's keen on keeping costs down.'

Lacy turned to stare at the rectangle of daylight behind her. The rain had turned from drizzle to a torrential hammering that hit the ground and flew upwards again.

'But…' she whispered. 'I'll *die*.' She gestured at the goosebumps already prickling up her bare arms. She couldn't be expected to survive the British summer in just a polo shirt and shorts.

She was about to ask if her job would also involve being transformed into a miserable forest creature, when there was a shriek from behind her.

A rabbit bounced into the storeroom.

Whoever was inside was so short that the costume hung off them in folds of grey that made Lacy think of a malnourished elephant. The way they skittered around and danced from one oversized foot to the other suggested they'd taken their method acting a little too far.

The bunny head was removed to reveal a blonde girl who looked like she was the antidote to the bear's wretchedness. She was so smiley that it made Lacy's cheeks ache just to look at her, and her round blue eyes glittered with excitement.

'Oh my god, there you are, Marc!' she squealed at the bear boy. Lacy felt a pang of guilt when she realised she hadn't even asked the bear's name.

'Yes, Rachel,' Marc sighed. 'Here I am.' He frowned at her. 'You're even chirpier than usual. What's going on?'

Rachel's teeth gleamed as her grin widened. 'A body has been found.'

CHAPTER 3

The manic grin on Rachel's face didn't waver, despite the stunned silence that followed her announcement.

'Eh?' Marc finally said. Lacy was relieved to see he was as thrown as she was.

'A body!' Rachel squeaked, bouncing merrily on her huge rabbit feet. 'A guest is dead!'

Lacy's gaze flitted between the forest creatures. Was this some kind of initiation prank? She pressed her teeth together and tried not to react, sure she was being laughed at.

But Marc didn't seem to be in on the joke either. 'OK,' he said slowly. 'And why are you practically giddy with glee over this fact?'

Rachel theatrically readjusted her face into a cartoonish upside-down smile. She brought her hands to her eyes, made dainty fists and moved them as though she were a crying toddler. '*Waah, waah,*' she said feebly. 'Is that better?'

Lacy and Marc gawped at her.

'Oh, for god's sake, lighten up, will you!' Rachel snapped, and Lacy saw a glimmer of something cold and hard beneath the bouncing bunny exterior. 'Nothing ever happens around here, so forgive me for being a little excited.'

Lacy's skin crawled and she rubbed the goosebumps on her upper arms. She wanted to scream at Rachel, demand she explain what was going on. But she cleared her throat gingerly and asked, 'How did they die?'

Rachel's cheeriness returned immediately. 'His head was bashed in.'

'Jesus,' Marc gasped.

Lacy's stomach clenched violently. She'd been thinking something along the lines of a heart attack. Or an unfortunate accident. But *murder*?

'You the new girl?' Rachel asked brightly, interrupting Lacy's morbid imaginings. 'I'll show you to the dorms.'

Before Lacy had time to respond, Rachel had shoved her bunny head back on and bounded out of the door.

Lacy's mouth dangled open as she turned to Marc for reassurance, but he looked as stunned as she did and shrugged helplessly.

Would the park be shut down? She couldn't go home before she'd even had the chance to earn a penny. She needed this job – rent in Paris was staggeringly high and there was no way she could ask her parents for help.

She hurried out of the storage room in search of the rabbit with a morbid curiosity for death.

Rachel was hopping, actually *hopping*, down the path that led away from the playpark and bar. She even stopped at one point to perform a cute little bum wiggle for a laughing family, who gathered around her to take a selfie. Lacy recoiled in horror as they moved their attention to her before realising Marc had followed them and it was him they were after. He performed a jaunty dance that made the baby in the pushchair cry.

Lacy felt as though she'd been sucked into some kind of *Alice in Wonderland* hellscape.

Their weird little procession continued away from the park and back into the maze of beige caravans. A police car drove slowly past them and its occupants waved cheerily as Rachel pranced along. The police weren't too concerned by the murder, it seemed.

Lacy hurried after Rachel, struggling to keep up with the surprisingly speedy rabbit.

Finally, as they left the busy hub of the park and reached yet more rows of beige caravans, Rachel slowed. Her oversized head swivelled, presumably checking to see if the coast was clear, before she lifted it off. Lacy eyed her hair jealously. It was sleek and smooth, the kind that could get wet and dry again without looking like it had been backcombed by a bramble. Just like Ali's hair had been, before her severed ponytail had appeared at the foot of Lacy's bed.

'Apparently, they found him underneath a caravan,' Rachel said, as though their conversation about the dead guest hadn't just been interrupted by a parade that belonged at Disneyland. 'He was probably killed last night, but they only discovered him an hour ago when his wife reported him missing.'

'Why'd she take so long to report him missing?' Marc asked, also taking his head off. 'It's already evening.'

Rachel shrugged and rubbed her button nose with a fluffy paw. 'Maybe she only just woke up. Apparently, there was a lot of heavy drinking at the bar last night, guests getting rowdy and that.'

Lacy flinched at the prospect of rowdy, drunk holidaymakers.

Whatever job she would be doing, she hoped it wouldn't put her anywhere near them. That was assuming she still even had a job.

'Will they close the park?' she asked, equal parts scared and hopeful.

Marc snorted. 'Not a chance. Last season we lost five caravans into the sea when the cliff collapsed. The affected guests got a voucher for a fiver to spend at the bar. There's no way they'd close the park and lose money just because of one dead guest.'

Lacy shuddered. Just how many dead guests did it take to close a holiday park?

They turned a corner into a wind tunnel that came straight from the sea. Lacy narrowed her eyes against the wet gale, but Marc and Rachel ploughed on, seemingly unbothered about their costumes getting soaked. The park was getting shabbier the further they ventured from the central plaza. The caravans looked older, the grass had been left to grow long and scruffy, and there was a fishy smell that Lacy suspected was a mixture of seaweed and drains.

She wrinkled her nose and cringed at the thought of her sister discovering where she'd been forced to get a summer job. It was the kind of place Winter wouldn't have been seen dead in, and she would mock Lacy relentlessly if she could see her now, flanked by a hyperactive rabbit and a depressed teddy bear.

But Winter was gone.

At first, Lacy hadn't tried to contact her, knowing that when Winter disappeared, she wanted space, not her little sister pestering her. But weeks rolled by, then months, and a cold knot of fear settled in Lacy's chest.

She'd been abandoned.

So she'd messaged Winter, texted her, even called her. But the messages went unread and the calls went straight to voicemail.

That didn't mean anything though – Winter often turned off her phone. Just…never for seven whole months before.

Lacy blinked rapidly, banishing the pain that thinking about Winter inevitably brought. Her sister may not have waited for her before leaving for Paris, but it didn't matter. Lacy would make her own way there, and they would finally be reunited.

But first, she had to survive *this*.

The park had completely given up on any attempt to be presentable now. The caravans either side of the road were stained with green lichen, and some were even missing doors. Lacy suspected even the keenest bargain hunter wouldn't pay for a holiday in one of these. She warily eyed the gap between the caravans and the ground, wondering how the dead guest had ended up wedged beneath the stilts.

They passed an empty pitch where, presumably, a caravan had once stood, judging by the leftover charred rectangular stain. The state the park was descending into as they got closer to the cliffs didn't give her much hope for the condition of the staff accommodation.

As Rachel and Marc steered her towards two large buildings framed by a bleak, grey horizon, she realised she had been right to be concerned.

'Home sweet home,' Marc sighed.

A sign reading **STAFF ACCOMMODATION** had been hammered into the verge, and someone had written *KEEP OUT* in Sharpie beneath it. The two large, blocky buildings in front of them were made from wood so dark they looked black. They made Lacy think of warehouses, or an American prison.

They reached the door of the closest block, and Lacy peered around the corner towards the second, the one closest to the edge of the cliff. It was identical to the one they stood in front of but looked derelict. Some of the windows were smashed.

'That one's empty,' Rachel said, noticing her looking.

Lacy couldn't stop staring at it. Why had it been left like that, hideously blocking the view to the horizon beyond? A feeling of dread crept up from the pit of her stomach. The windows were so dark…

'They're focusing on doing up the other side of the park,' Rachel explained, making Lacy jump. 'It's not worth the expense of knocking the old buildings down, so they're leaving this side to rot.'

'Yeah, or just waiting for nature to do its thing.' Marc laughed humourlessly. 'It'll crumble into the sea before it has a chance to rot.'

Lacy shuddered and wondered if that would be for the best.

'Come on.'

Lacy tore her gaze from the abandoned dorm and followed Rachel into the building labelled **Dorm Block A**, praying the inside was better than the exterior.

It wasn't.

A long, narrow corridor welcomed her. A sickly glow was cast by the green fire-exit signs hanging from the ceiling, highlighting the brown, flaking paint and the grimy carpet beneath Lacy's wet feet. Graffiti etched onto the wall showed just how old the building was.

Bae Peryg Massive 1991
Greg & Sarah 1979 ♥

They travelled deeper into the belly of the dorm block, and Lacy guessed there must be at least forty rooms on this level. The building was two stories high, so there had to be accommodation for dozens of residents, but surely there couldn't be that many staff working here? Just how many teenagers dressed as cutesy animals did a holiday park need?

'Come *on*,' Rachel said again, as though Lacy wasn't moving eagerly enough for her liking. 'Bathroom there,' she said, pointing to a door on the right. 'Toilets there and there.' Two more doors, and Lacy wondered how on earth she was supposed to know which were the toilets and which were people's bedrooms.

'Kitchen,' Rachel announced, opening yet another identical wooden door. 'You can use the food in the blue cupboard until you get your vouchers for the shop – they come out of your pay.'

The strip lights of the kitchen made Lacy flinch after the murkiness of the corridor. She glanced around, noting the cupboard doors hanging off broken hinges, the teetering piles of filthy dishes and the teenagers sitting on the counters, staring at her.

'Hi!' a voice cried before Lacy had fully entered the kitchen. A man who looked in his early twenties bounded towards her. He was shorter than her, with a stocky build and a ruddy, weather-beaten face, and he looked like he was born to wear the lime green of the park's uniform.

'I'm Andy, staff manager. You must be Lacy. So sorry I didn't get up to the station to meet you, but I was a little occupied with…well, things.' He grimaced cheerily, as though he'd been dealing with a broken washing machine rather than the death of one of the park's guests.

'Give us the deets then, Andy,' Rachel said eagerly, clambering up onto the kitchen counter to join the other staff members, resting the bunny head beside her. There didn't seem to be any chairs in the kitchen.

'Not much to tell, I'm afraid,' Andy said, attempting to rearrange his face into something sombre but failing to wipe away his natural jolliness. 'A male guest was found deceased beneath his caravan an hour or so ago.'

'*Murdered*,' a startingly pretty girl with a mass of thick brown hair and a Welsh accent said from the worktop.

Lacy glanced round at the other members of staff, but they all blended into one with their green polo shirts, black shorts and glum expressions. She quickly counted ten of them and assumed there were more still at work in various positions around the park.

'Who was it?' Marc asked from beside Lacy. 'I mean, do we need to worry about getting *our* heads caved in?'

Lacy nodded. Marc seemed to be the only one reacting in an appropriate way to the news – there was a distinct lack of panic around the fact that there was potentially a murderer on the loose.

Andy placed his hands on his hips and chortled. 'No, no. Don't worry – they've arrested the guy already. It was an altercation after a fight at the bar last night. Nothing to worry about.'

'Oh,' Rachel said, failing to hide her disappointment that the murder hadn't been something juicier. 'Don't the police want to interview us or anything?'

'Why?' Andy said sharply, his smile faltering. 'Did you see anything?'

'Obviously *not*,' she replied. 'I think I'd have told someone if I'd witnessed a guest getting his brains bashed in.'

Lacy winced at the image. She felt bad for Andy, whose enthusiasm seemed to have been dampened by Rachel's spiteful tone.

'No, no,' Andy stuttered, 'of course you didn't. Silly me.' His smile returned as he looked at Lacy. 'Let me show you your room.'

Lacy gave the other staff members a last glance before she left the kitchen, but the ones who returned her gaze looked disinterested. She groaned inwardly as she pictured what she must look like – a soggy, frizzy mess. The very opposite of poised.

Andy strode down the corridor in front of her, opening the doors to the minuscule shower and toilets to show her as he rambled on. 'There are only eighteen employees staying here at the moment – it's been a real struggle to find reliable staff this year. That's why we're so glad you've joined us.' He turned to give her a friendly smile, and Lacy couldn't help but return it. Andy was overenthusiastic and cringy, but he was a welcome respite from Marc's saltiness and Rachel's hot and cold behaviour.

'You're in room 27,' he said, pausing at a door. Lacy could just about make out the number carved into the wood. 'There's no one in the rooms either side of you. I've tried to space everyone out so there's plenty of privacy.' His cheeks reddened suddenly, and Lacy tried not to snigger at his embarrassment. He needn't worry – there was no way she'd be getting up to anything with anyone in this place.

He produced a key, unlocked the door and pushed it open, standing awkwardly so Lacy had to press up against him to get past.

'It isn't much,' he said unnecessarily as Lacy took in the single bed and wonky clothes rail, which were the only pieces of furniture in the prison-cell of a room. 'But, well, I hope you'll be comfortable.'

He dithered for a moment as Lacy tried, and failed, to hide her dismay.

'If you need anything, anything at all, I'm just down the corridor – room 25.'

Lacy looked at Andy in surprise. He lived here too? If she had worked her way up to a managerial position, there was no way in hell she'd still be staying in this festering dorm block with a bunch of teenagers.

'Is there anyone else?' she asked curiously. 'Other managers or…?'

'Nope, just me!' Andy said brightly, his chest puffing with pride. 'Well, there are managers above me, of course.' He laughed awkwardly. 'But they mainly manage the park from the head office, offsite. It's unlikely you'll see any of them.'

'Wow,' Lacy said. Even with just eighteen staff, that was a lot of responsibility for one guy.

'Don't worry, though,' Andy said, noticing her concern. 'I've worked here ever since I was sixteen – know the place like the back of my hand. You'll be safe under my watch.'

Lacy wondered if the dead guest was supposed to have been under Andy's watch too, but nodded bravely. Andy closed the door behind himself, and her fingers found the cold plastic of her camera. She tried to keep her wobbling lip under control as she took in the details of her bedroom.

The paint was flaking away from the walls, and black dots of mould crawled across the ceiling. She could smell its cloying dampness. The curtains were too small for the window and were moving in the draft that had somehow found its way in from outside.

At least Andy was nice, she tried to reassure herself. Winter would have dismissed him as a pathetic little man, wasting his life at a dilapidated caravan park. But Lacy was glad for the friendly face – she suspected she'd be needing it.

'Oh,' Andy said, bursting back into the room and making Lacy jump. 'I completely forgot to tell you – you'll need to be at the swimming pool tomorrow morning from seven o'clock. You'll be working as a lifeguard.'

CHAPTER 4

Lacy had thought Andy was playing some kind of sick joke on her when he'd told her what job she'd be doing. But here she was, perched on a plastic chair at the side of the indoor swimming pool, wondering what she'd done to deserve this.

She could barely swim, for god's sake.

She'd tentatively appeared at the pool that morning and dithered by the front desk, waiting to be acknowledged by the receptionist, who was yet another lime-green teenager. Lee, according to his name badge, looked like he hadn't slept in a month. He had a pinched, haunted expression and angry red pimples dotted across his cheeks. A blue baseball cap was wedged onto his head, which nodded to the beat of whatever was blasting through his headphones.

He told Lacy to sit at the side of the pool and make sure no one drowned.

She'd considered refusing, arguing that it was ridiculous, negligent, *dangerous*, even, to put her in this position. But as she'd been confronted by Lee's blank stare, her bravado had deserted her, and she'd meekly done as instructed.

She never thought she'd be grateful for her shorts and polo

shirt, but she nearly cried with relief when she realised she wouldn't be expected to sit in a swimming costume all day.

For the hundredth time since entering the humid glass building, she attempted to flatten her hair with her hands, knowing it was hopeless. No matter how hard she tried, she couldn't convince her wayward curls to be the sleek French-style bob she longed for.

You're getting paid for this, she reminded herself as she watched the timer laboriously count the seconds. She'd been there a grand total of twenty-two minutes, and her attention had been on the clock for most of that time. She cast a glance around the pool as she realised that she hadn't actually looked at any of the swimmers for a while now. But all was fine – no dead guests on her watch, yet.

The echoes of screaming children made her head throb. She'd slept terribly, unable to escape thoughts of the man who'd been stuffed beneath his own caravan. Every time she closed her eyes, her imagination forced her to picture the messy remains of his skull.

Then, when sleep had finally claimed her, she'd woken frequently, her senses alert to every unusual noise – the slamming of doors, the groaning of old pipes and…

At one point, she'd sworn she'd heard scrabbling in the walls. She'd sat bolt upright, unable to see much of anything in the pitch black of her tiny room. She'd shone her phone light towards the sound, and, for a fuzzy second, she thought she saw an eye staring at her through a hole in the wooden wall.

She'd leaped out of bed and flicked the light switch on, revealing that, yes, there was a small hole in her wall. But, no, there was no one staring through it, watching her sleep. She'd pressed her eye to the hole and could just about make out the dim outline of a bed in a room that looked identical to hers, but it was empty. She'd crawled back under her covers and cursed her racing heart for refusing to allow her to relax back into unconsciousness.

She sighed, the warmth of the swimming pool making her drowsy. She wished she could have brought her camera and worked on her assignment. There was plenty of 'movement' in here, not that she would have wanted to photograph one of the noisy brats ignoring the **NO RUNNING** signs, even if she wouldn't have been arrested for it.

She needed to think outside the box – they wouldn't want the students to take a photo of something literally moving, would they? Surely they were after something touching, something that moved in other ways…

Lacy's heart fluttered as she saw something that moved *her*.

He was tall, tanned, flaunting muscles that no teenager had any business owning. He somehow managed to make the lime-green uniform look like it belonged in a copy of *Men's Health* magazine, and he was walking straight towards her.

'Oh god,' Lacy breathed as he smiled and revealed two perfect dimples and creases at the corners of his eyes that made her legs feel like jelly despite the fact she was sitting down.

'You must be Lacy,' he said in a thick North-Welsh accent. The deep blue of his eyes twinkled as they reflected the shimmering pool surface. 'I'm Dylan.'

Lacy had forgotten how words worked and nodded stiffly at him.

'Do you mind if I pull my chair over here?' he asked, beaming at her. 'I get lonely sitting by myself.'

Lacy nodded again, wondering when the power of speech would return to her. She watched him walk to the other side of the pool, and her senses slowly returned to her as she was released from his hypnotising gaze.

This had never happened to her before, even with Cal, the first boy she'd ever kissed. She'd told her friends she'd had a crush on him, but she hadn't liked him, not really. Even when she and Cal had inexplicably taken things further after that fateful day, she'd never felt remotely bewitched in this way.

She swallowed, the thought of Cal making her feel queasy. She needed to cure herself of the instantaneous effect Dylan had had on her. This kind of thing happened to simple, ditsy girls who were bowled over by a pretty face and collarbones that travelled smoothly down to the rippling six-pack she imagined existed under Dylan's polo shirt.

'*Stop it*,' she hissed to herself as Dylan returned with his chair.

'Sorry I'm late,' he said as he sat close to her, *too close*. Lacy could feel the heat radiating off his body. 'I'm usually a morning person, but I went for a jog pretty late last night and it just wiped me out, you know?'

Lacy definitely did *not* know, but she was not about to tell caravan-park Adonis that the most physical exercise she did was lifting her camera to take a shot. She made a noise in her throat that sounded like she had a small rodent stuck in it.

'Are you OK?' Dylan asked, his beautiful face puckering with concern. 'Would you like some of my water?'

He held a half-empty bottle towards her, and Lacy willed her mind and body to get their shit together. This was ridiculous. The presence of an attractive boy should not have had this effect on her. She was done with boys – that's what she'd promised herself after the disaster that was her ex.

'I'm fine,' she said, clearing her throat. She kept her attention on the pool in front of them. Maybe if she didn't look at him, she wouldn't fall under his spell again.

She just wished he didn't have to *smell* so good.

Lacy had been plagued by a smell that seemed to be a mixture of raw sewage and Winter's lavender perfume for months now. She'd vaguely wondered if she was just missing her sister with an intensity that had its own scent, or if she had a brain tumour. Whichever it was, the fresh, outdoorsy aroma of Dylan was a welcome replacement.

She tried not to breathe him in too obviously. *It'll pass,* she told herself as their shift continued. She would get over the initial attraction and then Dylan would be nothing more than another side character in this brief chapter of her life.

But the more Dylan talked, the more she felt herself being pulled towards him like a stupid little moth towards a huge, gorgeous lightbulb.

He lived nearby and didn't stay in the staff accommodation, she discovered. He loved sports, unsurprisingly. He was good with kids, she saw, after he'd scooped a face-planting toddler off the slippery tiles.

But most attractive of all was his apparent fascination with *her*.

He reacted with such amazement when she told him about her place at the Paris School of Fine Art that she had to stop herself from kissing him right there, at the poolside. He asked her question after question, responding with an enthusiastic 'Woah!' at every answer. His attention occasionally diverted to check that no one was drowning, but it always returned keenly back to her.

He couldn't have been more different from her ex. Cal had barely looked into her eyes during their entire relationship.

Though, if she was being honest, Lacy had barely been able to look at him either. She'd spent every moment they were together waiting for the punchline, the big reveal that it had all been a joke at her expense.

She'd been walking home alone from school when he'd approached her. Ali hadn't exactly been desperate to continue their friendship after the hair-cutting incident. She'd tried to press charges, but there was no proof it had been Winter, who had somehow managed to lop the silky ponytail off and disappear without being seen.

But Ali had known – who else would do something so evil if not Lacy's twisted sister?

Christmas had been a bleak, lonely affair, Lacy's parents dejectedly poking at microwaved vegetables and wondering where Winter was. So Lacy had been raw and ripe for the picking when Cal had approached her. His fingers had been slightly sweaty when he'd linked them through hers as she'd passed the bench claimed by him and his friends. She'd stared at him, astonished, wondering if she should ask if he was lost.

But he'd walked her home, chatting as though they were already a couple, kissing her goodbye before sauntering away and leaving her spluttering on the pavement. She'd scanned the area, searching for Ali and the others, her ears straining to hear their cruel laughter.

But there was no one there. And before Lacy could understand what was happening, she and Cal were apparently a couple.

The thought of Cal burst Lacy's delicious Dylan-induced bubble, and she guiltily averted her eyes from him for the first time in hours. What was she doing, flirting with such wild abandon after everything…

The pool house suddenly felt too hot.

'You OK?' Dylan asked, noticing instantly.

Lacy gave a weak nod as the pool wavered dizzyingly in front of her. She needed to get out of there. She couldn't do this, not with Dylan, not with *anyone*.

Not again.

Lacy sucked air into her lungs and wrinkled her nose. That rotten, floral smell was back. Oh god, what if it was *her*? She tried to subtly sniff herself, but Dylan wouldn't stop staring. Her heart tapped out a warning on her ribcage, reminding her not to get distracted. Paris was all that mattered. Paris, and Winter.

She wrapped her arms around herself and tilted her body away from Dylan.

CHAPTER 5

'Come on!'

Lacy dropped her camera in surprise as Rachel burst uninvited into her room. Luckily, the strap stopped it from falling to the floor. Had it broken, Lacy wasn't sure she could be held responsible for her actions.

'What is it?' Lacy gasped. 'What's going on?'

Dylan had insisted she take the afternoon off after her embarrassing dizzy spell at the pool. She'd gone back to the staff accommodation via the disappointing on-site shop and used her meagre meal-allowance money to buy some bagels and cream cheese. Then, she'd shut herself in her room, hoping to turn her crappy first day around by cracking the assignment.

She'd been trying to capture a photo of the bracelet Winter had given her as it fell onto the bed, with little success. But now Rachel's urgency had pulled her focus back to the dead guest. Had they found the killer? Had there been another death?

'*Par-ty*,' Rachel said slowly. The way she put unwarranted emphasis on words was already starting to grate. It was as though she believed everything she said deserved italics.

'Oh,' Lacy replied. She tried not to grimace too obviously at the prospect of a caravan-park party. 'I'm good, thanks.'

The idea of having to strike up conversation with her colleagues made her stomach twist with dread. She couldn't think of other people her age without thinking of Ali and the girls she'd seen as her friends for so many years. As far as Lacy was concerned, friendship was sneering and cruel. She'd rather be alone.

She turned back to scoop the bracelet off her bed. It was impossible to get the timing right. What she needed was someone to drop it for her while she took the shot. But there was no way she was going to bring any of the other staff into her project.

'Oh, come *onnn*,' Rachel said from the doorway, stamping her tiny foot like a toddler being denied pudding.

Then, before Lacy could register what was happening, Rachel's sharp little fingers were gripped around her forearm. She dragged Lacy out of her room, knocking sharply on every door they passed and screeching, 'Party!'

Lacy was reminded of Ali shoving her towards Cal. What was it about Lacy that made girls like Rachel and Ali think she was a thing they could push around and do as they wished with?

If she were Winter, she would have fought her way out of Rachel's grip and dared her to touch her again.

But she wasn't her sister. No matter how hard she pretended – she was Lacy Stevens, the nobody, the loser, the pushover.

Rachel didn't release her even once they reached the kitchen. It was as though she was afraid she would do a runner the second her grip loosened, which was fair enough – Lacy was already eyeing up her escape route. Staff filed into the cramped room, some still citrus green and looking like they should be sliced and floating in a cold drink.

Lacy saw a couple of faces she recognised – Marc, who still looked surly despite being freed from his furry prison, and the striking dark-haired girl who'd sat on the kitchen counter yesterday. The rest of the staff merged into one featureless blur again as they jostled for places on the kitchen counters.

Cultureless.

The word hissed inside Lacy's head, seemingly from nowhere. That's what Winter would have called them. It was what she called just about everyone in the UK, and Lacy had to work hard not to get lumped into that category herself. She studied French fashion, art and culture, and attempted to replicate it – anything to stop Winter from looking at her with the same haughty disdain that she wore when she considered their own parents.

The rest of the staff's easy banter made Lacy feel like even more of an outsider. She wished she could learn to relax inside her own body, but she was always fretting about her hair or saying something stupid or whether she was managing to mask her accent. She would never be a girl who could sit on kitchen counters and chat without a care in the world.

Andy entered the kitchen and Lacy released a sigh of relief. At least there would be someone older, someone sensible, to oversee the party Rachel was insisting on.

But the bulging plastic bags he raised above his head to the cheers of the staff suggested that Andy wasn't such a responsible adult after all.

'How many did you get?' Rachel asked, finally letting go of

Lacy's arm and bounding over to Andy, somehow managing to appear cute and aggressive at the same time.

Lacy rubbed the red imprint Rachel's fingers had left on her skin and widened her eyes as Rachel pulled two large bottles of vodka out of the shopping bags.

'Only two?' she pouted, and Andy's cheeks reddened, clashing horribly with his lime-green polo shirt.

'Sorry,' he stuttered. 'They've put a limit on alcohol at the park shop. I think they're trying to stop people drinking as much after the murd—'

'Shh,' Rachel insisted, holding her fingers over Andy's lips. Lacy suspected the blush now covered his entire body.

Lacy studied him in surprise as Rachel placed the vodka on the countertop. Lacy was still seventeen and suspected many of the other staff were underage too. Andy looked to be in his early twenties himself. Wouldn't he lose his job if he was found to be supplying alcohol to minors?

Clearly, Rachel wasn't concerned with the risk Andy was taking, and she clambered onto the kitchen counter, nudging the other staff aside. Lacy wrinkled her nose at the dirty marks her trainers left on the space where they prepared their basic meals. 'Lee, music!' she yelled, and Lacy saw the boy who worked at the swimming pool reception hurry to follow her order.

The music came on deafeningly loud from a portable speaker in the corner of the kitchen, and Lacy winced, waiting for Lee to lower it to an acceptable volume. But he returned to the group, his body twitching to the distorted bass like a puppet having its strings pulled.

'Three second pass!' Rachel screamed as though addressing

a stadium full of fans. She stamped her feet on the kitchen counter, barking orders at her captivated audience. Lacy wondered whether she absorbed attention in the same way plants gained energy from the sun.

Once again, Lacy was unpleasantly reminded of Ali, someone she had hoped never to see again.

As a bottle of vodka was passed around, Lacy learned what a three second pass was. It was a simple game really – each person had to drink directly from the bottle for three seconds, and if Rachel decided someone hadn't had enough, she straddled them and tipped more down their throat as they gagged.

'Come *onnnn*, Ceri!' Rachel whined as the pretty, dark-haired girl spluttered, tears streaming down her cheeks.

Lacy had seen enough.

'Er, new girl,' Rachel shouted as Lacy attempted to slip out of the kitchen unnoticed. 'Where do you think you're going?'

'I'm not really a big drinker,' Lacy said apologetically, hoping Rachel would see that she was too boring to bother paying any attention to.

But Rachel was like a dog with a bone – a small, yappy little terrier who was coming at Lacy as though she smelled blood. 'That will soon change!' she laughed, gripping onto Lacy's arm as she brought the spit-laced bottle up to her lips.

'Ew, no!' Lacy objected, pushing the bottle aside.

But Rachel held her tighter and shoved the bottle into Lacy's lips, banging the glass against her teeth. *This is ridiculous,* Lacy thought as she wrestled with the small but terrifyingly persistent girl.

She registered the frantic chanting of the rest of the staff as they banged on the counters. 'Drink, drink, drink!'

It would be easier, she mused, as she bobbed and ducked, desperately trying to get away from the bottle, to just take a sip.

But she didn't drink. Not only was binge drinking uncultured, it was *dangerous*. If the others knew what could happen, what it could lead to…then they'd understand.

And she'd told Rachel no – she'd said *no*.

'I said NO!' Lacy screamed. She lashed out and backhanded the bottle across the kitchen. Lee only just managed to avoid the missile, ducking as it sailed past his head and into the wall, where it left a dent in the plasterboard before sloshing its innards over the kitchen counter. Lee rescued the upended bottle, then clutched his baseball cap as though he were more concerned about it than he was his skull.

The other staff stared at her in shocked silence, smirks tugging at their lips. Lacy gulped and glanced at Rachel, who stared up at her with such unbridled hatred that Lacy wondered if she was about to become the park's second murder victim.

'All right, guys,' a voice called over the thumping bass. 'Did you start without me?'

Dylan was in the doorway, beaming cheerfully, oblivious to the tension in the room.

His appearance had the benefit of distracting Rachel. 'Dylaaaaan,' she drawled, and Lacy noticed her stand a little straighter and plump her lips. Clearly, Lacy wasn't the only one Dylan's good looks had an instant effect on.

Lacy took her chance to escape and wrenched her arm away from Rachel. She scurried out of the room, avoiding the eyes of the other staff, especially Dylan. But she didn't miss the concerned look he gave her as Rachel pressed a beer into his hand.

Wiping away the slimy residue the bottle had left on her face, she marched away from the pounding music and shrieking laughter that had erupted in the kitchen.

Two months, she told herself. Two months until she could go to Paris and find Winter.

The wind hit her as she yanked the door to the dorm block open. It felt good after the stifling atmosphere of the kitchen, and she greedily sucked the air into her lungs. She kept walking, embarrassment rippling through her body and powering her legs. It was dusk, and the fading light made the park look colourless. She could see the sea just beyond the cliff edge, reaching out to the flat horizon.

She walked towards it, wanting to focus on something far away from here. Dorm Block B – the empty staff accommodation block – sat between her and the cliff, and she cast a wary glance at it, then paused.

It was identical to the one she had just come from, but just like the previous day, something about it drew Lacy in with a strange, magnetic pull while simultaneously making her want to sprint in the opposite direction. She wrapped her arms around herself, already regretting fleeing the dorm without a coat.

The windows were black and empty, and many of them were broken. Lacy wondered whether the staff parties ever made their way into the abandoned dorm. She could see Rachel as someone who liked to smash things up after a drink, or at least encourage others to.

There were filthy mattresses piled up against the windows in some of the rooms and Lacy wrinkled her nose in disgust. There was nothing to stop the park guests from wandering over to this side of the park. Surely the management would be keen to demolish such an eyesore.

But if they were never here, maybe they didn't even know how bad it was. Marc had told her how money-obsessed they were – it was probably cheaper to let the building gradually disintegrate. From the looks of it, the block the staff were living in wouldn't be far behind.

She shivered and willed her feet to get moving again. But as her eyes travelled over one of the few intact windows, her heart stalled violently in her chest.

There was someone inside the abandoned dorm, staring out at her through the dirty glass.

CHAPTER 6

Lacy was too far away to make out the face clearly, but she could see that their skin was deathly pale, their eyes dark and hooded. She stepped forwards to get a closer look, squinting through the dim evening light. Who the hell was hanging out in the abandoned dorm, their face pressed against the grimy glass as though they couldn't get out?

Something landed softly on her shoulder. Lacy's gasp turned into a scream as she spun and found someone standing close to her, their face obscured by a black hood.

Lacy staggered backwards, stumbling over the uneven ground.

'Whoa!' the figure said, holding out their hands as Lacy opened her mouth to scream again. 'Jesus, stop freaking out!'

They pulled their hood down, revealing a teenager, not the grim reaper after all. Lacy's terror was quickly replaced by embarrassment, and she tried to regain her composure as she took in the person before her.

They wore an oversized black hoodie, but Lacy could see the tiny black shorts poking out from beneath it, confirming that they were yet another member of staff. They had piercings running over the rim of one ear and an edgy undercut that perfectly complemented their smudged black eyeliner. Lacy noted a tattoo snaking out of their sleeve and over the dark-brown skin of their wrist.

A grin danced at the corner of their lips, and Lacy bristled. Yet another person laughing at her.

'You cool now?' they asked. 'Or do you need to get another scream out of your system?'

Lacy scowled before remembering why she had been so tense in the first place. She turned back to look at the abandoned dorm, but the figure at the window was gone.

'I'm Chan,' they said brightly, unperturbed by Lacy's lack of response. 'You're the new recruit, right?'

'Lacy,' she replied distractedly, her eyes still roaming the abandoned dorm, wondering where the person could have gone.

'It's my first season too,' Chan said, and Lacy was surprised by how friendly they were. They looked like the kind of person you wouldn't mess with – although Rachel looked like a Disney princess, so maybe first impressions weren't everything. 'I work at the bar, so I'm back late most nights. I don't mind, though. I get to sleep all day.'

'Hmm,' Lacy replied, barely registering a word. She narrowed her eyes as a cold gust of wind hurtled towards them from the coast.

'How are you finding it?' Chan asked. 'Have you met all the others yet?'

Lacy sighed. Whoever had been staring at her must have retreated into the depths of the building.

'Yes, I've met them,' she replied tersely as she realised Chan was still waiting for a response. 'And they're exactly what I expected.'

Chan made a soft, throaty noise. 'Oh yeah, and what's that, then?'

Lacy finally turned her attention to Chan and decided to swallow the words that had been forming on her tongue. She already had Rachel after her blood. She didn't need to make another enemy in Chan. 'Nothing. Never mind.'

Chan raised their eyebrows as though they knew exactly what Lacy was really thinking. That the other staff were scum, that they were beneath her.

'You not joining in?' Chan asked, nodding towards their block. The music was still blasting out of the kitchen, and Lacy shuddered at the memory of the bottle being forced against her lips.

'No. It's not exactly my scene.' She jutted her chin flippantly, hoping she came across as above it all, and not like a girl who had just run away from a party like it was on fire.

She'd promised herself that this job was just a means to an end and the people she met here didn't matter. But already she'd managed to make herself look like a complete fool in front of most of the staff. She thought of Dylan's cheery face as he'd arrived, ready to enjoy the *fun* she was so desperate to escape.

If she was going to make it in Paris, she really needed to work on her personality transplant. It clearly wasn't convincing anyone.

'Is there anyone staying in there?' Lacy asked abruptly, gesturing towards the abandoned dorms.

Chan looked puzzled. 'Nah – it's falling apart. And there

aren't even enough staff this year to fill our block. They'd put people in the top floor before they risked opening that one back up.'

Lacy turned to look at the dark windows of the upper floor of their accommodation, her skin crawling at the thought of the dark corridor and empty rooms. The kitchen on the ground floor was brightly lit, and she could see silhouettes of the staff passing back and forth. She wondered if Dylan had joined in with the drinking games.

'Losers,' she muttered.

'Huh?' Chan grunted.

Shit. Had she said that out loud?

'Nothing,' Lacy said, clearing her throat. 'Just…this isn't exactly the kind of place I would choose to spend time at, or the kind of people I'd choose to be around.'

Chan snorted, before pulling the hoodie back over their head. 'I see.'

Lacy clenched her teeth together as she noticed the unimpressed expression on Chan's face. She'd managed to make Chan hate her within two minutes of meeting her. Quite possibly a new personal record. Though she'd done fairly well with Marc too, in that respect.

'I saw someone,' Lacy said, unable to bear the silent dislike coming off Chan any longer. She pointed towards the window from where the person had stared out at her. 'In there.'

Chan paused and turned to follow Lacy's finger. 'You can't have—'

'I did,' Lacy insisted. 'They were in that room, right there.'

She pointed again. It was the same room as hers, she realised with a shiver – the fourth room from the kitchen.

Chan stared thoughtfully at the abandoned dorm, dark eyes looking dramatic and intense with the hood casting a shadow over them. Chan possessed the kind of effortless coolness Lacy could only dream of.

'It could be…' Chan started to say, before reconsidering. 'No, it couldn't be.'

'What?' Lacy said sharply.

Chan sighed, running a hand over the shaved hair above their neck. 'I dunno if I'm supposed to tell you this – it's not exactly public knowledge.'

'Tell me what?' Lacy pressed. She didn't understand why, but she wanted to know everything there was to know about the abandoned dorm block.

'Well…' Chan said reluctantly. 'A while ago, some staff died.' They raised a finger to mirror Lacy's, pointing at the abandoned building. 'In there.'

Lacy snapped her gaze back to the black wood of the abandoned block. Her imagination fired off various possibilities – had a party got out of hand? Alcohol poisoning? Some kind of stupid dare gone wrong?

'It's still a bit of a mystery,' Chan continued. 'I don't really know the details, just that…'

Lacy spun to face them. 'What?' she demanded.

Chan grimaced. 'You sure you want to hear this?'

'Yes! Tell me.'

'Well…they were found in their beds—'

'They died in their sleep?' Lacy interrupted. Maybe it was carbon monoxide poisoning?

'Er, kind of, I guess.'

Lacy sighed, frustrated by Chan's vagueness.

'But, well. They'd been decapitated.'

What?

'How...?' Lacy spluttered, unsure where to start. 'When did this happen? How many of them? Who did it? How is it possible I didn't know about this?'

Chan shifted uncomfortably, as though regretting telling Lacy anything. 'I think it was, like, ten years ago or something. And there were only two of them,' they said, implying it wasn't such a big deal after all. 'And they caught the guy. He was a guest here.'

Lacy's mind whirred as she tried to keep up. 'A guest murdered two staff members, and the park stayed open?'

What *was* with this place? Not only had everything carried on as normal after a guest was found dead under his caravan, but now *this*?

'Like I said, it wasn't exactly public knowledge.' Chan shrugged one shoulder.

Lacy wanted to shake Chan but didn't dare. Chan was tattooed, worked at a bar and would probably put Lacy on her arse before she'd even laid a finger on them.

'How can the brutal murder of two teenagers not be made public knowledge?' she asked, trying to keep her voice measured.

'Money,' Chan said lightly. 'The owners of this place are a big deal. They have loads of sites across the UK, but this is their biggest money-maker. Something about the location.' Chan gestured vaguely towards the ocean. 'I guess they paid the right people to keep it all hush-hush. It's not something people like to talk about now, either. So, you know – don't go reminding the other staff about it, yeah?'

Lacy nodded absently as she stared at the abandoned dorm with this new knowledge. Something had happened in there. Something more awful than she could comprehend. And they were living right next to it, carrying on as though there was nothing to worry about other than playing drinking games.

'Anyway, night!' Chan said suddenly, before casually walking away from Lacy, hands thrust into the depths of their huge black hoodie.

Lacy gawped after them. Was she the only one who was horribly disturbed by the fact two teenagers had been slaughtered in their beds just metres away from here? She watched Chan mooch towards the staff accommodation, furious with them for filling her head with the grisly story and then abandoning her to her morbid thoughts. Thoughts that centred on the face that had stared out at her from the window.

CHAPTER 7

'Shut up!' Lacy screamed into her pillow. The sound was swallowed by the lumpy material, not that anyone would have heard it if she'd bellowed into the corridor.

It was 9 p.m., and the party in the kitchen was already in full swing. This was the fifth night in a row now. Lacy still just couldn't understand the appeal of drinking, listening to crap music and crap banter and feeling awful the next day. Then repeating it again until the summer had passed in a blur of hangovers.

Despite managing to avoid the parties, she was exhausted. Sleep was difficult when the bass from the music made the walls vibrate, and she was woken frequently by slamming doors, pounding feet and shrill laughter. Working as a lifeguard had also been surprisingly tiring, even though she barely had to do anything, or even leave her chair, for her entire shift. No, it was avoiding Dylan's magnetism that was wearing her out.

She sighed and rolled over on her bed. Part of her yearned to flirt with him – he was the first boy she'd ever felt genuinely comfortable around. He was so…simple. Kind, uncomplicated, and he permanently wore a placid, open expression that made

Lacy sure he didn't have a hidden agenda or even know what one was.

But seeing him that night with beer in hand, relaxed and ready to join the party, reminded her how different they were.

She and Cal had been different too, but she'd ignored the warning signs – the great flashing red lights and sirens. And look how that had turned out.

Lacy groaned. They'd been listening to this awful song on repeat for the last fifteen minutes. There was no way she was going to be able to sleep until they shut up.

She reached for her camera, lovingly running her fingers over the cold black exterior. She'd exhausted all the options in her room. There was nothing she could think of to photograph in here that would capture the essence of the assignment. *Movement.*

What she needed to do was get outside and find her inspiration.

She'd only really left the dorm to walk to the pool and back since Chan had told her about the murders in the abandoned block. And even then, she'd made sure she left at the same time as another group, trailing behind so she didn't have to make conversation, but close enough that they'd notice if someone tried to kill her.

She knew it was ridiculous – the staff members had been killed ten years ago. But she couldn't shake the feeling of something being…off.

She never felt quite alone.

She'd tried to convince herself that it was her imagination going into overdrive and researched the murders to try to put her mind at rest. Perhaps seeing the cold hard facts of the case would stop her from thinking of the worst possible things. But Chan had been right – the park had done an excellent job of hushing the deaths up, and Lacy hadn't found a single piece of information online. There had been plenty of other scandals though – food hygiene failings, the serving of alcohol to minors, petty theft from caravans. And, apparently, the park was one of the most haunted places in North Wales, not that Lacy paid any attention to that.

Why would anyone be interested in ridiculous ghost stories when there was a very real murder just five days ago to add to the list of controversies at Bae Peryg?

Carl Jones had been thirty years old, married but childless. There wasn't much more to the story than Lacy already knew. His poor wife had found him after he'd been hit over the head and stashed beneath his own caravan by another guest he'd got in a fight with at the bar. Lacy wondered if Chan had seen anything that night but wasn't about to ask. She didn't want to be told another story that would scar her for life.

The killer, another guy in his thirties, with a shaved head and no neck, insisted he was innocent. But they always did, didn't they? It was an open and shut case, hence the lack of ongoing police presence at the park.

Lacy wondered if the police had left as quickly when the two teenagers were killed ten years previously.

A crash from the kitchen shocked Lacy out of her musings. Perhaps Rachel was antagonising someone else into throwing bottles.

She frowned. She could hear another noise, something beneath the music and the shouts from the kitchen. Something coming from outside her window.

She silently swung her legs off the bed and stared at the sliver of grey sky outside, framed by the tattered curtains. The wind rattled the thin glass urgently. Had that been what she'd heard?

Lacy's skin prickled. All she could see was the reflection of the lightbulb that hung from her ceiling. But if there was anyone out there, they'd be able to see her.

She stood abruptly and stepped towards the window, whipping the curtain back and pressing her face close to the grimy glass. There was no one there, but as she looked from left to right, a movement caught her eye.

A shadowy something darting around the corner of the abandoned block.

She stared, motionless, waiting.

But nothing else moved. The park was quiet and empty, the only signs of life coming from the mayhem in the kitchen. She shook her head, annoyed with her overactive imagination. There was nobody out there, nothing to be afraid of.

The previous night, some little brats had ventured over from the caravans and thrown rocks at the staff dorm block. They'd scarpered after Rachel had screamed at them. They clearly didn't recognise her as the bouncing bunny they frolicked with in the daytime.

Aside from that, Lacy barely saw the guests. Well, apart from the endless hours she spent staring at them as they screamed and splashed in the water. They kept to their area, and the staff kept to theirs. And despite the derelict creepiness of this side of the park, Lacy suspected it would be preferable to the chaos of the central bar area.

She gazed out of her bedroom window. There was something

intriguing about the fading light outside and the way it made the shadows of the ramshackle caravans warp across the ground. Lacy looked at her camera where it sat nestled in the duvet.

Sod it, she was going out. She would find her inspiration if it killed her.

She hoped it wouldn't *actually* kill her, though. As serious as she was about her art, she wasn't ready to become a martyr for it. Not yet. She shrugged on her coat over her pyjamas as she walked down the corridor. She wanted to go to the clifftop and catch the dusky colours of the sky before darkness fell completely.

But the abandoned dorm lay between her and the coast, daring her to walk past it. She thought of the face she'd seen in the window, which her imagination had merged with the decapitation story and turned into something twisted and terrifying.

She did a one-eighty and headed in the opposite direction. She'd take the scenic route.

The empty, run-down caravans flanked her as she walked, and she tried not to look at the windows too closely, not wanting to conjure up another image of a pale face staring out at her. It was going to take her a while, she realised, to get to the clifftop and avoid the dorms entirely. She wasn't sure which dorm presented the bigger threat – the abandoned dorm with its history of murder, or the staff dorm with, well, Rachel.

She bowed her head against the wind and tried to convince herself that it just added to the atmosphere, and that walks in this kind of moody weather were the kind of thing artists did to allow their true genius to emerge.

She tried to convince herself that she wasn't freezing and miserable.

She thought of Winter and her resolve finally hardened. This was all for her, so they could be reunited. Winter was in Paris, living the life they'd dreamed of.

Her eyes filled suddenly with tears and she blinked rapidly. *Why* hadn't Winter waited? Why hadn't she been in touch? She was quirky, unpredictable, downright weird even. But all the same, she must know that her silence was torturing Lacy.

Lacy pulled her phone out of her pocket. She still took it everywhere out of habit, despite the lack of signal on this side of the park. She opened her and Winter's chat, wanting to see the last words Winter had messaged her before Lacy's endless attempts to get in touch. It had been something inane about running late for meeting Lacy in town, back when Winter had cared enough to let Lacy know about that kind of thing.

Lacy gasped and stopped dead, digesting the words on the screen.

A message. From Winter.

Lacy, I need—

But Lacy didn't manage to read the rest of the message, as the text warped into meaningless symbols in front of her eyes. And then they disappeared entirely, replaced by two words:

Media Corrupted

'What?' Lacy gasped, staring at her phone in astonishment. There had been a message, an actual *message* from Winter. She hadn't even had the chance to see when it had been sent before it disappeared, but she was sure she hadn't felt her phone vibrate in her pocket. And now it was gone, replaced by some useless error message.

She typed out a message, her hands shaking violently.

Are you OK?

She pressed send and frowned. Her message disappeared as though it had never been written at all.

She tried again.

Where are you?

The same thing happened, and Lacy groaned with frustration. There was still no signal out here. It had to be some kind of weird glitch, her messages getting swallowed by the phone, or something.

A door slammed to her left, wrenching her attention away from her phone. She turned to see a haggard-looking man emerge from one of the caravans. There was no car parked outside, and the caravan looked as decrepit as its neighbours.

He was wearing an off-white vest with what looked like baked-bean juice splattered down the front and across his pot belly. He stared back at her, his gnarled hands limp by his side, and his face contorted with suspicion, as though *she* were the creepy one in this situation.

He couldn't be staying in there, surely. The door had partly broken off its hinges, and there were black bin bags full of rubbish piled around the perimeter of the caravan. Could he have broken in and be squatting?

'Piss off!' he barked, making Lacy yelp with fright.

She didn't need to be told twice and promptly pissed off. He watched her leave, standing motionless until she'd rounded the corner and out of his line of sight.

Lacy shuddered with her entire body. Did the park management know there was some kind of grouchy vagrant living in one of their derelict caravans? Would they even care if they did? Given what she knew of them so far, she seriously doubted it.

The realisation that there was absolutely nothing stopping people like that man wandering into the staff accommodation made her stumble over a pothole as she hurried away.

The cliff finally came into view, and Lacy noted gratefully that the dorms were a comfortable distance away. She'd tell Andy about the old man the next day, she decided. Andy may be a little corruptible by Rachel's bad influence, but he'd listen to Lacy, she was sure of it. He'd told her to come to her with any problem, no matter what, hadn't he?

The wind stung her cheeks as she approached the edge of the cliff. There was no fence, no sign, no warning that the land was about to give way into a precipice that would claim the life of anyone who stepped over it.

Lacy crept closer, obeying the irresistible tug to see just how high up she was. The cliff fell away sharply, and jagged rocks emerged from the black water below as it crashed against the shore.

If she could get a shot of the waves breaking against the cliff, would that fulfil the assignment brief? The way the water churned and swirled far below was making her feel dizzy, as though she might tip forwards and over the edge.

She twitched, shaking herself out of her trance. Even if she captured the most stunning shot the world had ever seen, it wouldn't do her any good to have the evidence lost to the Irish Sea.

She sniffed. There was a rank, rotten smell on the breeze – the same stench she'd caught wind of before but suddenly intensified. Her nose wrinkled in disgust as she thought of sewage pipes leading into the ocean. But shit-pipes or no, she still wanted to get closer to the sea, and so she glanced along the clifftop, wondering if there was a way down to the beach. And then she saw them.

Someone was standing on the edge of the cliff, a hundred metres or so from Lacy. They were staring out to sea, just as she had been moments before. Dark hair framed their head, although from this distance, it was impossible to see their face.

But Lacy could tell they were looking directly at her when they turned their head. And she could tell they were aiming at her when they raised their finger and pointed.

CHAPTER 8

Lacy willed her eyes to focus and make out the features of the figure standing by the cliff edge, but the last dregs of daylight were rapidly disappearing, making it impossible to see clearly.

Their finger was still raised, stark white against the dark material of their shapeless clothes. What if...what if they weren't pointing at Lacy but at something else, something...?

She turned slowly to look behind her, filled with a sudden dread that she wasn't as alone as she felt.

Lacy inhaled so sharply she nearly choked.

Dylan stood beside her, gazing out at the ocean with his hands in his pockets. 'Beautiful, isn't it?' he said calmly, before noticing her face, which was contorted with a mash-up of fear and fury.

'Are you OK?' he asked, his serene expression morphing into mortification. 'Oh god, did I scare you? I'm so sorry. I thought you knew I was here.'

Lacy took a few gasping breaths to replenish the oxygen that had abandoned her. How had Dylan managed to appear right next to her without her noticing? Had she been that distracted by...?

The figure. She turned to look back down the bay towards where they had stood. But the clifftop was empty. She and Dylan were alone.

She shivered and shoved her hands into her pockets. It had just been a guest who'd strayed away from the main section of the park. That was all.

'What are you doing out here?' she asked, trying to be civil despite the way her mind kept tugging her back to the figure. Where had they gone? And how had they vanished so quickly?

Had they even been there at all?

'Just, you know, going for a walk.'

Lacy raised an eyebrow sceptically.

'OK, I followed you.'

Lacy let her face tell him what she thought about being stalked through the caravan park at night.

'I'm sorry,' Dylan said yet again. He ran his hand through his brown hair, fluffing it up adorably. 'I saw you leave your room and, I don't know…I just wanted to check you were OK. This side of the park is so empty. It made me worry to think of you wandering around on your own.'

Lacy shivered and shrank into her coat. Did Dylan know about the two dead employees? She swallowed the question. She didn't want to think about them.

'I saw you have a run-in with Gary,' Dylan said.

'Gary?' Lacy replied, scrunching up her face in confusion. 'Wait, the terrifying old guy in the caravan? He's called *Gary*?'

Dylan nodded seriously. 'He's a regular. He's been coming here on his holidays for years. Always stays in the same caravan, even though it's falling apart. It's where he used to come with his wife. He likes to feel close to her – well, to somewhere he has happy memories with her.'

Lacy gawped at Dylan. Who knew bean-juice man had so much depth.

'Wow,' she said sombrely, guilt colouring her cheeks. She'd judged and dismissed him within seconds of seeing him. Though, to be fair, he had told her to piss off within seconds of seeing *her*.

'What are *you* doing out here?' Dylan asked, suddenly turning his attention away from the sea and towards her, his gaze on the camera hung around her neck. 'Taking photos?'

Lacy's blush deepened. She wasn't used to people taking an interest in her work. Her parents tried, but they didn't ask the right questions, and it was clear they didn't really get it. Winter had advised her to stop sharing it with them – they were too common to appreciate the finer things in life. What could a nurse and a bus driver understand about culture?

So Lacy had listened to her sister and closed herself off to everyone – except Winter, of course. It hadn't been difficult. Ali and the others would have ridiculed her to the point of tears if they'd known about her obsession with photography. But it now meant that someone asking questions made her feel awkward and self-conscious. She felt like an impostor, a fraud.

'Yeah,' she said, her attempted photoshoot seeming ridiculous now that it was practically dark. But Dylan nodded as though he understood perfectly.

'You must be so excited for Paris,' he suggested. 'I thought you were French when I first saw you, you know.'

Lacy fought to stop her joy from showing on her face. All her hard work had paid off – the style, the poise, the studying of everything French.

Winter would be proud.

They stood side by side, staring out towards the horizon, and Lacy released the tension she'd been feeling since arriving at the park.

Then Dylan brought it rushing back.

'Has anyone told you the ghost story of this place?'

Lacy closed her eyes. Of *course* there was a ghost story linked to the murders.

But Dylan's story went back even further than ten years previously.

'The cove got its name because of how dangerous it was for passing boats,' Dylan began, his North Welsh accent making the story more captivating. 'Bae Peryg, or Peril Bay in English. There are loads of old shipwrecks beneath the water.' He pointed out towards the sharp rocks protruding from the black waves, and Lacy's skin crawled as she pictured the tombs hidden below.

'Two hundred years ago, there was a local girl called Catrin Roberts. She was known in these parts for being a beauty with porcelain skin and masses of dark hair, and she had a kind heart too – always helping people in need,' Dylan continued in a pained way that made it seem like he had known this girl personally. 'Then one day, she saved some sailors who got washed ashore, welcomed them into her home and nursed them back to health. They returned her favour by…' He paused and looked nervously at Lacy. 'Well, they killed her.'

Lacy willed herself to stay calm.

'Her fiancé returned from working on their farm to find her headless body outside the front door of their home.'

Lacy flinched as the image of yet another headless body

flashed violently in front of her eyes. For god's sake, what was it with this place?

Dylan at least had the decency to look more disturbed by the Catrin Robert's story than Chan had by the staff members who'd died in the same gruesome way. In fact, he looked utterly wretched, and Lacy was startled to see that his eyes were wet as he gazed towards the horizon. 'He vowed he would avenge Catrin,' he said, his voice thick with emotion. 'But the sailors had already fled. He set out to sea to track them down and the villagers never saw him again.'

He let out a sorrowful sigh, and Lacy had to resist reaching out to hold his hand. She'd never met someone who wore their heart on their sleeve like Dylan did. The story of Catrin Roberts and her devastated fiancé seemed to genuinely upset him.

'It's said Catrin still wanders these cliffs today, searching for her lost love.'

'What?' Lacy said sharply.

Dylan pulled his gaze away from the horizon to look at her curiously.

'I thought I saw…' she started, but the intense look on Dylan's face made her hesitate.

'You saw something?' he asked, nodding at her to continue. 'Where?'

'Nothing,' Lacy said, shaking her head. 'Never mind.'

She noticed Dylan sag with disappointment. He'd told her he was local – maybe the legend of Catrin Roberts was a big deal around here. Maybe people genuinely believed her restless spirit still wandered the cliffs, desperate to be reunited with her fiancé.

But Lacy wasn't going to voice it – the idea that she'd seen a two-century-old ghost pointing at her. It was ridiculous, pathetic. Winter, after getting over her phase of exploring the occult, had insisted that anyone who believed in the paranormal was a simpleton with a low IQ.

Lacy peered at Dylan. Sweet Dylan, with his farmer's tan and his muscles and his open, honest face. She suspected that he would believe just about anything he was told.

Well, not Lacy. She was an intelligent person who absolutely did not believe in ghosts.

CHAPTER 9

Lacy stretched her pale legs out beneath the sun umbrella. She and Dylan were covering lifeguard duty at the beach for the first time, and she was glad to be out of the claustrophobic pool house. The sun had finally agreed that it was in fact summer and had thrown its energy into warming the pebbly sand and the bodies of the holidaymakers.

Despite the balmy weather, the beach was shrouded in a strange, shifting mist that seemed to rise upwards, out of the sand. Lacy had been disturbed by it at first, until Dylan explained that it was just water left over from the high tide evaporating. It gave the air a dense, cloying feeling, and the humidity was doing nothing for Lacy's hair.

But she found the more time she spent with Dylan, the less self-conscious she became. She'd already convinced him she was an elegant, potentially French sophisticate without even having to try too hard. And he was so easy-going and non-judgemental that concerns about her frizzy hair and lack of make-up seemed increasingly unimportant.

Out here, surrounded by sunlight and laughter, the haunting stories of the park's past felt like a distant memory. A week had passed since Dylan had told her about Catrin Roberts, and Lacy hadn't seen anything else that had made her question the safety of the park – or her own sanity.

Lacy sighed, enjoying the heat. She'd always been a sun worshipper. But after Winter had insisted a tan made people look tacky, she was careful to keep her skin hidden. Dylan clearly didn't have any such issue and his bronze body glistened with sweat. Lacy didn't miss the fact that he carefully reapplied his sun cream every hour without fail and frequently readjusted the umbrella to ensure she was always shielded.

Like her ex, Cal, Dylan wasn't the arty type she'd sworn was right for her. But that was where the similarities ended. She snorted at the thought of Cal caring, or even noticing, that her shade had moved.

She closed her eyes. A guilty, swooping sensation gripped her stomach every time she thought badly of Cal.

'Drink?' Dylan asked, and Lacy smiled gratefully at him. 'Black coffee, no sugar, right?'

Lacy nodded. Was there anything Dylan didn't notice?

'Just, um, keep an eye out when I'm gone, yeah?' He smiled as though embarrassed at having to remind her they were at work. But he had a point – she was treating this shift like a holiday when, in reality, there was potentially much more need for lifeguards out here than by the pool. The mist, in particular, was a hazard. Dylan had explained how much harder it would be to spot people in trouble through the thick air.

She nodded and sat up straighter, wanting to reassure him that no one would die on her watch. As he left, she realised that she would prefer something cold and sweet, like one of the Slush Puppies half the children on the beach seemed to be clutching.

But she'd been training herself to like coffee the way the French drank it. And if she closed her eyes and tried not to think about it, she could almost tolerate the bitter tar-like beverage now.

She cast an eye towards the ocean and reasoned that she could really do with the caffeine hit after all. She was feeling comfortably drowsy, which possibly wasn't the best state for a lifeguard to be in. She knew she was just there for show, though. It wasn't like she was expected to actually save anyone. She'd been given no training and would likely need rescuing herself if she entered the water.

Besides, the holiday park guests were doing just fine looking after themselves. She watched them with detached curiosity as they built sandcastles, licked ice creams and paddled in the gentle surf. This part of the beach was accessible via a sloping wooden walkway – a far cry from the sheer cliffs that plummeted into the water by the staff accommodation.

She stifled a yawn with the back of her hand and looked forwards to Dylan's return. Maybe a summer of flirting wasn't such a bad thing.

It wasn't like Winter would ever find out.

Her sister was still untraceable, but Lacy knew exactly what she would say about Dylan, and it wouldn't be kind. Winter had never met Cal either, but she would have smugly insisted that Lacy should have known better when it all came crashing down in the most awful way imaginable.

Her good mood soured, Lacy huffed and looked for a distraction. The beach was bustling, filled with happy family sounds and squawking seagulls looking for an opportunity to steal a sandwich. Her gaze travelled down towards the cliffs and the cove that gave the park its name.

It didn't look so perilous today, the calm waves lapping lazily against the rocks protruding from the water. But Lacy couldn't help her mind wandering to Catrin Roberts and her tragic story. She pictured the young woman beckoning the struggling sailors up the beach, helping them to safety before…

Lacy swallowed, sickened by the thought of their betrayal. How scared must she have been when she realised her kind gesture had been abused in the worst possible way. No wonder Dylan had been so affected by the story, Lacy thought, as she realised she was close to tears herself. Just thinking of Catrin walking towards the ocean, her long skirts trailing across the damp sand beneath her feet, made Lacy feel like she'd known the murdered woman.

Like she was still here, somehow…

Lacy sat up fully, squinting through the thick air, sure she'd seen something in the distance. *There* – down the beach, moving slowly through the shifting mist.

A woman. A woman with long, dark hair, walking so slowly it was hard to tell she was moving at all. Nothing strange about that, Lacy tried to tell herself. Just another holidaymaker enjoying the beach.

Only, what holidaymaker from this century would be wearing a full-length skirt on a hot July day? And why were people running so close to her as she made her slow journey away from the water and towards the looming cliffs, frolicking and kicking balls around her as though they couldn't see the woman, as though she wasn't there at all?

The sweat on the back of Lacy's neck cooled as if an icy wind had swept in from behind her. She stared hard at the woman, trying not to blink in case she lost sight of her.

Lacy frowned as she considered getting off her chair to find out if the woman was in fact a two-hundred-year-old ghost, the product of her imagination, or maybe just an eccentric tourist. But a sound caught her attention – something beneath the relaxed chatter from nearby beach dwellers. Something edged with fear.

She reluctantly turned her attention away from the woman in the distance. The mist was less dense here, and Lacy scanned the crowds, searching for the source of the noise. There, a man, shouting and waving. Waving at Lacy.

Lacy stood, staring towards the sea where the man was gesturing. She reached over to Dylan's empty chair and the binoculars he'd left there. Feeling ridiculous, she brought them to her eyes and scoured the horizon.

It took her a moment to find the disturbance, but when she did, the remaining warmth leeched out of her bones.

A child was in the sea, bobbing above the surface only to disappear beneath the waves over and over again. A child was drowning on Lacy's watch.

CHAPTER 10

'Shit,' she breathed, the binoculars shaking as she held them to her eyes. For a fleeting moment, Lacy considered turning her gaze to the left, cursing herself for not using the binoculars earlier to get a better look at the woman in the mist. But then the man bellowed for help again, and before she'd considered what she should do, Lacy dropped the binoculars and started sprinting towards the shoreline.

She screamed at oblivious holidaymakers to get out the way as she ran, jumping over sunbathing bodies and ploughing through sandcastles. She had no clue how to save someone struggling in water. Christ, why did this have to happen *now*, when Dylan – the one person who would actually be useful in this situation – was gone?

She felt the attention of the guests on her as she entered the ocean, still wearing her green polo shirt and black shorts. She awkwardly leaped over the waves until she was deep enough to swim and gasped as the water swept over her head. The cold of it took her breath away. The day may have reached a toasty twenty degrees, but it was still the Irish Sea. And it *smelled*. God, it was that awful, sweetly rotting smell again.

Lacy's entire body rippled with repulsion at the thought of raw sewage being pumped through pipes directly into the ocean.

She'd left the floaty thing back on her chair, she realised as she struggled through the water. She really was the worst lifeguard.

But she was the only chance the kid had. She could tell from looking at him through the binoculars that he was in serious trouble. When he'd dipped below the surface, he'd stayed down for a little longer each time.

She paused, her lungs aching as she trod water. She turned a circle, trying to get her bearings. Where was he? She'd kept him in her sights the entire sprint down to the ocean, but now that she was in the water, she'd lost him. She spotted the man who had alerted her in the first place, still standing on the beach, pointing urgently to Lacy's right.

There was the boy. Still floating, just.

She pushed forwards, wishing she was back on the shore shouting support for Dylan as he powered athletically through the surf. She should be the one waiting with the towel, not the one responsible for saving a child's life.

Sea water rushed into her open mouth as she took a gulp of air, and she choked, gagging as her throat constricted and forced the water away from her lungs. The salt burned.

She had to keep going.

She could see the boy now, see the panic on his face as he feebly slapped the water as though searching for something to hold on to.

Just a few more metres and she'd be there. Then what she'd do, she had no idea. She was exhausted herself, and the kid looked pretty big. She wasn't sure she'd have the energy to drag him back to shore.

A wave broke over her head and she was suddenly underwater. She circled her arms upwards, towards the surface, towards air. But something stopped her.

She opened her eyes in terror, and the saltwater stung horribly. There was something gripping her ankle. Something that felt like a hand.

Lacy thrashed, her legs kicking wildly against the vice-like grip that made her think of Rachel's bony little fingers on her arm. But the hold on her leg was relentless, and as she fought, it tugged her deeper into the depths of the ocean.

Lacy's arms spiralled uselessly as she tried to swim upwards. She kicked out at whatever was pulling her down, away from the light and the air her lungs so desperately screamed for.

The sun was getting further away, and the water around her darkened. Bubbles of air escaped her lips and floated upwards. Her eyes widened as a black shape moved quickly over the surface above her head. A boat.

A boat was there to save the boy. Did the driver know she was beneath it, that she now needed saving too?

The temptation to breathe sea water into her throbbing chest was becoming unbearable. She was going to die, and no one would even know she was there.

And then, just as suddenly as it had seized her, the grip around her ankle was gone.

Lacy found a last ebb of strength and kicked upwards. But the edges of her vision were blackening, turning the light from the sun into a narrow beam of feeble light. Was she really going to drown, just inches beneath the surface?

She realised with slow horror that she was starting to sink again. Gravity was winning, forcing her back down into the depths.

A hand plunged into the water beside her and grasped her forearm, wrenching her upwards, towards the surface. Her chest made an agonised groaning sound as oxygen flooded her lungs, burning them as they expanded.

She blinked her stinging eyes and tried to focus on the owner of the hand that had saved her life. Their outline was surrounded by a halo of sunlight, casting their face into shadow.

Dylan.

He heaved her up out of the water and onto the deck of the speedboat. She lay on her side, her body trembling with exhaustion, before she rolled over to spew saltwater onto the floor.

She dully noticed a little boy sat huddled beneath a towel, his face a pallid green.

Lacy closed her eyes. The child was safe.

Dylan's strong hands pulled her up into a sitting position, and her head lolled heavily against her chest. She just wanted to sleep, so why was he holding her up and gently tapping her cheeks, his piercing blue eyes so close she could see the flecks of orange that looked like flames dancing over water?

'Lacy,' he repeated. 'Lacy, look at me.'

'Mmm,' she mumbled sluggishly.

'Can you hear me?' he asked.

Lacy nodded, before allowing herself to tip forwards and into his chest. It felt good there, pressed up against his hot, bare skin.

'Did you get me a coffee?' she slurred, and she felt Dylan's laughter shake through his chest and into her face.

The boat bobbed gently on the waves, and Lacy's stomach

clenched, warning her that she might not have finished purging the sea water out of her body.

She sat bolt upright, her temple knocking against Dylan's jaw as she remembered.

'Someone tried to kill me,' she garbled, her words still distorted as though she were talking underwater.

'Shh,' Dylan soothed, stroking her hair and trying to coax her back down onto his chest. But Lacy resisted the temptation, adrenaline coursing through her veins again as she recalled the feeling of cold, hard fingers round her ankle.

'No, really,' she insisted, her senses returning to her. 'Someone grabbed my leg and tried to drown me.'

She noticed the boy's eyes widen, but Dylan was frowning.

'Someone tried to drown you,' he repeated slowly. 'Someone who was...waiting beneath the water?'

Lacy blushed, hearing the stupidity of her words. She frantically ran through the possibilities in her mind – an evil scuba diver lurking beneath the waves, waiting for unsuspecting girls to swim past? A mermaid? The ghosts of the many sailors lost to these waters?

She remembered the woman walking solemnly away from the water and towards the cliffs, her heavy skirts trailing over the sand. Perhaps now was not the time to mention her to Dylan, who was already looking at her with a deep wrinkle of concern etched into his forehead.

She shook her head helplessly.

'Seaweed?' Dylan suggested tentatively.

'No,' Lacy said, but heard the lack of conviction in her voice. 'They *pulled* me. They tried to stop me getting to the surface, they...'

Dylan nodded earnestly, but Lacy could tell he was humouring her. She didn't blame him – she sounded like a rambling idiot who had tried to rescue a struggling child and nearly died in the process.

'I can come back with some snorkelling gear,' Dylan suggested, nodding seriously. 'I'll have a look around. Something clearly happened, and we'll find out—'

'No,' Lacy sighed, her fingers moving to her wrist. The bracelet Winter had given her was gone she realised with a pang of sorrow. It was probably lying at the bottom of the ocean now, settling among the sand and rocks, where it would remain, lost and alone.

She sank into Dylan's arms, seeking the warmth and comfort she knew she would find. 'It was just seaweed, or rubbish or something, tangled around my leg. And I was so exhausted from swimming that it pulled me down…that's all.'

She wished saying it out loud would convince her that it was the truth, but her heart continued to beat haphazardly, alerting her to a danger that felt like it had yet to pass. She offered the half-drowned boy a watery smile, but his eyes remained wide and terrified. The poor kid had come close to drowning and was now traumatised by Lacy's story. He was never going to set foot in the ocean again.

'Let's get you guys back to shore,' Dylan said gently and pulled Lacy closer to him. She wearily considered that she should probably offer the boy some comfort but imagined she had scared him worse than his own encounter with death, so kept her distance.

She felt Dylan plant a gentle kiss on the top of her head, and the warmth of it trickled down her neck and into her body.

She stayed leaning against him as he powered the speedboat back towards the shore and wished he would kiss her again, and keep kissing her until she could no longer feel the imprint of the fingers around her ankle.

CHAPTER 11

'I've got you,' Dylan said for what must have been the tenth time as they navigated their way down the perilous cliffside path, the sunset making the slate beneath their feet glow.

Lacy gratefully accepted his hand on her elbow, steadying her as her legs wobbled over the loose rocks. She still felt like she was on the boat, bobbing sickeningly in the ocean, her chest burning and the salt drying on her skin.

The tide was out, so Dylan had suggested they get out of the dorms and walk down to the sea. There was a party on the beach, and Lacy's face must have given away how she felt about joining in, because he'd assured her that he'd stay by her side the entire evening.

She'd found herself agreeing. Normally, she'd have been glad for the opportunity to have the entire dorm to herself. She might even get to bed at a sensible hour. But tonight, after the incident in the sea, she realised that being near people might be just what she needed.

Being near *Dylan,* specifically.

The prospect of snuggling close to Dylan in front of a campfire, even more specifically.

The path clearly wasn't an official path – it had probably been made by staff doing exactly what they were doing now. Lacy wouldn't even have spotted it, snaking diagonally down the cliff towards a hidden cove, if Dylan hadn't pointed it out. It wasn't *the* cove – the one with the shipwreck and the murderous sailors and the possible ghost of Catrin Roberts endlessly wandering the shores. If it had been, Lacy may not have been so quick to agree to accompany Dylan down the cliffside.

He spoke as they walked, and Lacy listened to his description of the plants, the creatures, the tides and the stories of the land, impressed by how knowledgeable he was about the area.

'So have you always lived round here?' Lacy asked as she clung to a tuft of wiry coastal grass to stop herself sliding down a patch of scree. Her camera bounced against her breastbone, adding to the permanent bruise above her heart.

Dylan stopped, put his hand on her shoulder and gently guided her gaze towards the direction he was pointing. 'That's my family's farm – the little white house just beyond those rocks.'

Lacy gawped. Even from this distance, the cottage looked idyllic. Across the bay and nestled in the hillside, it was like something out of a romantic period drama.

'And is it, like, an actual farm?' Lacy asked, wincing at her use of the word 'like'. She worked hard to banish inane, common words from her vocabulary, but they occasionally snuck in when her guard was down.

'Sheep farm,' Dylan concurred. 'Wool, mainly. Not much money in it nowadays.'

'Will you take it over one day?' Lacy asked, suddenly filled with a burning desire to know more about sheep farming. She knew Dylan went home every night instead of staying in the staff accommodation. Now that she'd seen where he lived, she understood why.

'Yes. It's been in our family for centuries. And, well, I didn't finish school. Didn't really go to school much, if I'm honest.'

Lacy raised her eyebrows in surprise. Was that even legal? She'd thought everyone had to go to school nowadays.

'So I don't exactly have a lot of options,' Dylan continued, and Lacy noticed his cheeks had reddened, as though embarrassed about his lack of education. 'But I'm fine with that – this place is my home. I can't think of anywhere else I'd rather be.'

Lacy was quiet as she digested the information. She had been desperate to escape her own hometown for as long as she could remember, so it was hard to imagine being content with where you were. Would it be so bad, she mused, to stay somewhere like this your whole life?

She paused and stared across the ocean and the grey cliffs that plunged into its depths. The sun was close to dipping below the horizon, and the water sparkled as it reflected the last warm rays of the day. She looked at Dylan's little white farmhouse and thought that, no, it wouldn't be so bad at all.

She wanted to ask Dylan more about his life, his parents, his dreams, but the sound of raised voices interrupted their conversation.

'Ceri, you're being ridiculous.'

Lacy froze and felt Dylan do the same behind her. She recognised that voice.

Rachel.

And Ceri – the striking girl with masses of dark-brown hair whom Lacy had seen in the kitchen a few times.

The path had reached the beach, but Lacy couldn't see anyone yet. Rachel and Ceri must be standing behind one of the many clusters of rocks that were usually underwater. Clearly, it was a private conversation, not that Rachel was bothering to lower her voice.

'You got drunk, you passed out, that's all. Now stop being so dramatic. You're really starting to kill the mood.'

Lacy raised her eyebrows. Rachel was a class-A bitch, that was clear. But she was usually more subtle about it, playing her little games that looked inclusive and fun but were actually designed to assert her dominance. She'd been unnervingly friendly to Lacy since the vodka incident, smiling at her whenever their paths crossed in a way that made Lacy wonder if she was plotting to kill her in her sleep.

'Rachel, please,' Ceri said in a Welsh accent that was similar to Dylan's. She was crying, Lacy realised. No, not crying, *sobbing*. 'I'm trying to tell you, something happened to me—'

'Eugh!' Rachel shouted, making Lacy jump. 'This is the first beach party of the year. Did you really have to pick this moment to make it all about you?'

Rachel appeared from behind the rock, her usually sunny face clouded with annoyance. Her step faltered as she saw Lacy and Dylan, and she snorted softly through her nose at the sight of them before quickly plastering a smile onto her face. 'What have we done to deserve the pleasure of *your* company?' she asked, beaming at Lacy.

Lacy sighed. She had no idea how to respond to niceness that was very clearly an attack.

'You know you wouldn't be able to get the fire lit without me.' Dylan laughed, and Lacy felt a pang of jealousy as Rachel hungrily turned her gaze to him.

But at least he'd defused the situation. Rachel demanded they follow her with her trademark 'Come *onnnn*!' and they continued along the beach. The other park staff were clustered around a pile of driftwood and various other items that might burn.

Lacy snuck a glance over her shoulder as they walked and saw Ceri peering anxiously at them from behind a rock. Her eyes were red and puffy, and her fingers picked at the inside of her elbow as she watched them leave.

Lacy shot a concerned look at Dylan, who nodded, his brow furrowed. 'I'll check on her,' he mouthed so Rachel couldn't hear. He silently retreated back towards Ceri like a panther moving stealthily through the rainforest.

Lacy dithered, wondering if she should go with him. But she heard him mutter something in Welsh, and Ceri reply in their mother tongue – she'd be intruding if she inserted herself into the conversation.

So she continued walking and watched Rachel's face twist with disgust when she realised she'd been left with Lacy.

'He's checking on Ceri,' Lacy explained.

Rachel could hardly control the sneer her lips curled into. 'Of course he is.' She cocked her head to one side as she looked at Lacy. 'Dylan is such a sweetheart – he never could resist a damsel in distress.'

She smiled sweetly before joining the others, leaving Lacy with a blend of unwelcome thoughts swirling through her head. What had Rachel meant by that? Did she see her as some kind of charity case? Or, even worse, did Dylan have a history of getting with girls who seemed a bit lost, a bit useless?

She swallowed, remembering the way he'd literally saved her life that morning. She didn't want to be some pathetic damsel in distress. But most of all, she didn't want to be played by a guy she allowed herself to develop feelings for. Not again.

'She's gone back to the dorm,' Dylan said as he appeared at Lacy's side, barely breathless despite running over. 'She said she'll be all right, but…' He stared after Ceri as she slowly trudged up the cliffside path, his forehead still wrinkled with worry. 'She was really upset. I'll check on her later – maybe she'll want to talk more then.'

Lacy nodded and tried to smile encouragingly, hating herself for how jealous she felt of the sobbing girl for being the focus of Dylan's attention.

'Is here OK?' Dylan asked. He indicated a spot of sand that was a comfortable distance from the rest of the staff, who were already passing bottles around, swigging and wincing as the fiery liquid hit their throats.

'Yes, perfect,' Lacy agreed, glad Dylan had set them up somewhere before darting off to get the fire lit.

The others were loud and obnoxious, as usual, but Lacy found she didn't care this evening. Marc sat slightly away from the group, sipping his drink and occasionally smiling in a way that didn't reach his eyes. Lee, the boy who worked at the reception of the swimming pool, had forgotten his portable speaker and looked devastated to be at the receiving end of Rachel's scorn. Andy was laughing too loud, trying too hard. Lacy wondered if he was aware of how desperate he looked and whether he had any friends his own age. Surely he had better options than hanging around with a bunch of teenagers?

She sipped from her water bottle and turned her attention to Dylan as he carefully selected and arranged sticks into a little pyramid. Her skin was warm from the walk and the humidity, and she could feel her hair defying gravity one strand at a time. She tried not to think about it – Dylan didn't change the way he looked at her depending on the frizz level of her hair.

She allowed herself to smile and pushed away the seed of insecurity Rachel had planted. Dylan *liked* her. She waved her fingers at him as he looked over at her from where he crouched, blowing on to a tiny flame nestled among the kindling. There was no way he could be faking it.

She gently touched her camera, suddenly hit by an itching desire to take a picture of him. She never took photos of people. People were messy and inelegant and generally not what she considered art. But looking at Dylan, his face glowing from the light of the flames and the sunset, she wondered if there had ever been anything more picturesque.

The fire lit and crackling, he hurried back to her.

'Why don't I ever see you taking photos?' he asked as he sat beside her, yet again displaying his uncanny ability to read her thoughts.

She shifted her weight in the sand, awkward as ever when it came to talking about her work. 'I don't know. I guess…it's always been kind of a private thing.'

Dylan nodded seriously. 'Yeah, I get that. If you ever do feel like sharing though, I'd be honoured.'

Lacy smiled, warmth heating her from within.

'How's your assignment going?'

Lacy sighed. 'Badly,' she replied.

'Hey, if you need a willing participant, I'm game,' he said, grinning at her.

Lacy moved her eyebrows quizzically, and Dylan leaped to his feet with a spray of sand. 'Movement, right?' he asked, bouncing with energy. 'I like to move – photograph me!'

Lacy laughed as Dylan did a goofy jig in the sand, waving his hands as though he were in a West End musical. God, he was adorable.

But as she watched him, she felt something stir inside. Maybe Dylan had a point. The sunset was highlighting the dark rocks of the cliff behind him, casting them in an orange glow that looked serene and dramatic at the same time. And Dylan was…well, Dylan was beautiful.

Lacy stood, not bothering to brush the sand off her trousers. 'Could you…?' she said breathily. 'Could you do something different, maybe?'

Dylan stopped fooling around and nodded. He stood straight, before exploding off the ground and executing a perfect standing backflip.

Lacy gasped at the image she'd captured.

It was perfect.

'Oh my god,' she squealed, hearing her accent forcing its way through but too excited to care. 'Can you do more?'

'Whatever you desire, *madame*,' Dylan said in a terrible attempt at a French accent.

Lacy tried to ignore the way Dylan saying the word 'desire' made her feel and concentrated on capturing his photo. He flipped and tumbled over the sand, and Lacy followed him with her lens, clicking frantically as she crouched to get every possible angle. She could feel the attention of the others on them but didn't care. She felt alive.

The light was fading, but Dylan didn't seem to be getting tired. Lacy stepped backwards to get a wider shot. She wanted the top of the cliff in the frame to show just how dramatic the scene really was.

She pressed her eye to the viewfinder and focused.

But her gaze was dragged away from Dylan. She squinted through her camera, tilting the lens upwards.

Someone was standing on top of the cliff, scarily close to the edge. Lacy adjusted the zoom to get a better look at them. Their features were blurred, but she could see white skin and thick dark hair, billowing in the wind. It was the same person she had seen the evening Dylan had told her the ghost story of Catrin Roberts and the murderous sailors. She was sure of it.

Her heart plunged into her stomach as the figure stepped forwards and plummeted off the edge of the precipice.

CHAPTER 12

Lacy screamed and let go of her camera. It thudded painfully against her chest, but she barely registered it, her gaze fixed in horror at the spot the person had jumped from.

Dylan was next to her in an instant, his hand on her shoulder, his face creased with concern. She felt the bodies of the rest of the staff pressing closer, their curious gazes on her rather than the cliff.

Which meant she was the only one who had seen the person fall. The person who, she'd only just realised, had a startling resemblance to Ceri.

She gulped, swallowing the tang of bile in her mouth. Her eyes reluctantly travelled down the cliff towards the ground, but she couldn't see anything. The body must be hidden behind the rocks.

'Lacy?' Dylan murmured.

'Someone fell,' Lacy breathed. She closed her eyes as the ground swayed beneath her feet.

'What?' Dylan gasped. 'Where?'

Lacy raised a trembling finger to point at the bottom of the cliff, around thirty metres from where they stood. Mutters and gasps rippled around the group.

'They could still be alive,' Dylan murmured. He gave her shoulder a gentle squeeze before removing it. Lacy fought the urge to reach for his hand and cling to it. 'I'll check.'

Lacy nodded gratefully but felt horribly guilty for standing there, frozen and useless.

The other staff were silent for once and Lacy peered blurrily at their shocked, still faces. Like her, they were all rooted to the spot, watching Dylan as he approached the rocks.

Lacy blinked and shook her head. He shouldn't have to do this alone.

'Wait!' she called as she ran after him.

He looked surprised to see her but let out a sigh of relief as she took his hand. He looked terrified, and Lacy remembered he was an eighteen-year-old farmer, not the action hero hunk she sometimes saw him as.

'Here?' he asked shakily, pointing at the jagged rocks that must be concealing the body.

Lacy nodded. She still couldn't see anything. Shouldn't there be some kind of evidence of what had happened? Some kind of...splatter?

She clenched her teeth against the vomit that threatened to rush up her oesophagus. She had barely eaten since her near drowning and her stomach felt like it was filling up with sea water again.

They crept closer, and Lacy promised herself that she would be the first to look. Then, if it was as awful as she imagined, she would insist Dylan turn away. There was no need for him to see too. Especially if, god forbid, it really was Ceri who had gone over the edge of the cliff.

She squeezed his hand and stepped around the rocks.

There was nothing there.

Lacy frowned and looked up at the cliff looming above them. She was sure this was the spot they had fallen – she recognised the grassy ledge just below the rim. So where was the body?

She looked behind every rock, between every crevice. She jogged along the base of the cliff in case she had completely misjudged where the person had landed.

'Lacy,' Dylan said softly.

'I don't understand,' Lacy said, turning to face him. 'They fell. I saw them fall – I watched them through my camera.'

Dylan opened his hands helplessly. 'Could it have been, I don't know, a speck of dirt or something on the lens?'

Lacy shook her head. It had been a person. Her brain had tried to make sense of it by suggesting it was Ceri, but the more she thought about it, the more she was sure it had been the same person she'd seen a few nights previously, standing on the edge of the cliff, pointing at her. And again on the beach this morning, walking mournfully away from the water.

'Has she gone mental?' Rachel asked cheerfully as she appeared at the base of the cliff.

Lacy's cheeks reddened. Rachel was the last person she wanted to see right now, just when she was wondering the same thing herself.

'Rachel, don't,' Dylan snapped, and Lacy looked at him in surprise. It was the first time she'd heard him raise his voice.

Lacy appreciated him defending her, but she inwardly thought Rachel might have a point, not that she'd choose to phrase it in such a crass way herself. This wasn't exactly an isolated incident – first the face in the window, then the figure by the cliff and on the beach. Then this morning she'd been certain some kind of malicious sea spirit had tried to drown her, and now…imaginary people plunging to their death?

Lacy closed her eyes. She never should have come here. She'd pretended that everything was fine, that her life could carry on as normal after the momentary blip that was Cal. But what happened four months ago, leaving her suddenly single, had clearly affected her more than she'd realised. She should go crawling back to her parents and apologise for how she'd left things with them. She should…

'What are we looking at?'

Chan had appeared. They looked the same as when Lacy had last seen them – their body swamped by a giant black hoodie. They hadn't been present at the bonfire, so must have just finished work at the bar. Chan followed the gaze of the others, placidly scanning the area to find whatever had them all transfixed.

'Lacy can see dead people,' Rachel whispered loudly, to the sniggers of the other staff members.

Lacy's cheeks grew hot.

But Chan didn't laugh and turned questioningly to Lacy. A concerned frown tugged the corner of their pierced eyebrow.

'I thought I saw someone fall,' Lacy muttered, wishing everyone would stop staring at her like she was a curious sideshow at a fair.

'Shit,' Chan said, both eyebrows shooting upwards. 'That's horrible. Do you know where—'

'Oh, come *onnnn*,' Rachel drawled, as though irritated by the attention Lacy was getting. 'This is boring now. Let's get on with the party.'

She physically tugged the sleeves of the other staff, dragging their attention back to the campfire and to her.

But Chan stayed with Lacy and Dylan by the cliffs. Lacy noticed Marc lurking too and wondered if he and Chan were friends. That would explain why Marc always seemed somewhat awkward when he was with the rest of the group alone.

Lacy could sense the worried glances they exchanged behind her back.

'I wonder,' Chan said thoughtfully, scanning the clifftop. 'I wonder if you saw me walking down the cliff path? I literally just got here from the bar.'

Dylan nodded as though he liked that theory, and Lacy didn't want to disappoint him, so agreed. 'Yeah, that would make sense.'

But she knew that wasn't what she'd seen, unless Chan had got to the beach by launching themself off the cliff.

'You OK?' Chan asked, clearly unconvinced by the brave smile Lacy was attempting.

Horrified, Lacy realised she was close to tears and turned her head away, wishing Dylan would stop staring at her so intensely.

'I just…' she gasped, cursing her voice for wobbling. What was she doing crying over figments of her imagination?

'Lacy had a tough day,' Dylan said gently. 'She nearly drowned this morning. It was scary. Really scary.' He rubbed her upper arm affectionately and Lacy couldn't decide whether she hated him for revealing her vulnerabilities, or loved him for stepping in to save her, yet again.

'God,' Chan replied. 'No wonder you're shaken up.'

'That sounds horrible,' Marc added, and Lacy was surprised

by what seemed to be genuine sympathy on his usually surly face.

Lacy nodded, relieved to have got the tears under control. Chan was right, she realised. The giddiness Dylan made her feel had been masking the fact that she was extremely shaken, and not just by the events of this morning.

'I know someone who fell,' she blurted, then clamped her mouth shut. Where had that come from? She'd never spoken to anyone about it and barely allowed herself to *think* about it.

The three of them stared at her silently, and Lacy couldn't blame them. How did you respond to someone revealing something like that, so out of the blue?

'Do you want to talk about it?' Chan asked gently.

Lacy peered at them from beneath her lashes. Everything about Chan's appearance said edgy, aggressive even. But from what Lacy had seen of them so far, they were kind and gentle – almost a parental figure compared to the rest of the shrieking teenagers grouped around the campfire.

So Lacy considered the question rather than automatically dismissing it.

Did she want to talk about it?

She thought about Cal and Winter and her parents, and how she'd never spoken to anyone about how she was feeling, not for a long time.

'No,' she replied finally. 'No, I'm fine. Thanks, though.'

She smiled at Chan, Dylan and even Marc and wondered if maybe this was the start of that statement becoming the truth.

CHAPTER 13

Lacy had chewed her thumbnail so low that the skin around it was raw and painful. She checked the time on her phone yet again. It was nine o'clock.

So where was Dylan?

He'd asked her to come for a walk to watch the sunset, which must be close to ducking below the horizon by now.

Since he'd saved her life the day before, Lacy had dropped her guard entirely and decided to let Dylan in. She had finally pushed away Winter's persistent voice in her head, telling her that she didn't need anyone apart from her. She'd had enough of being alone.

And she suspected this walk was more than a walk. It was a date.

She stared at her bedroom door, willing him to knock on it and apologise for being late. Maybe he'd been caught up in something after work? He was the kind of guy who would leap to help if he saw someone struggling, so that wouldn't be a bad guess.

But what could possibly be taking this long?

She'd showered then spent an age getting ready, trying on

various outfits and rejecting them all because they didn't feel right. They felt like the person she was trying to be, and she was starting to question if that was who she really wanted to be after all.

She sighed and drummed her fingers on the thin mattress. Maybe there had been a misunderstanding. Maybe he'd thought they would meet in the kitchen. She stood abruptly, filled with the certainty that he'd been waiting for her all evening while she sat there like a chump.

The sheer volume of the music hit her as she stepped into the corridor, and her ears throbbed in protest. Surely no one could actually hold a conversation in this din. Although, as she squeezed past a couple snogging against the wall, she wasn't sure any of the other staff were particularly interested in conversation.

Rachel was standing on the kitchen counter, grinding her arse an inch away from Lee and Andy's faces. Lee's eyes were obscured by his baseball cap, but his mouth was slack and practically drooling, while Andy looked close to spontaneous combustion. Marc moped in the corner of the kitchen, gloomily swigging from a bottle of rosé. Lacy suspected he was missing Chan, who must be working at the bar. Ceri wasn't there either, which was strange – she was usually glued to Rachel's side. Maybe their fight on the cliff path the previous evening had damaged their friendship beyond repair.

The rest of the staff watched Rachel, and Lacy realised why she insisted on having the music so loud. If no one could make conversation, they had no choice but to stare at her.

Lacy made a beeline for Marc, remembering his comforting presence on the beach. He'd been there for her, as well as Dylan and Chan.

'Have you seen Dylan?' she screamed, her mouth pressed up to his ear.

Rachel must have had some bat DNA in her as she somehow heard Lacy's question and leaped off the counter. Lacy could see her glossed lips moving as she approached but couldn't hear a word she was saying.

Rachel reached out and smartly whacked Lee on the thigh, gesturing for him to turn the music down.

'Finally,' she breathed, rolling her eyes as Lee fumbled with the volume. She turned her attention to Lacy and looked her slowly up and down. Then a delighted smile spread across her mouth. 'Have you been stood up?'

God, Lacy couldn't be bothered with this, not now. 'No,' she sighed, before turning back to Marc. 'Have you seen him?'

Marc opened his mouth to reply, but Rachel got there first.

'Maybe he's with Ceri,' she chirruped. 'I haven't seen her since yesterday. I thought she was just moping in her room, but it would make sense if she's with Dylan, what with, well, their *history*.' She smiled slowly, watching for Lacy's reaction.

Of course Ceri – beautiful, raven-haired and from around here – had been involved with Dylan. That explained the concerned look on his face when they'd found her crying, the way he'd run after her to see if she was OK.

They had history. History that had potentially gone back for years, long before Lacy arrived on the scene.

Lacy kept her back turned to Rachel and closed her eyes. She wouldn't rise to it.

'I think I saw them together,' Andy agreed. Lacy's eyes snapped open to see Marc staring pityingly at her.

'Where?' Lacy asked, wishing the attention of every staff

member wasn't directed at her. Somehow, this was even worse than last night at the beach, when they'd witnessed her freaking out over her overactive imagination.

Andy squirmed beside Rachel, and Lacy died a little inside. She wouldn't trust a word Rachel said, but Andy wouldn't lie to hurt her.

Which meant…

'They were walking by the cliff,' Andy said softly. 'I think he…likes to take girls there.'

Lacy's chin wobbled. Of course he did.

'Right,' she said smartly, trying to mask the tremor in her voice. 'Thanks.'

She marched out of the kitchen, her head bowed, but couldn't miss Rachel's expression as she passed. She looked as though all her dreams had come true.

'Lacy, wait!' Andy trotted after her. 'I'm sorry,' he said, sounding as if he was about to burst into tears. 'I wish you didn't have to find out like that.'

'It's fine,' Lacy said, wishing he would stop looking at her like she was going to break.

'You deserve so much better, you know,' Andy murmured, his face creased with pity as Lacy stared at the space beside his head. He was still wearing his lime-green uniform. She wasn't sure he even owned any other clothes.

'Thanks,' Lacy said thickly, turning to slope back to her room and nurse her wounds.

Had she read this completely wrong? Perhaps Dylan's arm around her shoulder after he'd pulled her out of the ocean was purely a way to comfort her, in the same way he'd comforted the shivering, scared kid who'd nearly drowned. Why on earth had Lacy thought she could compete with Ceri, his beautiful ex-girlfriend?

But he'd kissed her, hadn't he? Granted, it had been on the top of her wet, salty hair. But still, it had been a *kiss*.

She sighed as she flumped onto her bed. She should have listened to Winter. She'd promised herself that she wouldn't lose focus on Paris, but yet again, she'd been lured by a pair of pretty eyes.

Her gaze fell on her camera, and she wished she could have seen the sunset. Maybe it wasn't too late. Maybe she didn't need Dylan there to enjoy it.

She grabbed her camera and marched out of her room.

'You want some company?' Andy called from behind her. Had he been waiting in the corridor for her?

'No,' Lacy shouted, waving his concern away with her hand. She winced – she saw how Rachel treated Andy, and now she was being just as dismissive. She turned and paused for long enough to smile at him and say, 'Thanks though.'

Andy raised a pudgy hand to wave sadly at her.

Lacy squirmed, hating the feeling of being pitied.

The fading remains of the gorgeous sunset Dylan had promised were bleeding into the horizon. Had he enjoyed it with Ceri instead? Had they walked hand in hand along the clifftop?

Stop it, Lacy.

It didn't matter. He was just a boy whom she would never see again once the season was over.

The breeze gently teased her perfectly straightened hair. She'd fantasised about Dylan running his fingers through it as she'd got ready. Pictured him sweeping it away from her face as he kissed her in the pink glow of the sunset.

And all that time, he'd probably been thinking about Ceri. It was mortifying.

Her step faltered as she drew closer to the cliff. There was someone standing there. No, two people.

Her cheeks flamed with embarrassment. Dylan and Ceri were still on their date.

The dying light turned them into silhouettes, locked in an embrace that was so passionate Lacy felt like she should avert her eyes. She could barely tell where one body ended and the other began as they stood next to the edge of the cliff, their limbs tangled, their faces pressed together.

Lacy wished she could have shrugged it off, walked away and convinced herself it was nothing. But seeing him kissing another girl hurt her more than she cared to admit. She should have listened to the voice in her head, the voice that sounded like her sister, warning her to stay away from dumb, pretty boys.

They were moving in a way that looked almost aggressive. They must really like each other, she mused. She should really stop staring at them.

But as she turned to go, she realised there was something wrong about the way the silhouettes were moving. The larger one, the one she was sure was Dylan, was sagging to the ground, staggering as the smaller shadow loomed over him.

Lacy squinted, willing the sun to dip below the horizon so she could see them properly. The gentle breeze blew the familiar rancid smell of drains towards her.

Dylan was on his knees now, and Lacy realised with a slow horror that Ceri's hands weren't clasped tenderly around his face.

They were around his neck.

Without thought, Lacy started running, sure now that this wasn't some kind of graphic display of public affection and something was very wrong.

The dying sun threw a sudden beam of blinding, orange light across the horizon and Lacy shielded her eyes with her arm. And then it was gone, the day finally complete. Lacy moved her arm away, blinking the blobs of warped patterns out of her eyes until she could see properly again.

Dylan and Ceri had gone.

CHAPTER 14

'Dylan?' Lacy breathed, a horrible sense of déjà vu bubbling up from the pit of her stomach.

But this hadn't been a figment of her imagination. She'd seen the pair of them only seconds ago. They had been *right there*.

And there was only one place they could have gone.

'DYLAN!' Lacy screamed.

She ran, her thoughts coming at the same frantic rate as her pulse as she desperately searched for an explanation that didn't mean Dylan was lying broken at the bottom of the cliff.

The last streaks of red in the sky were fading as the day turned to night, and a gentle breeze blew Lacy's hair across her cheeks as she reached the cliff edge and dropped to her knees.

She gripped the grassy rim of the cliff, feeling loose dirt and stones crumble beneath her fingers. The tide was in. She could hear the waves crashing against the rocks far below.

She closed her eyes and braced herself for what she was about to see.

She slowly peered over the top. Despite the calm weather, the water looked black and angry, swirling and frothing at the base of the cliff. She scanned the shoreline, searching for the white of Dylan's T-shirt.

There was no one there.

A strangled cry escaped her lips and she forgot the hurt she had felt towards him moments ago. Dylan was *gone*.

Ceri had pulled him over the edge, not seeming to care that she had plummeted to her death with him. What had happened to make her so furious that she would kill them both?

Lacy dug her fingers deeper into the ground as she sobbed. This couldn't be happening, not again.

Dylan.

Had it somehow involved her? Had Ceri been upset because of Dylan spending time with Lacy? Had she snapped, deciding that if she couldn't have him, no one could?

Lacy shook her head – none of it made sense. They were teenagers, for god's sake. People split up and dated other people all the time. Ceri couldn't have been so distraught that she'd…

Lacy shrank away from the drop, and as she shifted her weight, something caught her eye below. There was a ledge – a rocky outcrop just to the left of where she was, not too far from the top of the cliff. Curled in a foetal position on the ledge was a body. A body wearing a white T-shirt.

Lacy hesitated for a moment as her brain tried to catch up with what she was seeing. 'Dylan!' she screamed, barely daring to believe that he was there.

But he wasn't moving. Even if he hadn't been lost to the sea, he might still be…

He groaned.

'Dylan!' she shouted again, willing him to sit up, turn his

tanned face towards her and tell her that everything was all right.

He started to roll onto his back, and Lacy gasped as she pictured him slipping off the ledge and into the water below.

'Don't move!' she cried, thankful that the wind was quiet for once so that her voice wasn't swallowed by it. 'Dylan, keep still. I'll…'

She looked around in desperation. What could she do? She wrenched her phone out of her pocket, knowing already that she wouldn't have signal out here. It was a complete dead zone – the only place you could reliably find signal in the park was by using the WiFi at the bar, which might explain why so many of the customers spent all their time there.

'Shit,' she breathed.

She was going to have to leave him.

'Dylan,' she called. She could see his face now. His forehead was puckered with pain. 'I'm going to get help. Just…don't move, OK?'

She stared at him a moment longer, wishing she could pull him up to safety with just the force of her gaze, then stood.

But as she was about to sprint back to the dorm block, she heard him speak.

'Lacy,' he groaned.

She dropped back to her knees to peer over the edge. 'I'm here.'

'Don't leave me,' he whispered, his eyes still closed. 'Please.'

Lacy's heart tugged towards him. He looked so alone, so scared. And he was slurring as though he'd hit his head. Her eyes darted around frantically as she tried to decide what to do.

It wasn't safe to leave him. What if he was gone when she returned?

'OK,' she said. 'OK, I'll stay.'

She looked over her shoulder. She could just make out the murky outline of the accommodation block in the distance and fired desperate thoughts in the direction of the building.

Help me.

But she knew no one would notice if they failed to return. They'd be too busy partying, then passing out drunk. She never usually joined the parties, so her absence wouldn't be noticed, and everyone thought Dylan was off on a romantic stroll with Ceri.

Lacy closed her eyes. Ceri was gone, but it was up to her to save Dylan.

She clenched her jaw and studied the ledge. It was around four metres below her. It must have hurt like hell when Dylan landed on it and she prayed he hadn't broken any bones. She crawled to her left until she was directly above him.

It wasn't a vertical drop here, she realised. There were little ledges, holes and sloping sections of grass, leading down to where Dylan lay.

She could get down to him.

And then what?

She pushed the thought away. She was going to have to take it one step at a time. At least she'd be able to see how injured he was and whether she would be forced to leave him and go for help.

Her leg trembled violently as she lowered it over the edge of the cliff. She was aiming for a small ridge just below the rim, but it still felt like she was climbing off the edge of a sheer drop, not helped by the rapidly fading light.

Her foot made contact, and she tested her weight, prodding the rock as she lay on her stomach, her upper body folded over the grassy cliff edge. It held.

She gripped long tufts of grass, tugging them firmly before trusting them to support her weight, and started climbing.

A seagull shrieked as it flew alarmingly close, and she gasped as her feet slipped over a patch of loose scree. She slid downwards and scrabbled to save herself, then pressed her body against the cliff, trying not to think about how close she'd come to falling.

She steadied herself. She needed to keep calm, hold it together. She couldn't panic like she had in the sea. Dylan wouldn't be saving her this time.

She lowered herself onto the ledge Dylan was lying on. It was barely big enough for the both of them, and Lacy wondered if she'd made a terrible mistake. Would her weight send the platform crumbling into the sea?

Crouched by Dylan's feet, she scanned his body, searching for injuries. He seemed intact, thank god, but remained motionless. She reached over his body and touched his cheek with her fingers. He smiled, but his eyes stayed shut.

'Hey,' he breathed.

'Hey,' Lacy replied, longing to pull him further away from the ledge, but not daring to move more than necessary. Why hadn't Ceri landed on the ledge too? Their bodies had been so entwined when they'd gone over, they'd have fallen as one. But Ceri was nowhere to be seen, nor was she visible in the churning water below when Lacy dared to peer over the side of the ledge.

But she couldn't think about that, not now. She had more than enough to worry about.

'Can you move?' she asked softly. 'Do you think you've broken anything?'

'I'm fine,' Dylan said cheerily, though his eyes were still closed and his voice was thick and distorted. He was quiet for a moment, then spoke suddenly as though only just registering Lacy's presence. '*Iawn – be di'r plan ta?*'

He was speaking Welsh, Lacy realised, wishing she could understand him. But he knew she didn't speak Welsh, so why was he suddenly talking to her as though she were fluent? He must have hit his head. How was he going to climb back to the top with a concussion?

She raised her eyebrows in alarm as he suddenly attempted to sit up. She reached towards him, gripping his hands so he could pull against her. Finally upright, he leaned wearily against the cliff and opened his eyes.

The deep blue still made her heart flutter, even now.

'Hey,' he said again, and Lacy noticed some of the colour had returned to his cheeks. Maybe they could do this.

She crouched beside him as he rested, her eyes never leaving his face. She wanted to wait for him to regain some strength, but she eyed the horizon nervously. The last of the light was rapidly disappearing. Climbing the cliff in the dark would add a whole new level of danger to the situation.

'Dylan?' she said gently after she'd left it as long as she dared. 'We need to try and get back up.'

'Mmhmm.' He nodded sleepily. Lacy opened her mouth to repeat his name and his eyes suddenly flew open. He lurched to his feet in one movement, swaying so precariously that Lacy had to grab the waist of his jeans to pull him back towards her.

'Careful!' she gasped.

Maybe she should leave him here and go for help after all. But he clearly wasn't himself. Could he be trusted to stay put on the ledge?

She didn't have time to make the decision. Dylan had started scaling the cliff, casually searching for handholds as though he were climbing a low wall that wasn't dangling over a deathly drop.

'Wait!' Lacy insisted. 'I'll show you where to go.'

She shouted up directions to him, but he ignored her instructions and scrambled clumsily upwards, sending stones and dirt showering down on her. If he hadn't been so athletic, he would have fallen, she was sure of it. But luckily his body took control, even if his mind seemed to be struggling to function.

When he finally made it to the top, Lacy's legs shuddered with exhaustion and relief. She had to steady herself against the rocks as dizziness threatened to pitch her over the edge.

It was her turn.

She didn't have the adrenaline that had helped her on the climb down – her body felt tired and sluggish as she heaved herself up, hand over hand, foothold by foothold. But at last her fingers grasped the grassy clifftop, and she hauled herself over, rolling away from the edge.

She'd done it.

She turned her head to the side as she caught her breath, searching for Dylan.

He was gone.

CHAPTER 15

Lacy sat bolt upright, a rush of panic restoring her depleted energy. A squeak of fear escaped her lips. Had he staggered off the edge while she was climbing up?

She scrambled to her feet, spinning as she squinted through the gloom.

There. He was lurching across the grass, back towards the accommodation block, his white T-shirt just visible in the near dark.

'Dylan!' she shouted, jogging after him.

He didn't react to his name. As she reached him, she touched his upper arm and he spun to look at her. His face was slack and expressionless.

Then realisation hit him and a surprised smile slowly spread across his mouth. 'Lacy! Whatta you doing here?'

Lacy frowned. His slurring was even worse now and he swayed as he stood, his eyes focusing on a spot just to the right of her face.

'You fell,' she explained, holding his arms to keep him steady. 'Dylan…Ceri pushed you.'

Dylan frowned, and Lacy's heart ached for him. Did he

really not remember? Maybe it was for the best.

The confusion slowly disappeared from his face, replaced by his sunny smile. 'Lacy!' he repeated as though seeing her for the first time. 'Can I have a kiss?'

He lurched forwards, his lips pressing towards her face. Lacy recoiled, holding him away from her and staggering backwards under his weight.

'Dylan!' she exclaimed as she tried to stop him from sending them both crashing to the ground. And then she smelled it…

Alcohol, on his breath.

'Dylan, have you been *drinking*?'

He swayed, only just managing to stay upright. 'Few beers,' he hiccoughed, before swallowing as though they were about to make a reappearance.

Lacy screwed up her face in disgusted realisation. He didn't have a head injury. He was wasted out of his mind.

'Sorry,' he continued. 'I was nervous, about our date.' He giggled. 'I didn't think I'd get *this* drunk, though.'

'But…' Lacy breathed as her thoughts scrambled to catch up. 'You were with Ceri.'

Dylan shook his head, his entire body tipping from side to side with the motion. 'Ceri? I haven't seen her since yesterday, at the beach party.'

Lacy turned to look at the cliff, willing her memory to replay the scene. She'd seen them – Dylan and Ceri, struggling next to the edge.

Hadn't she?

'She pushed you,' Lacy insisted, but Dylan shook his head again.

'I just had a little stumble, that's all!' He smiled inanely at her, his eyes failing to focus on anything.

Lacy's lip curled. She'd climbed down a cliff for him. They'd nearly *died*. And he was acting as though nothing had happened.

'Shall we go for our date?' he slurred.

He reached for Lacy again but was so disorientated that he managed to cuff her painfully around the head, before his hand fell heavily on her chest.

'Get off!' she shouted, pushing his hand away. This wasn't the Dylan she'd pictured going for a romantic stroll with. She didn't want anything to do with this drunken, obnoxious mess.

He was just like the others, she realised. Just like the rest of the staff, partying back at the dorm. Just like Cal and all the lowlife idiots her sister had warned her about.

'Sorry,' he mumbled, holding his hands up as he backed away from her. 'Sorry, Ceri.'

Lacy gawped at him.

What the hell had happened tonight? Was Dylan telling the truth? Had he really just drunkenly staggered off the edge of the cliff? Had Ceri been a figment of Lacy's imagination, just like the figure walking across the beach in the mist and later plummeting off the clifftop? The person who had a startling resemblance to Ceri, with their pale white skin and masses of cascading dark hair?

She closed her eyes and tried to steady herself. If she was losing it and seeing things that weren't there, then at least that meant Ceri was still alive, wherever she was.

'Everything OK here?'

Lacy snapped her eyes open to find Chan standing a few

metres away, wearing their trademark oversized hoodie. They looked awkward, like they were reluctant to interrupt. Lacy could have hugged them.

'Can you help me get him back to the dorm?' she asked, suddenly struggling to fight back tears.

'Of course,' Chan said, stepping forwards without hesitation and draping one of Dylan's arms around their shoulder. He dwarfed them both, but Lacy suspected Chan was seriously strong, despite their small frame.

Lacy took his left arm, grimacing at the dead weight of it across her neck and the smell on his breath.

They struggled silently, Dylan barely helping and mumbling incoherently. Lacy tried to figure out what she should tell Chan, who must be returning from a shift at the bar. They always seemed to arrive just in time to witness Lacy having some kind of ridiculous issue.

'I've never seen him like this,' Chan wheezed, finally breaking the silence.

'Me neither,' Lacy said. She wished she'd never had to.

Chan didn't say another word and Lacy was glad. She had no idea what to say. The more she tried to focus on the memory of Dylan's silhouette struggling with another's, the more she suspected it had just been Dylan all along, drunkenly thrashing about.

Maybe she needed an eye test. She almost laughed at the thought. It would certainly explain most of the weirdness she'd seen recently.

'We'll put him in a spare dorm room,' Chan panted. 'He can sleep it off here. There's no way he can walk home in this state.'

Lacy nodded and wondered if his mum would be waiting for him at the pretty white farmhouse across the bay.

The kitchen door was shut, so they managed to avoid attention as they heaved Dylan down the corridor, pausing to rest him against the wall, before staggering the final stretch towards an empty room, far from Lacy's own. His body hit the bare mattress with a thump and within seconds he was snoring.

'Should we make him more comfortable?' Chan asked carefully, and Lacy snorted softly.

She was tempted to leave him there, twisted, with his legs half dangling off the bed.

She sighed and tugged his shoes off, dumping them on the floor.

'We'd better put him in the recovery position,' Chan said, and showed Lacy how to manoeuvre him onto his side and wedge a pillow beneath his back. 'Hopefully, any puke will go thattaway.' They motioned towards the floor and Lacy shuddered.

She wasn't feeling particularly fond of Dylan right now, but she didn't want him to choke to death on his own vomit.

'I'll check on him before I go to sleep,' Chan said, catching the concern on Lacy's face. 'I stay up late anyway, so it's no bother.'

Lacy nodded mutely, still staring at Dylan. Thank god Chan had arrived when they had – Lacy had no idea how she'd have managed him on her own. She had a sudden urge to hug Chan.

As though sensing it, Chan gently rubbed Lacy's upper arm. Lacy smiled gratefully, but was still unable to banish the sick, unsettled feeling swamping her chest.

'Have you seen Ceri today?' Lacy blurted, unable to ignore

the fear that she had in fact witnessed a death tonight.

Chan pulled a confused face. 'No. Why, what's wrong?'

Lacy took a faltering breath. She should say something. What if she *hadn't* imagined it?

'It's just…' she began, knowing she was probably about to make herself look even more unstable than she already had. 'Rachel and Andy said they'd seen Ceri walking by the cliff with Dylan this evening. And…when I got there, I thought…I thought I saw the two of them. And then they fell. But there was no sign of Ceri, and I'm not actually sure I didn't imagine the whole thing, just like last night.'

She laughed nervously, and Chan frowned.

'Lacy,' Chan said slowly. 'Ceri's gone.'

Lacy widened her eyes.

'No,' Chan said hurriedly. 'I mean, she left. I think her dad picked her up earlier today. I don't know the details. Maybe Rachel—'

'No,' Lacy said quickly. The last thing she wanted was for Rachel to get involved in this.

'She lives locally, I think,' Chan continued. 'So she'll probably be home now. We could get her number from the office tomorrow if you want to give her a call to check?'

Lacy gave Chan a grateful smile and shook away the creeping feeling of dread. It wasn't that implausible to think that Ceri had left. She worked alone in the on-site shop, so the other staff wouldn't have noticed her absence until this evening. She'd have thought Andy would know though. He was supposed to be the manager.

So why had he insisted he'd seen her walking with Dylan?

Maybe Lacy wasn't the only one seeing things, getting

confused. It must be hard to keep track of all of the staff, working different roles with different hours. Andy had simply been mistaken, that was all.

She watched Dylan's chest as it rose and fell and confirmed what she knew: Ceri was alive, men were trash and Lacy was slowly losing her mind.

CHAPTER 16

Lacy's thumb hovered over the button that would delete the photos of Dylan backflipping on the beach from her camera. They really were stunning. She'd captured the light just right and the moodiness of the black rocks in the background added a captivating drama.

But could she really make Dylan the subject of her assignment now that she knew that beneath the attractive and sweet surface lay just another disappointing teenage boy?

A familiar bubble of guilt lodged itself in Lacy's throat whenever she thought poorly of Cal. He'd got his comeuppance and then some.

He deserved it.

Lacy blinked, surprised by the ferocity of the thought. She had stopped channelling her sister quite so much recently, distracted by a Welsh boy with dimples and a surprising talent for gymnastics.

But now that she was pushing him away, Winter was back, reminding her of what she should be thinking and who she was.

She sighed and scrolled to the next photo.

With a gasp, she let go of the camera as though it had burned her. It fell heavily onto the bed and she stared at it, her heart drumming against her ribs.

There had been something, *someone*, in the last photo with Dylan. She swallowed, unable to look away from the camera but too scared to pick it up and check the image. Not that she needed to – she could still see it now, engraved into memory.

Dylan had been centre stage, his legs tucked close to his chest, as he'd twisted athletically in the air. But behind him, lurking at the base of the cliff…

That dark, indistinguishable figure. The same person she'd seen in the abandoned dorm, on the clifftop and walking on the beach. The person she had seen fall that night at the party. They were in the photo of Dylan, standing behind the rocks, staring directly at the camera, at Lacy.

Which was impossible, because they were at the *top* of the cliff moments after this photo had been taken. Lacy had watched them through her viewfinder, seen them step forwards and plummet off the edge.

At least, that's what she *imagined* she'd seen. There hadn't *really* been anyone, had there?

So who was in the photo?

Lacy reached her trembling hand out towards her camera.

There was a tentative knock on her bedroom door and she gasped, snatching her hand back to her chest.

'Who is it?' she called, her voice shaking as violently as her fingers.

'It's Dylan.'

Lacy closed her eyes. He hadn't shown up at the pool for his shift today, and she'd been filled with the certainty that he was dead, lying in a pool of his own vomit. Lee, who was somehow her superior, had allowed her to jog back to the dorm to check on him. He had been sleeping soundly and hadn't reacted when she'd called his name.

She didn't want to talk to him. She didn't want to talk to anyone, not right now. But the knock at the door had snapped her out of her scared trance, at least, and she snatched the camera off the bed.

The photo was gone. All that remained was a black screen, and a message: Media Corrupted.

Lacy stared vacantly at the camera. They were the same words that had appeared on her phone when she'd tried to message Winter.

What was happening?

'Please, Lacy, can we talk?'

Lacy's eyes remained glued to the camera screen. There was nothing to talk about, but maybe speaking to him would be preferable to staring at the weird message.

She gently placed her camera on the bed and unlocked her door, opening it enough to make it clear she wasn't inviting him in.

'I…' Dylan started, before running his fingers through his messy hair. He looked awful – blotchy skin, puffy eyes and none of his usual sparkle. 'I'm so sorry.'

Lacy sighed. She didn't want to hurt Dylan. He was a sweet guy and he'd be perfect for someone else, someone like Ceri, perhaps. But Lacy should have stuck to her guns when she'd promised herself she wouldn't go near boys again for a good long time. She should have learned her lesson after what had happened with Cal.

'I'm not angry with you, Dylan. I just…I don't think we should hang out anymore.'

She'd been going for the gentle approach, but Dylan looked like he'd been kicked in the chest.

'I don't understand,' he said, his eyes darting around in despair. 'I mean, I understand why you wouldn't want to see me…but I don't understand what happened last night. I had a drink while I was waiting for you to get ready, and then…I can't remember anything. Just flashes, like…I think I fell? And you…I think you helped me?'

Lacy nodded. 'That's pretty much it.'

She left out the part about her original conviction that Ceri had tried to push him to his death. He was supposed to be the one with the unreliable memory in this situation, not her. She'd spoken to Andy that morning, who had apologetically confirmed that Ceri had indeed gone home, citing personal reasons as her excuse for quitting. He'd blamed his mistake on the dusk light, but Lacy suspected he'd just gone along with what Rachel had said, as always. And she suspected that Rachel had outright lied about seeing Ceri and Dylan together, just to mess with her.

'It was like I lost time.' He shook his head and frowned. 'I've never been like that before, ever.'

'I know,' Lacy said gently, realising she really wasn't angry with him. He'd miscalculated how much alcohol he could handle, that was all.

'Please,' he said, and Lacy's heart tugged towards him as he trapped her with his ocean-eyes. 'Let me make it up to you. I'm not that guy. I'm really no—'

'I know, Dylan,' she repeated, wishing he would stop. Her

resolve was weakening, but she couldn't let it happen, not again. 'But I'm not interested, OK?'

Yesterday, she had been very, very interested. But dangling off a cliff to save a drunk boy had served as a stark reminder that she had bigger things to focus on.

She closed the door on him, turned and rested her back against it. Dylan had been a momentary distraction, and now she was back on her path of becoming who she was supposed to be.

So why did she feel so awful?

She jumped as another knock pounded on the door, louder this time. She frowned. Dylan struck her as someone who understood that no meant no. Surely he wasn't trying to win her over again?

'Dylan,' she sighed as she opened the door.

But he had gone, and Marc and Chan stood in his place, grinning sheepishly. They both wore their own clothes. Like Lacy, they seemed eager to shed the lime-green monstrosity of a uniform the second they finished work for the day. Marc was stylish in ripped jeans and a tight T-shirt, and Chan, as always, looked effortlessly cool in their huge black hoodie.

Despite the difference in height, style and personas, they somehow looked like a perfect pair.

'Trouble in himbo paradise?' Marc asked cheerily.

'Himbo?'

'Yeah, you know,' Marc said impatiently, his hand gesturing vaguely in the air. 'A bimbo…who is a him.'

'As in, very pretty to look at,' Chan added, 'but not much going on between the ears?'

Lacy couldn't help but bristle at their judgement of Dylan.

He was pretty to look at, that much was undeniable. But to suggest he was stupid…

She bit back her retort – he wasn't hers to defend.

'I knew there had to be some flaw.' Marc nodded sagely. 'No one can be that perfect – the universe doesn't allow it. If he'd been gifted a brain as well as a chiselled body and dreamy eyes, the cosmic balance would be thrown out of whack, you know?'

'God, Marc, you do talk some shite,' Chan said, but a playful smile tugged at the corner of their mouth.

Marc grinned back, and Lacy felt like an outsider peering in on the energy Chan and Marc's friendship generated. She resisted the urge to inform them that even though Dylan didn't have much of an education, he was probably the most emotionally intelligent person she'd ever met.

'Shouldn't you be at the bar?' Lacy asked Chan, wincing inwardly. As always, she'd managed to sound rude without trying.

But Chan didn't seem offended and beamed at Lacy. 'Night off!'

Marc was smiling like a child who was being allowed to play with a toy that was usually kept locked away for special occasions. Lacy wondered if he felt as alone as she did when he was forced to hang out with the others without Chan.

'But seriously,' Chan said, smile fading as their voice lowered. 'Are you OK? Last night was pretty intense.'

The genuine look of concern on Chan's face made Lacy pause. It had been intense. And she still wasn't fully recovered from the emotional rollercoaster – rejection turned to terror turned to irritation. She was doing all she could to ignore the creeping feeling that she was losing her grip on reality.

But she wasn't about to admit to Chan and Marc that she'd imagined a fictional person falling over the cliff, again.

'I mean, yeah,' she sighed. 'It was less than ideal.'

'Drunk boys are the worst.' Marc nodded in exaggerated sympathy. 'They revert into the cavemen they all are underneath.'

'And you don't?' Chan scoffed.

'Darling, please. I get more fabulous with every shot.' Marc flipped his fringe away from his eyes with such sass that Lacy couldn't help but grin. He seemed so different from the surly character who usually lurked on the edge of the parties. Maybe he had more than one personality, depending on the situation. Maybe he didn't even know who he was, just like Lacy.

'Sooo,' Chan said. 'You gonna let us in then?'

Lacy hesitated, her hand still on the door. 'Don't you want to join in with that?' She nodded towards the direction the music had just started from, mingling with cheers from the kitchen.

Marc pulled a face and shuddered. 'Eugh, I am so done with Rachel's godawful parties. I've decided – I'm doing a three-day juice cleanse. Nothing but goodness shall pass these lips.'

Chan snorted. 'You literally just ate a tub of ice cream for your dinner.'

'Starting tomorrow, obviously,' Marc sighed, flouncing into Lacy's room and flopping onto her tiny bed.

Chan joined him, scooching up close enough to make room for Lacy.

But Lacy stayed standing, still unsure what they were doing here. 'Why do you do it then?' she asked.

'Do what?' Marc replied.

'Join in with the parties if you don't enjoy them?' He always looked miserable, granted, but he was always there, sitting on the edge of the action with a glass of something in his hand.

Marc exhaled softly. 'What can I say? I'm a sucker for peer pressure.' He stared meaningfully at her. 'We can't all have your resolve.'

Lacy felt the heat rise to her cheeks. She'd assumed the others all thought she was some uninteresting prude, but something in Marc's voice made her feel like he admired her.

She closed the door softly behind her.

'Marc's terrified of being boring,' Chan explained, ignoring Marc's poisonous glare. 'Though, if you ask me, Rachel is the most boring out of all of us.'

Lacy snorted, agreeing completely. She lowered herself onto the bed, her legs angled to the side so she wasn't touching Chan, whose own legs were draped casually over Marc's.

'So, what happened last night?' Chan asked, and Lacy groaned inwardly – she'd hoped they'd moved on from the topic. 'You looked more than pissed off. You looked...well, like you'd seen a ghost.'

Lacy felt her pulse rise. She'd furiously quashed the nagging thoughts that she had seen just that. But her imagination had been unleashed by Chan's story about the murdered staff, Dylan's old story about the murdered village girl and the very recent murder of the guest, Carl Jones.

'I guess...' she said reluctantly. 'I guess there's been a lot of death around here and it messed with my head a bit.'

Marc's face appeared from the other side of Chan, his eyes wide with alarm. 'What do you mean, a lot?'

'You know,' Lacy squirmed, loath to admit how much the

stories had affected her. 'The abandoned dorm block, and Catrin Roberts.'

Marc's face crumpled in confusion. 'Who the hell is Catrin Roberts?'

Lacy had assumed it was local folklore and something all the staff would know about. But then again, none of the staff apart from Dylan and Ceri seemed to be from around here. They were all like her – travelling from cities like Liverpool, Manchester and Birmingham to work for the holiday season before returning home. None of them actually left the caravan park. They stayed trapped within their little bubble for months.

'A girl who used to live here, like, two hundred years ago,' Lacy explained. 'She was murdered by some sailors.' She gestured weakly at her neck to indicate she'd died in the same grisly way as the two murdered staff members.

Marc and Chan raised their eyebrows as they took in what was clearly new information.

'And what about the abandoned dorm block?' Marc asked. 'What's wrong with that, apart from being utterly rank?'

Lacy frowned. Didn't he know about that? It had been Chan who had told her the story, and the murders had only been ten years ago. The park may have kept it out of the public eye, but the staff would be aware of it, wouldn't they?

She looked at Chan, waiting for them to explain. But Chan was gnawing their thumbnail and resolutely avoiding her eye.

Lacy opened her mouth to tell Marc what she knew – that two staff members had been slaughtered not too far away from where they sat. Just thinking about it was making her heart flutter against her ribs like a panicked bird. She pressed her hands between her knees to stop them from shaking, knowing her imagination would inevitably play out the murders in her brain as she described them.

But as she formed the first word on her tongue, something hammered against her bedroom window and the word morphed into a scream.

CHAPTER 17

Chan squealed and launched at Marc, who clutched them to his chest as though he was drowning and they were a lifebuoy. Lacy had sprung to her feet the moment the banging had started and faced the drawn curtains, every muscle in her body taut with alarm.

The banging continued.

'What the hell?' Chan spluttered from beneath Marc's gangly limbs.

Lacy's shock quickly flared into anger. It was one of the others, trying to scare her. It wasn't the first time she'd heard scuffling feet outside her window.

She marched forwards and snatched the curtain back.

There was a face pressed up close to the grimy glass.

Lacy shrieked and stepped backwards. The face was like a Halloween mask, contorted into a grizzled snarl, the eyes bloodshot and staring straight at Lacy. They raised a gnarled finger and tapped it furiously on the glass.

Chan appeared by Lacy's side and squinted at the window. '*Gary?*'

'Eugh,' Marc groaned loudly and flumped heavily onto the

bed, still clutching his heart. '*Of course* it's pissing *Gary*.'

Lacy tried to fight the adrenaline that had flooded her body. Gary, the old man who lived in the decrepit caravan not far from the dorm block, was hammering on her bedroom window.

'What does he want?' she whispered, trying not to move her lips in case he could read them.

Gary's eyes still glared at her, and he raised his hand to continue his banging. Lacy flinched as the single-pane window rattled threateningly. He could put his fist straight through it. And then there would be nothing stopping him from climbing into her room and—

Chan stepped forwards and tugged the window open.

'Chan!' Lacy scream-whispered. 'Don't let him in!'

But Chan ignored her and leaned out of the window, asking placidly, 'Hi, Gary, how may we help you this fine evening?'

Gary responded with a tirade of abuse. Something about the bloody volume of the bloody music and the lack of bloody respect kids had nowadays.

Lacy peered around Chan's back to watch his furious hand gesturing. His fist was clenched and he darted it threateningly in Chan's direction a few times, but Chan didn't flinch.

Lacy looked urgently at Marc, who was still lying on the bed as though bored already. He gave her a thin-lipped smile. 'Don't worry – Chan's used to it.'

Lacy turned her attention back to Chan, who was nodding sympathetically at Gary. 'I know, mate. I know,' they said softly beneath Gary's ranting. Lacy noticed his words getting quieter and his movements less violent. Was Chan letting him tire himself out, like a stampeding bull charging again and again until he finally collapsed with exhaustion?

'It's the same every bloody year!' he shouted, his finger jabbing towards the staff accommodation. 'If you want to get shagged, then get shagged – just turn the bloody wireless down!'

Marc stifled a snort of laughter.

'Gary, love,' Chan sighed, 'no one is getting shagged in here, trust me. And look, I'm on your side. I really am. But you might have noticed, the music isn't coming from in here.'

Lacy saw the rage on Gary's face fade slightly, and he shifted his weight awkwardly. 'I know,' he muttered. 'But I was hammering on the kitchen window for ten minutes and no one could hear me.'

Marc pulled his T-shirt over his face to hide his laughter, and Lacy wished she could find the situation as amusing as he did. But she still felt horribly on edge. The one sliver of privacy she had in this place was being violated by a raving lunatic with about four brown teeth to his name.

'I know,' Chan said gently. 'Why don't you head back to your caravan and pop your own music on? That'll be nice, right?'

The way Chan said it almost made Lacy feel tempted to go to Gary's caravan and listen to music.

She watched in amazement as the rage melted from Gary's grizzled face. He nodded with a serene expression before shuffling meekly away.

'You're a wizard,' Lacy breathed as Chan closed the window and clapped their hands together.

Chan laughed. 'Plenty of practice dealing with upset customers, that's all.'

'Why doesn't he move to a different caravan?' Lacy asked, peering out of the window to watch Gary trudge back towards his grotty caravan. 'Then he wouldn't have to worry about any of this.'

Chan collapsed onto the bed beside Marc and shrugged. 'We all have our idiosyncrasies.'

Lacy looked at Chan in surprise. They looked like someone who would enjoy getting into a scrap on a night out, but here they were, throwing around words like 'idiosyncrasies'.

'Doesn't it freak you out?' Lacy pushed, watching Gary walk away until she was sure he'd definitely gone. 'That there are people like Gary, right there…people who could get into the dorms if they really wanted to?'

'Ah, Gary's harmless,' Marc insisted as he emerged from inside his T-shirt.

'But what if…?' Lacy chewed the inside of her lip. 'What if something happens again, like it did ten years ago? What's to stop someone coming in here and—'

'Wha—' Marc began, before Chan abruptly cut him off.

'Lacy, don't worry about it, honestly.' They stood and placed a comforting hand on Lacy's shoulder. 'I know what it's like, being somewhere like this – it's intense, claustrophobic. Your imagination can start running away with you a bit.'

Lacy flushed, remembering Chan's concerned face the evening she'd freaked out on the beach.

'I worked in Blackpool for the Christmas season and, trust me, that was much worse than here. You had to perform for customers all day. Pretend to be this happy, smiley person, when really you were sick of the sight of them, and everything was shit.'

Marc nodded viciously and Lacy wondered if it was really so bad working here. But then again, her job involved staring at the water with a hot lifeguard all day. She might not feel the same if she was dealing with angry drunks or dancing around dressed as a bear.

'In Blackpool we had people just not turning up for work because they couldn't hack it anymore,' Chan continued.

'Like Ceri?' Lacy said quickly, hoping for some intel on why she might have fled.

'Yeah.' Chan nodded thoughtfully but didn't offer anything further.

'Andy said she was close with Dylan,' Lacy pressed, wincing at how obsessive she sounded. It was clear Dylan and Ceri had history, even if she hadn't been anywhere near the cliff last night. But that wasn't what bothered her. She just wanted to reassure herself that Ceri had really been picked up by her parents and wasn't floating dead in the sea somewhere.

'They're both local,' Chan said.

'I know Ceri was upset because of something that had happened during a pretty heavy night,' Marc piped up, and Lacy wondered how much he saw from his brooding perch on the outskirts of the parties. 'I dunno what it was. Some drama with her and Rachel, I think. But I know for a fact Dylan wasn't there that night, so it can't have been anything to do with him.'

He gave her a small, sympathetic smile, and Lacy gratefully returned it. She found herself wishing she'd been less snooty when she'd first met him – maybe if she'd been more pleasant he'd have been quicker to show her the sweeter side of his personality. She got the impression they could both have done with a friend, especially on the evenings Chan spent working at the bar.

'Try to remember,' Chan said softly, staring intensely at Lacy, 'this place isn't real.'

Lacy frowned. What did *that* mean?

But Chan grinned, and Lacy felt stupid for feeling creeped out by their words. 'It's a weird little Groundhog Day bubble. We get up, we go to work, we get drunk. Repeat.'

'Isn't that just what being an adult is?' Marc quipped, and Lacy snorted. He was right – that was exactly how she would describe her parents' lives.

But her amusement suddenly turned sour, replaced by something closer to anger. 'It's not how my life will be,' she said firmly, her thoughts spilling out of her mouth.

'Oh, yeah?' Chan asked curiously. 'Destined for bigger things?'

Lacy blushed and wished she hadn't spoken. She hadn't even *meant* to say anything. It was bad enough when random Winter-esque thoughts burst unbidden into her head. But to have them coming out of her mouth as well made her feel as though she had no control over herself.

She turned her gaze back to the window and wished Chan would sit back down on the bed instead of standing so close and staring curiously at her. If she was Winter, she would have proudly told them about her place at the Paris School of Fine Art, and that, yes, she was destined for much bigger things than the majority of people she knew.

But she wasn't her sister. And, truth be told, she wasn't sure she really was destined for greatness.

'I'm moving to Paris in September,' she mumbled into the threadbare carpet beneath her feet.

'*Niiiice*,' Marc said, looking impressed. 'You speak French and stuff?'

Lacy's blush deepened. She hadn't exactly been practising lately. 'Kind of.'

'You got family there?' Chan asked. 'Or a holiday home or something?'

Lacy squirmed. She knew Marc and Chan's questions were well intentioned, but they made her feel like she was being scrutinised.

'Um, no...' Lacy replied reluctantly. 'I, um. I've never actually been there. I've never actually been out of this country.'

She'd hardly been anywhere, in fact. Her parents both worked shifts and never seemed to be off work at the same time. And even if they had been, she doubted they'd have been able to afford to stay at Peril Bay, let alone Paris.

She froze, waiting for the ridicule of being obsessed with a place she had never even visited. She was a fraud.

But the mockery didn't come. 'Nor me,' Chan said brightly. 'I've always wanted to go to Eastern Europe, though. I'm saving to buy a car, and then I'm going to drive all the way over to Slovakia and just, I dunno, explore.'

Marc shuddered dramatically. 'I'm still not going with you unless you take a detour to do some *sightseeing* on the beaches of Italy.'

He waggled his eyebrows suggestively, and Chan grinned as she punched him on the arm. 'Perv.'

Marc's hand darted out to grip the back of Chan's neck, making them shriek and squirm. Before Lacy could understand what was happening, they were full on play-fighting, Chan straddling Marc and making him slap himself with his own hands as he giggled wildly.

Lacy allowed the laughter to bubble up from her chest and

out of her mouth. Seized by a sudden inspiration, she grabbed her camera from where it hung on the back of her door and snapped photos of them as they wrestled.

As Chan and Marc lay panting on the bed, barely able to breathe through their hysterics, Lacy flicked through the images she'd captured.

They were messy, with terrible lighting and wonky frames. But she'd captured something in Chan and Marc's faces – something alive, something that screamed 'movement'.

Maybe she'd been approaching the project all wrong. Maybe she'd be better off if she let go of everything she thought she knew about photography – about what she thought she knew about *everything*.

CHAPTER 18

'So, why France?' Marc asked as Lacy shoved her feet into her ballet pumps. It had been two weeks since Dylan's tumble off the cliff, and, miraculously, Marc and Chan had stuck around. They seemed to actually like her. 'I mean, why *specifically*?'

Lacy wished she had a profound answer, something about how she'd felt the call of brie and baguettes in her bones for as long as she could remember. But, in truth, Winter had become obsessed with Paris, so Lacy had followed suit.

And Lacy would never admit this to anyone, but she hated cheese.

'Dunno,' she mumbled. 'Just…reasons.'

'Ah, yes,' Marc said. 'I understand now.'

He rolled his eyes and nudged her in the ribs with an elbow that felt like a sharp stick. Lacy smiled shyly and followed him out of her room and down the corridor. She still couldn't quite believe that he and Chan had adopted her as a friend.

Never being one to mince his words, Marc had admitted that he'd seen her as stuck-up and rude when he'd met her. But he'd come to realise she was actually 'all right', he'd told her, as though this were the highest form of praise. It had certainly felt that way to Lacy.

The longer she'd spent at Peril Bay, the more Lacy was losing sense of who she was. When she'd arrived, she'd known she was sophisticated, confidently aloof, *poised*. At least, those were the things she strived to be. Now, she was mumbling words like 'dunno' into her shoes and smiling at someone who had definitely just bruised her ribs.

And even stranger was the fact she had agreed to accompany him to the bar to meet Chan.

'Lacy.' A voice came from behind her as she trotted down the corridor after Marc.

She turned to see Dylan standing outside her bedroom door, watching her with a doleful expression.

'Yes?' she asked, trying to keep her voice completely devoid of emotion.

Getting the balance of repelling him without being cruel, but also not encouraging him into thinking there was still something between them, was exhausting. They'd continued working together, but they sat apart now, whether they were stationed at the pool or the beach. Dylan hadn't been his usual sunny self since the accident. He stared broodingly into the water for hours on end, and Lacy couldn't help but wonder what he was thinking about.

'I…' Dylan faltered, his gaze drifting to Marc, who hovered by Lacy's side. Whatever he wanted to say, he clearly didn't want to say it in front of Marc.

'Dylan, babes,' Marc said firmly. 'I think it's time you moved on. If Lacy wants to talk to you, she'll talk to you. Is that fair, Lacy?'

Marc looked pointedly at her, and she hesitated. Is that what she wanted, for Dylan to stop even trying to talk to her?

'It's just…' Dylan began, his blue eyes flitting between Lacy and Marc. 'There's something I need to—'

'Dylan,' Marc said, his voice sharper this time. 'I saw you trying to look into Lacy's room earlier, pressing your eye up against the crack in her door. It's not cool, man. Just back off.'

The colour rushing up Dylan's neck to his face revealed the truth of Marc's words, and Lacy's jaw dropped. She turned and raised her eyebrows at Marc, who shrugged apologetically.

'I didn't want to freak you out,' he explained.

What had Dylan seen? She'd been getting changed out of her uniform not long ago. Is that what he'd been trying to get a glimpse of?

'It's not like that!' Dylan insisted, his entire face reddening in response to the look of horror on Lacy's face. 'I was—'

'Marc's right,' Lacy snapped, finally finding her voice. 'Back off, Dylan.'

She turned on her heel and marched down the corridor, tugging Marc with her.

'Eugh!' she cried as they stepped into the night. She rubbed the goosebumps that crept up her exposed arms. 'I can't believe he was watching me!'

'Hmm.' Marc nodded as he met her stride. 'It's not the first time me and Chan have noticed him lurking.'

Lacy stared at Marc in surprise. She'd thought Dylan had backed off the second she'd told him to, but clearly, he hadn't gone far enough.

Rachel's words rushed back to her: *He's always been a sucker for a damsel in distress.*

She was beginning to feel like she'd dodged a bullet.

'Ah, shit,' Marc groaned as he stopped walking.

'What is it?' Lacy asked, casting her eyes around in the fading light.

'Forgot my phone. I'll be right back.'

He loped away on his long, slender legs, leaving Lacy standing in the evening light between the staff accommodation and the abandoned dorms.

She curled her lip in distaste as she stared at the dark building, sickened by her anonymous employers for leaving the site of such a horrific crime standing. It was more than disrespectful to keep the dorm blocks, it was unethical. How would the parents of the dead teenagers feel, knowing that nothing had changed since their kids were murdered? That it could easily happen again if some psychopath decided to walk straight into the block that the current staff called home?

There was a lock on the only door into the staff accommodation and it required a code to open. But it was often left on the latch so Rachel's gang could nip out to smoke and do stupid dares that involved running in and out of the building, screeching and banging on the doors as they passed.

And, Lacy realised as she craned her head towards the entrance of the abandoned dorm, there was the exact same lock on Dorm Block B too. Not that it had stopped the killer ten years ago.

'This place is so messed up,' she muttered, hoping to rid herself of the unease that crept over her chilled skin.

Her gaze was pulled towards the black window that stood opposite hers. The window she'd seen a face staring out of.

The window she'd *imagined* she'd seen a face, she corrected herself. There had been nothing there then, and there was nothing there now.

Except...

Lacy held her breath as she tried to focus on the gloom of the bedroom behind the grubby glass. There were mattresses piled in the far corner, and it was difficult to see anything past the crack that snaked across the window. But she swore there was...

A shadow. A *person-shaped* shadow standing in the corner of the room.

Lacy sucked air into her lungs, barely daring to move, torn between wanting to investigate and wanting to run the hell away. She squinted through the fading light and into the deeper dark of the room.

It really did look like a person. But unless they moved, she just couldn't be sure. She wrinkled her nose. That rancid, floral smell was back.

A noise to her right stole her attention and she tore her gaze away from the window.

'Jesus,' she hissed. Standing next to the entrance of the abandoned dorm was Marc, and he was wearing the huge, brown bear mascot.

'Hilarious,' she sighed.

She tried to laugh, but the feeling of unease remained. She wrapped her arms around her middle as a howling gust of wind hurtled between the two dorm blocks.

Marc didn't move. He just stood there, his giant bear head slightly askew, looking like he'd been draped messily in the skin of a dead animal.

'Are we going to meet Chan, or what?' Lacy snapped, irritated by this juvenile game.

She turned back to the window but couldn't see anything inside that resembled a person this time. Which meant she was either experiencing yet another sinister hallucination, or there had been someone in the abandoned dorm, and now they were gone.

Lacy wasn't sure which option she preferred. Once again, she found herself hoping that her terrible eyesight was to blame and a trip to the opticians would solve all her problems.

Just as she was about to see if Marc had finished dicking about in his bear suit, a hand landed heavily on her shoulder. She gasped and turned. There was Marc.

CHAPTER 19

Lacy swivelled back towards the entrance to the abandoned dorm, where Marc had been standing in the bear suit moments before.

'How did you get changed so fast?' she asked him, pointing at the now-empty spot.

'Eh?' Marc's forehead puckered in confusion.

Lacy sighed. She didn't have the patience for unfunny pranks. 'The bear costume?'

'What about it?' Marc said slowly.

'You were wearing it, like, ten seconds ago,' Lacy replied, noticing the slight hysteria in her voice. 'You were standing over there!'

She jabbed her finger at the entrance of the abandoned dorm. But even as she did, she knew it was impossible. He couldn't have taken the suit off and somehow teleported to stand behind her so quickly.

'Lacy,' Marc said carefully. 'I promise, I—'

'OK, so it wasn't you,' Lacy agreed. 'But someone has stolen your costume and is creeping around the park in it.'

Marc frowned. 'I mean…it seems unlikely. Apart from

Andy, me and Rachel are the only ones with a key to the cloakroom we keep the suits in.'

'There you go then,' Lacy said, glad there was a mundane explanation. 'It was Rachel.'

But Marc was shaking his head. 'Rachel is like, five feet tall. The bear suit is made for a lanky giant like me. I don't see how—'

'One of the others then!' Lacy snapped.

Marc widened his eyes at Lacy in surprise before asking tentatively, 'Why are you so rattled about this?'

Lacy pinched the bridge of her nose and sighed, suddenly exhausted. It was just one of the other employees, probably doing some kind of stupid dare. She wouldn't have felt so unnerved if it had been the only thing that had happened, but the bear was the icing on a really weird cake.

'I just…' she said, wondering how much to tell Marc. Did she really want to risk ruining one of the first friendships she'd ever had that felt like it could be genuine?

She peered at Marc, who was studying her with a concerned frown. She decided to tell the truth.

'I keep seeing things. That night Dylan got drunk, I could have sworn I saw Ceri push him off the cliff. And just now, I thought there was someone in my room, watching me. Well, not *my* room, but the room that would have been mine in the abandoned dorm.'

She pointed and her finger trembled in the air.

'And now, I'm being stalked by a giant teddy bear.'

Lacy could see Marc fighting a smirk but appreciated him not straight out laughing in her face. She knew she was being oversensitive, maybe even delusional. But an unnerving feeling that she was never alone had been creeping her out since she arrived at Bae Peryg.

'All right, you two.' Chan's voice came suddenly from their side, making both of them jump. 'Did you decide that standing here staring at an empty building was a more exciting prospect than meeting me after work?'

Chan stood facing them, cutting off Lacy's view to the abandoned dorm and the empty window.

'Sorry – I had to run back for my phone,' Marc said, waggling it in the air to show Chan. 'And, er…Lacy had a, um, mild hallucination?'

Chan looked questioningly at Lacy.

'It was nothing,' she muttered, feeling more foolish by the second. 'Just someone being an idiot.'

Chan's eyes narrowed, clearly not convinced. 'You OK, Lacy?'

Lacy worried the inside of her lip as she peered around Chan towards the empty building. She'd already admitted to Marc that she was seeing things – she may as well get all her concerns out in the open. 'Has anyone been in there since…you know? I mean, is it all properly locked up? There's definitely no one squatting in there or anything?'

'Since what?' Marc asked, looking baffled.

Lacy still couldn't believe he hadn't heard about it when he seemed to know everything about everyone in this place. How was it possible Chan hadn't told him? 'Since the *murders*,' she whispered.

Marc straightened, looking like an alarmed giraffe. 'Someone was *murdered* in there?'

'Ah, shit,' Chan sighed.

Lacy turned slowly to look at them. 'What?'

Chan grimaced and reached beneath their hood to rub the soft stubble of their undercut. 'OK, before I tell you, please know that I feel really, really bad about it.'

'*What?*'

'No one was killed in the abandoned dorm. I made it all up.' Chan winced and waited for Lacy's reaction.

'But…' Lacy spluttered, her brain whirring in confusion. 'But…'

Chan had *lied*. And Lacy had been a gullible fool. She'd swallowed Chan's bullshit story without hesitation. She'd even accepted it when there was absolutely nothing online mentioning the murders. She'd been stupid, completely stu—

'Chan!' Marc gasped, his hand over his mouth in glee. 'That's not like you!'

Chan shrank further into the hoodie. 'I know, and I feel really bad. It's just…well, you were kind of rude when we first met. And it just…came out.'

Lacy's eyes grew damp. She *had* been rude. But did she really deserve to have such a sick joke played on her? And did Chan really feel bad about it, or had they been laughing at her this whole time?

But Marc tutted loudly and looped a long arm around Lacy's shoulders, pulling her towards his bony chest. 'God, Chan, you've traumatised the poor girl!'

Chan peered at her, their face creased with guilt. 'I wouldn't have said anything if I'd known it would mess with your head, I promise. I've felt awful about it ever since, especially since you started…you know.'

'Freaking out over things that aren't there?' Lacy suggested, and Chan smiled apologetically.

Maybe Chan was genuinely sorry for sending her imagination into overdrive so that it had dreamed up a menacing figure that haunted her wherever she went.

Another thought occurred to Lacy. Was that why Chan and Marc had befriended her? Chan must have felt awful after witnessing Lacy freak out over ghostly figures on multiple occasions. And it wouldn't have been difficult to convince Marc that the two of them needed to look out for Lacy – Marc clearly worshipped the ground Chan walked on.

This wasn't friendship. This was pity.

Lacy pressed her tongue between her teeth, biting back the tears.

Winter had insisted that it didn't matter if she didn't have friends, that there was no one from their hometown worth being friends with anyway. Lacy had agreed, not admitting that she was lonely as hell.

And besides, she had Winter.

It's you and me forever. I'm all you need, OK?

Marc gave her shoulder a gentle squeeze and brought her back to the present.

'Sorry,' she muttered. She wondered if Chan and Marc would stop hanging around with her now.

'Let's go for a walk,' Chan suggested brightly, and Lacy's heart soared with hope.

'Yeah,' Marc agreed. 'Even if no one was murdered in there, it's still bloody horrible.' He nodded darkly towards the abandoned dorm, and Lacy nodded.

But it wasn't haunted, at least, and she took a shuddery breath. Now that she knew nothing awful had happened in the dorm, maybe she could finally stop seeing things that weren't there.

CHAPTER 20

Lacy gazed down at her feet as they shuffled across the tarmac. She yawned noisily, not bothering to hide it – there was no one around as she trudged back to the accommodation block after a long shift at the pool. It amazed her how exhausted doing nothing all day was making her. She spent hour after hour staring mindlessly at the shimmering water, the shouts and screams of the swimmers blurring into a continuous white noise that made her horribly drowsy.

During her shifts, she tried not to dwell on the fact that life was short and she was wasting it literally watching a clock. But this was a means to an end. In six weeks' time, she would have saved enough money to pay the first month's rent on her tiny Paris apartment.

She just hoped her brain wouldn't rot from inactivity in the meantime.

There was a thump from inside one of the occupied caravans, followed by a shout, a slammed door and someone else shouting from another caravan to keep the noise down. She shuddered and tugged her jacket over her green uniform. She'd learned to keep it hidden when she was off duty.

Guests had a habit of demanding things whenever they saw a member of staff. Two days ago, someone had angrily insisted that she personally compensate them because the park shop had run out of WKD.

She forced her eyes back to the path. Now that the story of the abandoned dorm had been exposed as untrue, her mind had returned to the very real murder of Carl Jones. She couldn't help thinking of the way his body had been stashed beneath his own caravan. Were there new guests in there now, carrying on as though nothing had happened?

Stop it, Lacy.

She shook the morbid imaginings out of her head and yawned again, stretching her arms. As she tipped her neck from side to side, easing the ache of a day of inactivity, she caught a glimpse of movement out of the corner of her eye.

Dylan was walking behind her.

He faltered as he realised he had been spotted, shifting his weight from one leg to the other as though considering diving behind a caravan to hide from her.

Lacy went through the usual cycle of conflicted emotions when she laid eyes on him. A tug of affection, exasperation and now...unease.

She remembered her first night at the park, and the eye she'd seen staring through the hole in her bedroom wall that she'd convinced herself had been a figment of her imagination. She remembered Dylan suddenly appearing on the clifftop the night she'd gone for a walk to clear her head. And she remembered with a shudder when Marc had told her about him peering through the crack in her bedroom door.

Maybe she had imagined most of the weird incidents that

had happened since arriving at Peril Bay. But what if some of them had been real?

A sudden, sickening thought occurred to Lacy.

Ceri – that night on the clifftop. Lacy had been sure the striking Welsh girl had wrestled Dylan over the ledge, then had been just as sure that she hadn't been there at all, existing only in her overactive imagination.

But what if...what if she *had* been there? What if she *had* fallen to her death, and Dylan had chosen not to remember it because he'd wanted her gone? Because *he'd* pushed *her*?

No. Lacy shook her head as she walked. No, there was a big difference between some potentially dodgy behaviour and murdering a girl he'd known for years. It was just her stupid head spiralling and conjuring up the worst possible things, yet again.

But then why was Dylan walking towards the dorms now? Did he enjoy Rachel's parties so much that he'd rather be here than relaxing in his cosy farmhouse after a long day at work?

'Dylan,' she said sharply, stopping to confront him. 'Have you been following me? Have you—'

'Laaaacy!'

Lacy jumped as Marc appeared at her side and wrapped her in an elbowy hug. '*Happy birthday to you, happy birthday to you, happy birthday, dear LAAAACY...*'

As Lacy squirmed free of Marc's gangly arms, she noticed Dylan's eyebrows rise with surprise. 'How did you know it was my birthday?' she muttered.

She frowned at Marc's golden face, which she'd since learned came from a bottle. Spending the day inside a bear suit made opportunities for tanning limited. Lacy was sure she hadn't told anyone about turning eighteen. She wasn't exactly big on birthdays. Winter said they were just another way for big corporations to make money, when all we were really celebrating was getting a step closer to our inevitable deaths. Her words hadn't exactly instilled a celebratory feeling in Lacy, so she'd simply started pretending her birthdays weren't happening.

'It's your birthday?' Dylan asked tentatively, cowering as though expecting to be shooed away.

'How do you know?' Lacy repeated to Marc, ignoring Dylan.

'If I tell you, I'll destroy my international man of mystery persona.'

Lacy now raised her eyebrows too and stared at him.

'*Fiiiine*,' he sighed. 'I saw it in your file.'

Lacy blanched. They had a *file* on her? She thought back to the cramped room full of boxes that Marc had taken her to on her first day, when he'd given her the acid-green uniform. There had been files in there, hadn't there? Had Marc been poking around, reading private information about her and the other employees?

'What did it say?' she asked, folding her arms and turning slightly away from Dylan, making it clear that he wasn't invited into this conversation. But he continued to lurk awkwardly.

Marc shook his head impatiently. 'Oh, it's just your CV, your personal profile, et cetera. Your application was very fancy.' He winked at Lacy. 'It read like you were applying for Oxford, not a position at Wales's worst caravan park.'

Lacy shrank into her lime-green polo shirt, mortified. She'd spent an embarrassingly long time on her job application for this place, detailing what she would bring to the team, her unique skill set and her five-year plan. She knew now that it would probably have been sufficient to say she wasn't an axe murderer.

'I'm just messing with you.' Marc grinned and threw his arm back around her shoulder. 'You're clearly a lot smarter than me, and it makes me insecure, and I therefore have to tease you… The great circle of adolescent life.'

Lacy snorted. She suspected Marc was a lot more intelligent than he gave himself credit for.

'Happy birthday,' Dylan said softly, giving her a watery smile.

Lacy returned it warily. 'Thanks.'

'Come on,' Marc said smartly and steered Lacy away from Dylan and towards the staff dorm.

'Where are we going?' Lacy asked, itching to peer over her shoulder to see if Dylan was following.

'To celebrate your birthday, of course!' He must have felt her tense beneath his arm, as he said, 'Don't worry – it will be classy and sophisticated.'

'*Really?*' Lacy asked disbelievingly as she struggled to walk in time with his huge, loping strides.

'I promise. There won't be a single shot in sight. And –' he paused for dramatic effect as he pushed the dorm block door open '– Chan has bought *premium* alcohol.'

Lacy opened her mouth to object, to tell him that she didn't drink, that she wouldn't ever drink, that drinking could end horribly. If he knew… If he knew what could happen, what *had* happened just four months ago… But Chan was waiting in the kitchen to greet them and broke out into a deafening rendition of 'Happy Birthday' when they walked in, distracting Lacy from her spiralling thoughts.

There was no one else there, thank god. Lacy would have died on the spot if the whole team had been shouting and singing her name. Not that they would have – she'd hardly made herself popular. She still avoided everyone apart from Chan and Marc. Though she returned Andy's polite chit chat when they ran into each other, which was surprisingly often.

'Look!' Chan shrieked, more animated than Lacy had ever seen them. 'Red, pink *and* white!' Chan gestured grandly at the three bottles of wine on the kitchen surface. 'I assumed you'd want the red, cos that's the most French.'

'This one's mine,' Marc insisted, plucking the rosé off the counter and clutching the bottle to his chest.

'Guys,' Lacy said, overwhelmed by their eagerness to celebrate with her. 'I don't...'

Chan stepped towards her, and Lacy was comforted by the kindness in their eyes. 'What's the worst that could happen?'

Lacy's lips twitched as she struggled to contain her answer. She knew all too well what could happen, and her story would horrify Chan and Marc.

But as she looked at their grinning, hopeful faces, she hesitated. She wasn't going to drink so much that she lost control. She wasn't going to do anything she regretted.

She wasn't Cal.

Her fingers wrapped around the bottle of red wine.

'Did you steal this from the bar?' she asked, turning the bottle over in her hands. She really should start learning about wine if she was going to make a true Parisian.

'Er, I'll have you know this is the Pitstop's finest vintage,'

Chan said, referring to the on-site mini supermarket that stocked an array of essentials, such as plastic cheese, beer and inflatable rubber rings. The staff had to survive off its stock, and Lacy was starting to fear she'd get scurvy from the lack of nutrients in her diet.

'Well,' Lacy said awkwardly. 'Cheers, I guess.'

Chan and Marc linked arms with her and, much to Lacy's relief, marched her towards her bedroom. She may have agreed to a drink with them, but she'd have drawn the line at being the centre of attention at yet another trashy kitchen party.

'Right then,' Marc said, his focus on his phone. 'Music. Lacy – your birthday, your choice. And if you suggest Rachel's playlist of party bangers, then we are no longer friends.'

Lacy hesitated. She knew she despised the music that usually came thumping through her wall every night, but didn't know what she *did* like.

Her cheeks flamed as her mind desperately searched for the name of a suitable song suggestion. She'd tried to educate herself on French music, but it was difficult to know what was considered cool without an actual French person to discuss it with.

She had no taste of her own, she realised with horror. She just liked what Winter told her to like.

'Too late, I've chosen,' Marc declared, tapping his screen.

Lacy nearly sagged to the floor with relief. She twisted the screw cap off her wine bottle and took a swig.

Chan and Marc laughed as she spluttered, her face twisting in disgust at the bitter taste. 'This is awful!' she gasped once she'd finally recovered. The obsession everyone had with drinking was now even more of a mystery to her.

Ali and the other girls would drink occasionally, but Lacy never seemed to be invited when they got together and shared the booze they'd managed to convince someone to buy for them. Maybe they didn't consider her worth sharing their precious supply with.

And Cal drank. Cal drank like he'd been born in the pub, despite only being seventeen when…

Lacy blinked and took another swig of the wine, which was somehow sweet, sour and off-tasting at the same time.

She'd never got into drinking because Winter didn't drink. It was as simple as that. Winter was so vehemently against drinking that her face would contort with disgust at the mere mention of it. Sometimes Lacy considered asking why she felt so strongly about it, but she'd been scared of the answer, so had kept quiet.

That was because Winter hadn't always been so against drinking. The hatred had come at the same time as the name change, the fashion change, the complete personality change. And it was like Lacy had something blocking her brain from remembering other details of that time. She'd been the one to find Winter sobbing on the bathroom floor, powerless to the violent vomiting that shuddered through her body. She'd been the one who'd listened to her sister's wails of pain that had made no sense to her thirteen-year-old brain – something about a house party, something about not knowing what happened. Something about being scared.

Lacy flinched, the memory bringing a physical reaction with it so strong that it felt like she'd been shoved hard in the chest.

Don't think about that.

She tuned back into Chan and Marc's chatter, suddenly missing Winter more than ever.

She drank again.

The taste was still disgusting, but as the evening continued, she found herself relaxing. Maybe it was the wine, or maybe she was finally starting to feel more comfortable in her own skin, but for once, she wasn't weighing up every word she said, trying to figure out how it would make her come across.

She almost missed the sound of knocking as she was struggling to regain control after Marc's frighteningly accurate impression of Rachel. She opened the door, hoping it wouldn't be Dylan.

When Rachel was revealed, wearing the exact same pouty expression Marc had been imitating moments before, Lacy burst out laughing in her face.

'Care to share the joke?' Rachel asked, fighting to keep the smile on her face despite clearly being furious.

'Sorry,' Lacy spluttered, feeling genuinely guilty but unable to stop the laughter from coming.

'I was wondering where my speakers were,' Rachel said brightly, her teeth gleaming.

'They're Lee's speakers actually, babes,' Marc replied, still using the voice he'd adopted to do his impression of her. 'And he said we could, like, totally borrow them.'

Lacy was powerless to the giggles that wracked her body, especially once she'd noticed the silent tears of mirth streaming down Chan's face. A tiny voice in the back of her head told her that they should stop. This could hardly be making Rachel feel great.

But then she remembered the way Rachel had made *her*

feel on many occasions, and she stopped fighting the laughter.

'Well, why don't you bring them to the kitchen.' Rachel smiled, trying a different tack. 'Then we can have a *proper* party instead of being in this poky little room.'

Lacy snorted. Like Rachel's room was any less poky than hers.

'Nah, we're good, thanks,' Chan said.

Rachel's eyes narrowed as the smile dropped off her face. 'You'd rather be in *here?*'

The emphasis in her voice and the way her eyes flicked towards Lacy made it clear that what she really meant was, *You'd rather be with* her?

Lacy swallowed, her muffled laughter suddenly sounding forced. She'd been asking the same question herself, ever since Marc and Chan had shown an interest in her. And, apparently, she wasn't the only one.

Perhaps she'd been right in assuming they'd only befriended her out of pity, but surely they hadn't been able to continue the façade for this long? They were still here, laughing *with* her instead of at her, noticing and celebrating her birthday.

Like real friends.

'Yup,' Chan said cheerily, not offering anything further.

Rachel was actually shaking now, Lacy realised. Was this how badly not having complete control affected her? She must really hate Chan, in that case. Lacy couldn't imagine Chan had ever gone along with any of Rachel's orders.

'Marc?' Rachel said, turning her frenzied smile towards him and holding her hand out as though he were a toddler. 'Come on!'

Lacy willed him to stay put. He'd admitted to being a

sucker for peer pressure, and Lacy couldn't think of a force with greater pressure than Rachel. But he wouldn't be sucked into her games, not tonight, would he?

'Come *onnnn*,' she wheedled. 'Don't be so *boooorrring*.' Marc twitched – Rachel clearly knew how to play on his deepest insecurities. 'Honestly, you've been like an old woman lately. Going to bed early, barely drinking. It's like you're turning into Lacy!'

Her laugh was musical and would have been infectious if her words hadn't sent a bolt of shame through Lacy. She felt the pressure start to build behind her eyes and wondered for an awful moment if she was about to burst into tears over some pathetic comment from the park's resident rabbit entertainment.

Lacy knew she was at best boring and at worst rude. But did that really make her deserving of Rachel's spiteful comments and attempts to turn everyone against her?

No, Lacy decided as her fingers moved to the wrist that Winter's bracelet used to encircle before being lost to the sea. No, she didn't deserve this.

But she *deserves what's coming to* her.

Before Lacy's thoughts could turn towards how Rachel might be made to pay for being a vindictive bully, Rachel's mouth opened to give a whining command of, 'Come *onnnnn*!'

And to her own surprise as much as everyone else's, Lacy interrupted, watching with satisfaction as Rachel's mouth snapped shut in surprise. 'Oh, why don't you just PISS OFF, RACHEL!'

CHAPTER 21

Rachel blinked rapidly, and Lacy felt like she'd just drop-kicked an innocent forest creature. But just as she opened her mouth to apologise, the bunny rabbit morphed into a rabid chihuahua.

'*What?*' she hissed, her teeth bared and worryingly pointy. 'What did you just say to me?'

It was Lacy's turn to freeze. Her eyes darted between Rachel and the bodies that had filled the corridor behind her, lured by shouting and the promise of drama. Lee was gawping, bouncing on the balls of his feet, while Andy looked more serious than Lacy had ever seen him.

She could save this. She could take it back and apologise profusely. She could scuttle back into her little mousehole and spend the rest of her summer trying to avoid Rachel even more than she did already.

Or…she could actually stand up for herself for the first time in her life.

'I said, why don't you just piss off,' she repeated, slowly and deliberately.

Her voice was surprisingly steady, despite the thumping of her heart. What was she *doing*? She glanced at the wine bottle on the floor, but there was barely an inch gone from it, which meant that this wasn't the alcohol talking.

This was *her*.

Rachel was vibrating alarmingly, and Lacy wondered if she would go straight for the jugular when she attacked. She hoped her new-found confidence didn't desert her the moment she had to fight for her life.

'How…how…' Rachel was struggling to speak, and Lacy was suddenly afraid she might have broken her for good. Had anyone ever stood up to her before?

She hadn't expected Rachel to burst into tears.

She cried noisily, without shame. Lacy's fingers curled around the door as she recoiled from Rachel's unbridled anguish.

'You're horrible!' Rachel wailed, shielding her face behind her hands. 'All I do is try to be kind to everyone and make sure they have a good time!'

Lacy looked over her shoulder at Chan and Marc for some kind of help. But they were frozen, looking as astonished as she felt. Even Rachel's friends were transfixed, as though watching the climax of a terrible TV soap that Lacy had somehow been given a leading role in.

Lacy self-consciously patted her hair to check for wayward frizz. 'I didn't…' she began, but Rachel sobbed harder.

'You've been mean to me since the second you got here!' she shrieked. 'You're nothing but a horrible bully!'

Lacy turned again to check Chan and Marc's reaction to Rachel's hysterics. Marc's mouth was dangling open, and Chan only shrugged, making it clear they weren't going to be any help.

Lacy peered through Rachel's fingers, which were still held over her trembling face. Her cheeks were dry. There were no tears. Rachel was full of shit.

'I'm not a bully,' Lacy said firmly. 'I just don't enjoy your parties.'

Rachel's hands disappeared from her face, which wasn't even blotchy. Her devastation apparently gone, she pulled a face as though Lacy had just gravely insulted her mother.

'You don't like my *parties*?'

'No,' Lacy said, then added, 'sorry.'

Rachel narrowed her eyes. 'What the hell is *wrong* with you?'

Lacy widened her eyes in exasperation. This was getting ridiculous. What were they even fighting about? 'Jesus, Rachel, it's not that big a deal. Just…accept it and move on.'

Even before Lacy finished making her suggestion, she knew Rachel was not the *get over it* type. She was more of a *flog it to death* kind of girl.

And that might be exactly the treatment Lacy was about to get.

'You think you're so much better than me, don't you?' Rachel snarled, her eyes bulging like a pet hamster being squeezed too hard. 'You think we're all beneath you, that we're stupid, that we're going nowhere.'

Lacy dithered. It wasn't that straightforward. She didn't think particularly highly of them, no. But she didn't think particularly highly of herself either. She didn't think highly of *anything*, in fact. Whenever she got enthusiastic about something, Winter's voice piped up in her head, mocking it.

The only thing she'd felt permitted to enjoy was Paris, or Winter's vision of Paris, at least.

'Well, I'm not stupid!' Rachel squeaked. 'I'm going to university in September!'

Rachel's eyes were genuinely wet now, and Lacy bit her lower lip, suddenly embarrassed by how she'd assumed she was the only one who would be going into higher education.

'Yeah!' Lee bellowed from behind Rachel. 'And I'm—'

'Shut up, Lee,' Rachel snapped, without looking at him. 'You actually are stupid.'

Lee's face fell and he shrank in on himself, hiding his face beneath the peak of his baseball cap. It was the same as Marc's reaction when Rachel had turned her attention on him.

Lacy didn't feel uncertain anymore. Rachel was a nasty piece of work, regardless of whether Lacy was particularly great herself. And Lacy was done with being made to feel small and worthless.

'I'm not the bully here,' Lacy said, clenching her fists as she fought to control her shaking hands. '*You* are. You belittle people, you make them feel like they don't have any choice, that they can't be themselves. You don't even give them a chance to learn who they are!'

Rachel's face screwed up in confusion. 'What are you going on about?'

Lacy frowned. She'd been talking to Rachel as though…as though she were her sister. For a moment, she'd even imagined Winter's black eyes.

Was *Winter* really the same as girls like Rachel and Ali – girls who made Lacy feel like she was nothing? A wave of dizziness made her grip the doorframe.

'Nothing,' Lacy muttered, clawing herself back to reality. 'Just that your parties suck.'

Rachel's own fists clenched in response to Lacy, and she stood on her tiptoes and pushed her face towards her. 'You take that back!'

'I will not!' Lacy shouted.

'Take it back!'

'No!'

'Girls!' A pleading voice came from the corridor.

Lacy took her eyes off Rachel to see Dylan standing in the background, a head taller than the others. She blushed furiously. She would really prefer him not to see her engaging in this pathetic argument.

Rachel snorted in disgust as she followed Lacy's gaze. 'What the hell does he see in a boring bitch like you? You're not even pretty.'

Lacy didn't care what Rachel thought of her, but god, that hurt. Especially when she knew that Rachel was right. She tried to be interesting and sophisticated, but underneath she knew she was some boring, ugly—

'I believe Lacy told you to piss off out of her room,' Chan said, appearing at Lacy's side, their shoulder pressed comfortingly against hers.

Rachel's ferocity waned as she looked at Chan, and Lacy couldn't blame her. Even if Chan was staggeringly kind most of the time, Lacy was sure they could rip Rachel in half if they felt so inclined.

Marc stood to flank Lacy from the other side. 'So off you piss, *now*.' His voice was shaking, and Lacy knew it must have taken a lot of nerve for him to finally stand up to Rachel.

Lacy almost felt sorry for Rachel as her eyes flicked wildly between the three of them. None of her vast cohort of friends seemed to be willing to step forwards and defend her. Not after the way she'd treated Lee for speaking up.

'You can shut the door behind you,' Lacy said calmly.

She turned her back on Rachel, feeling a rush of power as she dismissed her. She sat back down on her bed, trying to look casual, and hoping Rachel couldn't tell how fast her heart was beating from where she stood.

Chan and Marc joined her, leaving Rachel spluttering in the corner.

One by one, the others slowly peeled away. Lacy had to stop herself from checking if Dylan had also gone.

She finally allowed herself to look up and rolled her eyes when she saw that Rachel was still there, her lips twitching as she tried to think of a killer parting line.

'You'll pay for this,' she finally settled on, before flouncing out of the room with the little dignity she had left.

CHAPTER 22

'That was *epic*,' Chan breathed, gazing at Lacy with unfiltered awe. Lacy's cheeks pinkened with delight.

'I particularly enjoyed how you stuck to your key message throughout.' Marc nodded. '"Piss off" has such an elegant simplicity to it.'

'Don't forget "your parties suck",' Chan added.

'Ah yes, the pièce de résistance.'

'You do know she might actually murder you now, though?' Chan said.

Lacy chewed her lip as she eyed the empty doorway. Would Rachel really seek revenge on her? She didn't want to spend the rest of the summer looking over her shoulder. She was finally finding her place at Peril Bay and starting to feel comfortable in her own skin. But the feeling was fragile, and she knew it would be all too easy for Rachel to shatter it.

'Don't worry, Lacy,' came a male voice from the corridor.

Lacy snapped her head up, wondering if Dylan had come to check on her and unsure how she felt about the prospect.

But it was Andy. He'd got sunburned and his head looked like a glacé cherry perched on top of a slice of key lime pie.

'I'll look after you,' he said, holding his hand earnestly to his heart as he stepped into the room. 'Rachel won't be able to do anything to you. Not on my watch.'

'Um, thanks, Andy,' Lacy replied awkwardly, wondering what Rachel might do and how Andy expected to prevent her from doing it. He might be their manager on paper, but he clearly wasn't the boss around here. The complete absence of any other responsible adult at Peril Bay had already led to a bar fight that left a man dead and stuffed beneath his own caravan. Staff grievances weren't exactly going to be top of management's list of priorities.

She broke eye contact with him, hoping he would take the hint and leave.

But Andy clearly wasn't the hint-taking type.

'Having some drinkie-poos?' he asked. Chan visibly shuddered.

Andy was in his early twenties but somehow managed to come across as the park's embarrassing uncle.

'Um, yeah…' Lacy said flatly, praying he wouldn't ask if he could join them. She could hardly say no, but his presence was already killing her high from telling Rachel off.

'Well, it's no use over here, is it?' He chuckled and bent to pick up the bottle Lacy had left near the door.

She turned to roll her eyes at Chan and Marc as Andy strode merrily across the bedroom towards them.

'Here you go,' he said. He held the bottle out for Lacy to take, like a dog proudly bringing a stick to his master.

'Thanks, Andy.'

And before Lacy could understand what was happening, Andy had draped himself over her in the most uncomfortable hug she had ever experienced. He rubbed her back in a way that made goosebumps run up her entire body and she had to fight the instinct to squirm out of his embrace.

'There, there,' he whispered, his breath moistening her ear. 'Let it all out.'

Lacy glared furiously at Chan and Marc over Andy's shoulder. They were barely managing to contain their hysterics.

'Andy,' Lacy said, tapping him on the back, her voice muffled by his shoulder.

'It's OK,' he soothed. 'I've got you.'

A strange squeak came from Marc as his face turned dark purple. He looked like his head might explode from the effort of holding his laughter in.

'Andy, I'm good,' Lacy insisted, but Andy just squeezed tighter. 'Andy, I don't need a hug!'

He let her go and Lacy sighed with relief, then felt instantly guilty when she saw his embarrassed expression.

'Sorry.' He laughed awkwardly, running his hand over his sunburned cheeks, which had turned even redder.

'No, it's fi—'

'I'll leave you to it then, shall I?' He dithered, rocking on the balls of his feet as he stood next to the bed, his eyes locked unblinkingly on Lacy's.

She could hardly tell him to go now, could she? Lacy opened her mouth to insist he stay, but Marc trod sharply on her foot.

'Ouch! Um, yeah, sorry. I mean...thanks, Andy.'

She cringed as Andy scuttled out of the room with his tail between his legs.

'That guy is so nice he makes me do a small sick in my mouth,' Chan declared once he had closed the door behind him.

The three of them settled back onto the bed, and this time Lacy didn't make an effort to keep a gap between them.

'He should be the one in the bloody bear suit,' Marc growled, and Lacy nodded her agreement. He really was a sweet, bumbling teddy bear…who smelled slightly of stale sweat and cheap aftershave.

'Gotta keep your eye on the nice ones,' Marc said darkly and raised his eyebrows suggestively at Lacy.

Lacy brought the bottle to her lips and swigged before slumping back against the wall. 'Do you mean Dylan?' she asked softly.

'Hmm,' Marc said.

Was there more that Lacy didn't know, other than Dylan trying to peek through the gap in her door that night? Lacy couldn't decide whether she wanted to know, or if she'd rather remain ignorant. What did it matter, anyway? Whatever she had going on with Dylan was over, whether he was a nice guy or not.

'He was nice to me,' she mused. 'Which is more than I can say for my ex, who was a dick from day one.'

She swallowed, instantly wishing she hadn't mentioned Cal. She never understood her emotions when he came up – sadness mingled with self-loathing for making such a disastrous relationship choice.

'Why did you get with him if his dickishness was so apparent?' Marc asked, resting his head against the wall as he waited for Lacy to answer.

Lacy squirmed on the mattress, unsure how much to reveal. 'My sister had just left and my friends had ditched me,' she explained. 'I guess I was feeling pretty low. I probably would have gone on a date with Freddy Krueger at that point.'

Marc nodded knowingly. 'We've all shagged a Freddy.'

Lacy looked at him sharply. 'I didn't *shag* him.'

'OK,' Marc said, holding his hands up defensively.

Lacy closed her eyes, embarrassed. Her carefully concealed emotions were bubbling dangerously close to the surface tonight.

'Sorry,' she said. 'I just... I'm a bit sensitive about it. He, um...' She sighed slowly. 'We were together for a few months, and he wanted to do stuff, but I wasn't, you know, ready.'

She felt Chan tense beside her.

The wine tasted rotten and sweet on Lacy's tongue as the memory she'd tried so hard to banish flooded her thoughts. Cal in her bedroom, his mouth over hers, swallowing the words desperate to be voiced: *No. Wait. Stop.* Knowing she should push him off, scream and fight and make it clear that she didn't want this. But Cal was her boyfriend. She didn't understand the rules, let alone the repulsion she was feeling as his hands tugged at her jeans.

And why *didn't* she want him? Was there something wrong with her? Maybe she should just close her eyes and get it over and done with.

But just as she'd been trying to convince her body to relax, Cal had screamed and leaped off her as though he'd been burned by her skin. Something that made no sense at all as she'd felt cold and stiff beneath his touch.

'What the hell?' he'd shouted, his eyes bright with fury, his hand clamped to his cheek.

Lacy's eyes had widened as blood trickled down his jaw.

'I fought him off,' she told Chan and Marc, although she still didn't understand how it had happened. She didn't remember bringing her fingers up to claw at his face.

'But he told everyone that I did stuff with him…like, nasty stuff. Stuff I wouldn't ever…' She swallowed, her face reddening from the memory. 'I had loads of random guys calling me, asking if I would do it with them too. I think he must have given my number out, not that he would admit it.'

'Jesus,' Chan breathed. 'What an utter scumbag.'

'Hmm,' Lacy agreed, still reluctant to speak badly of him, even now. She had asked him to slow down, moved her face away from his and tried to squirm away. But had she been clear enough, loud enough?

Cal certainly hadn't got the message at the time, given his furious reaction when her nails had left their mark. *Bitch. Psycho. Tease.*

'Girl, you must have some pretty major trust issues,' Marc suggested.

'Yeah.' Lacy laughed. 'Just a tad.'

'Well, screw him,' Chan said loudly. 'Not literally, obviously. But let's toast to, I don't know –' Chan gestured in the air with the wine bottle, thinking of a suitable toast '– his balls falling off.'

'To his balls falling off!' Marc hollered, clinking his bottle against Chan's, and then Lacy's.

Lacy tried to smile with them, but a wave of hatred tightened her fingers around the wine bottle. If Ali hadn't pushed her into Cal that day he would never have noticed she existed. She took a large gulp of wine to wash the memories away. She didn't want to go back there. She wanted to be right here, celebrating her birthday with Chan and Marc.

'Where'd your sis go then?' Marc asked, and Lacy wished she'd never brought Winter or Cal up.

'Paris,' Lacy said as casually as she could manage. 'She'd always wanted to move there.'

Though, Lacy realised, this wasn't necessarily true. Winter had been fixated on various locations over the years. At one point she'd talked very seriously about joining a commune in rural Scotland. Paris was just the latest of many obsessions.

'We had a plan,' Lacy continued. The wine seemed to be loosening her tongue, making her reveal things she would never usually disclose. 'But we had to wait for me to finish college so I could get a place at art school.'

The image of her and Winter living in the flat they'd dreamed up was so vivid that Lacy felt her room transform around her as she visualised the elegant furniture and stylish artwork they would decorate it with.

'But I guess…' She took a breath, the pain still raw. 'I guess she decided to go on ahead without me.'

'You mean,' Marc said cautiously, 'she just left?'

Lacy nodded. 'Just before Christmas.' She nodded towards the note Winter had left her, scribbled on the back of the card with the hospitality temping agency details, the one that had found her this job. She'd pinned the note on her wall as a reminder of why she was here.

See you in Paris.

Chan and Marc were still staring at her, so she shrugged and tried to make her voice light. 'Winter was always like that, though. She was a free spirit, you know? She'll be settling down somewhere now, ready for when I can join her in September.'

'So you haven't heard from her since?' Marc asked. 'How will you know where she is? Has she even been in touch with your parents?'

Lacy laughed flippantly, but it sounded high-pitched and forced. 'Oh god no, she didn't get on with them. My parents are...' She stopped herself before she uttered the word Winter would use to describe them.

Common.

'What did you say her name is?' Chan asked suddenly.

'Winter,' Lacy repeated. 'It's as unique as she is.' She smiled softly, proud of her sister and the name she had chosen – yet another thing to ensure she was different from everyone else in their crappy little town.

Chan made a strange throaty noise, and Lacy snapped her head round, ready to defend Winter against any kind of mockery. But Chan wasn't laughing and just looked horribly uncomfortable.

They must have thought Lacy pathetically tragic, obsessed with fleeing to a country she'd never been to, chasing after a sister who didn't care enough about her to wait.

'I love this song!' Chan said suddenly, diving forwards and cranking up the volume on the speaker.

Lacy let out a sigh of relief, glad she wasn't going to be forced to reveal any further intimacies. She gulped more of the red wine and wished she had kept her mouth shut. She'd felt giddy and full of adrenaline after her encounter with Rachel. Now she felt exposed and embarrassed.

'Dance!' Chan insisted, clambering off the bed and tugging Lacy to her feet.

Lacy tried to resist. She'd never been someone who danced, even as a small child. But Marc grabbed her other hand before turning around so he could twerk rigidly in her direction, and she felt a smile cracking the frown that had been fixed on her face since she'd started talking about herself.

It was a good song, she conceded as she tried to give her limbs permission to move to the beat. Winter's mocking laughter echoed in her ears. She would never let Lacy live this down if she could see her.

But she wasn't here. She'd left.

And Chan and Marc *were* here, laughing and making sure she wasn't left out as they threw their bodies wildly around her tiny room.

Lacy took another swig of wine, raised her hands above her head and danced.

CHAPTER 23

Lacy was drunk.

Horribly, uncontrollably drunk.

She was outside but couldn't remember how she'd got there. It was so dark she could barely see, and the wind howled as it hurtled towards her from the sea.

She was alone.

A low groan rose in her chest. She felt sick, dizzy and like she needed someone to take care of her.

Why was she outside?

She blinked heavily, willing the dark shape in front of her to solidify so she could figure out where she was. Slowly, it swam into focus, looming over her. Dark, empty windows and shattered glass. The abandoned dorm.

Another wave of nausea hit her as she stared at it, its presence simultaneously drawing her towards it and making her want to sprint in the opposite direction. Not that she would be capable of running – she could hardly stand.

'Chan?' she slurred. She tried to search for her friend, but the world seemed to move at the same speed as her eyes, spinning away from her so she couldn't focus on anything.

'Marc?'

They weren't there.

It was night, she realised blurrily as she craned her neck upwards. It had still been light when she'd been in her room with Chan and Marc. She remembered the sunset casting a pink hue into the room and matching the warm feeling that was blossoming in her heart.

So what had happened between then…and now?

She pressed the heel of her hand against her pounding head and tried to remember. They had been in her room, talking, drinking, dancing. But she'd only had a small amount of the wine, hadn't she? She knew what happened when people got too drunk, so she wouldn't have drunk enough to get into this kind of state…would she?

Clearly, though, she had. And now she was paying for it.

A nagging memory tugged at the edges of her mind, just out of reach. She'd come out here for a reason. There had been something…something she'd seen.

She couldn't remember.

Her head felt heavy, like it was pulling her to the ground, urging her to lie down and close her eyes. She stared at the grass, which, despite being squashy with moisture, looked soft and inviting. It was so, so tempting to slump down into oblivion.

But no, she couldn't be found like that. Not after the way she had judged the others for their partying. It would be mortifying if she was found passed out on the ground between the two dorm blocks.

She suddenly felt a deep regret for the way she'd scorned Dylan for getting too drunk. Clearly, it was easily done.

She staggered sideways as she attempted to return to the staff dorm block. She needed to get to bed.

God, she felt sick.

That must have been it, she decided. She'd felt sick and come out here for some fresh air, that's all. And now she needed to get to bed and sleep it off.

She urged her legs to obey her and took a lurching step forwards. They twisted and trembled beneath her weight, and she foggily prayed that no one was watching her.

Nearly there. She mentally rehearsed the route back to her room, daunted by the simple task of putting the keycode into the door. Hopefully it would be propped open. Usually, the knowledge that anyone could get into the dorm filled her with dread, even since Chan had revealed that the story of the murdered staff members wasn't real. But tonight she was grateful for the shoddy security. She wasn't convinced she'd even be able to see the numbers on the lock, let alone punch them in. She'd have to curl up outside, huddled against the rotting wood of the dorm block, and wait for morning.

The door was even less secure than usual, though. Lacy frowned at the keypad, which was hanging off as though someone had repeatedly smashed it with a heavy object. A thought crept slowly into her head – had she done this? Gone on a drunken rampage and smashed her way out of the building?

She stared at her hands as she swayed on the spot, despairing at her lack of memory. The door was smashed too – a hole kicked through the lower pane of glass.

She pushed her face closer and peered into the building.

There were no lights on, meaning it must be very late.

Rachel's parties usually kept going until the early hours. And…

She squinted and pressed her forehead against the glass so she could see better.

There was someone there, standing in the corridor.

Lacy couldn't make out their features. They were just a dark, shadowy outline.

The figure wasn't moving. Could they see her? Was it Chan, or Marc?

They raised an arm and pointed directly at Lacy.

She recoiled, the sudden realisation hitting her as she took in the things she'd previously missed – the shattered glass on the floor, the filthy mattresses leaning against the walls in the corridor, the peeling letters above the door, identifying the building.

Dorm Block B.

She was at the wrong dorm block.

Lacy's eyes widened in horror as she stared into the gloom. She waited for the figure to disappear, to prove to be yet another figment of her imagination. But they remained, motionless.

Their hand hung in mid-air, pointing.

Then, with no warning, they rushed towards her, inhumanly fast. Lacy staggered backwards, but her legs felt as though they had been disconnected from her brain and buckled beneath her. She landed heavily on the ground, fragments of broken glass cutting her palms.

She trembled, too terrified to move, braced for the figure to descend upon her. They were real. There was no way she had imagined them, not this time. She realised that, despite all her previous curiosity, she now had no desire whatsoever to see who the person was.

She waited, paralysed with terror. She had no idea how much time had passed. Her eyes became dry and sore, but she didn't dare blink in case whoever was waiting in the abandoned dorm appeared the second she reopened her eyes.

As she sat on the grimy concrete, she realised with panic that her senses were fading again, her memory blurring at the edges. She had to remind herself why she was on the cold ground, staring at a broken door.

Her eyes grew heavy and her body sagged.

She just wanted to let go and sleep.

Her gaze finally dropped as unconsciousness lured her in.

It was too tempting. She was too tired. And if she was asleep…she wouldn't have to deal with any of this. She wouldn't have to be afraid anymore.

As her eyelids drooped, there was a sharp noise from behind her. Using the last of her strength, she sluggishly raised her face towards the sound.

CHAPTER 24

It was her birthday.

She didn't usually celebrate birthdays, but this one had been good. There had been friends, and dancing, and laughter.

And wine.

The wine had not been good.

Lacy groaned. The sound sent a lightning bolt through her brain.

Only a few hours could have passed since her birthday celebrations – it was pitch black in her room, blacker than she remembered it ever being before. She tried to recall the events of that evening, but there was just a jumble of images and faces. Rachel, Andy, Chan and Marc, and…

She frowned and tried to get her mind to stretch and grasp the thing she was trying to remember, something she felt like she really *should* remember.

It was no use. Perhaps things would feel clearer in the morning? She just hoped she hadn't made a fool of herself.

Her mouth was disgustingly dry and she moved her tongue around, desperately searching for moisture. She was going to have to go to the kitchen for a glass of water.

She stood gingerly and realised that she was still fully dressed. She could feel the familiar material of her favourite shirt and jeans over her body, which felt strangely achy. She didn't have any covers over her either. She must have passed out before getting properly into bed.

How embarrassing.

There was a smell too – a musty, damp smell. She scrunched her face up in disgust. Had she been sick?

God, she hoped it had been after Chan and Marc had gone back to their own rooms. She remembered Chan putting Dylan into the recovery position the night he'd had too much to drink. Had they done the same to her?

No one was going to see her as the poised, sophisticated soon-to-be-French student that she was trying to emulate now.

She would have to do some damage control in the morning. But first, water.

She held her hands out in front of her face, wondering if it was always this dark at night. She didn't usually make a habit of being up in the early hours. She'd made the walk from her bed to the door hundreds of times, but without light she felt disorientated and unsure of her surroundings.

Her fingers tapped the air as she shuffled forwards, and, finally, they made contact.

Lacy frowned. Something was wrong. The surface beneath her fingers was hard and smooth, just like a door. But it was also cold and… She tapped it with her fingernail.

It was glass.

Lacy stepped backwards and closed her eyes, lurching sideways as her balance wavered. Had she somehow gone the wrong way when she'd got out of bed and arrived at the window instead of the door? She recounted her steps. She was sure she'd turned left, as she should have.

She must be mistaken. People did weird things when they were drunk. Apparently, Lee had pissed all over his laptop one night after opening the lid, thinking it was the toilet.

She shook her head, glad no one was there to see her foolishness. She could make out the faint outline of her reflection in the window now. The clouds must have shifted to allow a pale sliver of moonlight to peer through. She could also see the other person, standing directly behind her.

Lacy screamed and stepped backwards away from the reflection, before realising she would be stepping into whoever was in her room. She staggered to the side and crashed into her bed.

Only…the bed shouldn't have been there. It should have been on the other side of the room.

A burst of memory bolted through her aching head. This wasn't the first time she'd felt raw terror tonight… She'd seen someone looming over her. Someone with…

But the memory evaporated as a fresh horror demanded her attention.

She wasn't in her room.

She was in the abandoned dorm.

Lacy whimpered as she perched on the bed, a bed that wasn't hers, a bed that reeked of damp and rot.

How had she got there?

And who was in the room with her?

She froze, her teeth chattering with fear, too terrified to move. The silence was thick, but she could still sense the person in the room with her. She could *smell* them – a thick, cloying scent that sat at the back of her throat and made her gag.

'Hello?' she whispered, her voice barely a squeak.

There was no reply.

She remembered the figure she had seen on her second day at Peril Bay, staring out at her from the abandoned dorm, possibly from this very room. Yet again, the glimpse of their reflection in the glass moments before had been hazy. It had been impossible to make out any features – just a pale face and dark circles for eyes. But she was sure it was the same person who had haunted her since the day she'd arrived.

'Hello?' she tried again, unsure if the silence was more terrifying than someone replying.

She held her breath and willed her heart to calm down so she could listen. The silence was stifling, but…

There – a slow, rattling intake of breath.

A deep feeling of dread crept through Lacy's entire body and her instincts finally kicked in.

Run.

She sprang to her feet, praying she wouldn't collide with her stalker. For a stupid moment she headed back towards the window, still disoriented by the mirror-effect room. Then she changed direction and crashed into the closed door, her fingers scrabbling wildly for the handle, screaming a silent prayer that it wouldn't be locked.

She wrenched the door open and staggered out into the corridor.

The hallway was lit by the emergency exit signs that were inexplicably still working. Dark smears of black mould were illuminated in a greenish hue and the yellowing wallpaper was peeling itself to the ground. Lacy gagged as the stench intensified. The smell of stagnant air and something sickly sweet that made her stomach clench in disgust.

She cast a glance over her shoulder at the room she had come from, but no one had followed her out…yet.

She had woken in *her* room, she realised as she scrambled to her feet. It was the room opposite hers – the one she could see into from her actual room, in the occupied building.

As she ran, she tried to remember the last thing she had seen before blacking out. It had been a face…a face that had terrified her. But even now, the image danced on the edge of her memory, refusing to solidify. Had she passed out because she'd been hit around the head, or had the booze finally sucked her down into oblivion?

It didn't matter. All that mattered was getting the hell out of there.

Her legs were still wobbly and she lurched down the corridor, wincing as she touched the rank walls for support and her hands came away slick with slime.

All the bedroom doors were shut, and she pushed against them to steady herself as she staggered forwards. She knew, with a certainty that made her whimper with fear, that if she fell down, she wouldn't be getting up again.

The corridor stretched tauntingly in front of her, like some kind of sickening hallucination. Would she ever reach the outer door at the end, or was she doomed to stumble down the hallway until whoever had been in the room with her finally decided they were done playing?

Her breath came in panicked gasps and her legs protested as she forced them forwards. The green emergency exit sign above her head flickered urgently, making Lacy's head pound, each flash of light bringing blindness with it once it died.

Her hand slammed against another door. But, she realised with a sickening jolt, this one wasn't locked. It flew inwards and Lacy tumbled into the room.

She landed heavily on her elbow and cried out as red-hot pain shot up her arm.

Get up.

But she'd seen something as she'd fallen…something in the room.

The flickering green light was feeble, and Lacy prayed it was making her see things that weren't there. But every time it offered a glimpse of the room, the image became more concrete.

There was someone on the bed.

Lacy whimpered from where she crouched on all fours. She could keep running. She could get away and pretend she hadn't seen.

But she crawled forwards, her breath squeaking as she wheezed. Her hand landed in something wet and thick. It was *warm*.

She snatched her hand to her chest, reeling backwards onto her knees. As her attention returned to the bed, the blinking light revealed a pair of gore-streaked trainers.

Bile rushed to Lacy's mouth as her eyes travelled up the length of the filthy mattress, away from the trainers and towards the motionless body lying flat on its back.

Darkness again. The next flash of light showed a hand flopping limply off the side of the bed, the fingers still curled and beckoning Lacy to come closer.

Darkness, and Lacy considered keeping her eyes clamped shut. She didn't want to see. *She didn't want to see.*

But her eyes refused to obey her command, and she finally took in the rest of the torso, her gaze lingering on the place where the head should have been.

CHAPTER 25

'I need you to be straight with me, Lacy. Do you think you could do that?'

Lacy stared into the depths of the lukewarm cup of tea on the desk in front of her. Her fingers were tightly clamped between her thighs and the hard plastic chair, where she'd trapped them to stop the trembling.

Her elbow throbbed and she had cuts on her palms that stung savagely. Lacy couldn't remember how she'd got them. It hardly seemed important.

'I am,' she said, for what felt like the hundredth time.

Officer Johnson, a stern-looking woman who was clearly fed up with Lacy's monosyllabic answers, gave her colleague an exasperated glance.

They'd been in this cramped office in the park's reception building for what felt like hours. The walls were plastered with rotas, health and safety notices and details of upcoming park events. Lacy hadn't been in here before, and it occurred to her just how little of the park she was actually familiar with. The only areas she frequented were the pool, the beach, the dorm block and now…the abandoned dorm.

A woman in a business suit had ushered them in here before disappearing, and Lacy wondered if she was one of the mysterious owners she'd heard about. Lacy had found herself glaring at her glossy blonde hair, hating her. What gave her the right to swan around like she was in charge, when she probably managed the park from a fancy office somewhere? She didn't know this place, not really. She didn't know the people who kept the park going, who worked all hours, keeping up with the demands of the guests.

Maybe if management had been a bit more interested in their staff, Rachel would still be alive.

Rachel. *Rachel* – the whirlwind of energy whose voice had penetrated Lacy's walls every night, making her feel small and boring in comparison. *Dead.*

'Lacy,' the other officer said from where he stood in the corner of the room. He can't have been much older than she was and was clearly there to do as he was instructed by his senior officer, Johnson, who had been grilling Lacy since the Gwynedd police force had arrived at the park that morning. He had gentle eyes. 'You see why we're struggling here, don't you? Your story… It just doesn't add up.'

Lacy sniffed. She didn't need telling that – she was the one who had lived through the confused horror of it.

'There must be more you can tell us, Lacy,' Officer Johnson insisted. 'One of your colleagues has died in a horrific way and you were the one to find her. Why were you in the abandoned dorm in the first place?'

'*I can't remember,*' Lacy insisted for the hundredth time. Tears spilled out of her eyes as she finally raised them to look at the police officers.

She knew what this looked like. She'd had a fight with Rachel. Then she'd found Rachel dead. And that's all she could tell them. The facts had been lost in a terrifying blur and Lacy had no idea what was real anymore.

Officer Johnson stared down at the papers on the table in front of her and tapped them with her pen.

'Have you seen anything strange since getting here? Any disturbances, arguments?' she asked in a resigned voice, as though she'd read the question off the paper but had no faith it would unearth any important information.

Lacy blinked in panic. There had been plenty of strange things, but the police weren't going to want to know about the freakish events Lacy's overactive imagination had conjured up. And the only argument she could think of was the one she'd had with the girl whose headless corpse she'd found in the abandoned dorm.

She squeezed her eyes shut, wishing she could banish the image of Rachel's mutilated body from her memory. She could barely remember anything from last night, so why did that have to be the thing that stood out so vividly it was as though she was still kneeling over the bed, Rachel's blood soaking into her jeans?

She was wearing a spare park uniform now. Her clothes had been taken – evidence, apparently.

Evidence of what, Lacy had no idea.

'Have there been any visitors to the dorm? People who didn't live there?' Johnson continued, her eyes still on the paper. Lacy thought of Dylan, but the next question came too quickly for her to answer. 'Any exes with grudges?'

'No, he's dead,' Lacy said, her mouth offering the information before her brain could engage.

Johnson suddenly looked interested. 'Excuse me?'

Shit. Why had she said that? It was completely irrelevant – the police officer had clearly been asking about *Rachel's* exes, not hers. But Lacy could hardly gloss over it now.

She shook her head, exhausted by everything. 'My ex – he died a few months ago. He…' She dug her fingernails into the bottom of her thighs. 'He was at a house party, and he got drunk and fell.'

Officer Johnson's eyebrows raised as she digested the information, and Lacy tried to guess what she must be thinking. For a moment, she hated the policewoman for forcing her to recall the tragedy – she'd been working hard to keep it suppressed.

She and Cal had split up two weeks previously, but she was still getting awful messages and calls from his mates. When rumours of him falling off a balcony at a party and dying had spread, she had assumed it was a sick joke. Until the story had appeared in the local news.

Teen dies in balcony fall at 'out of control' house party.

'Can I have a glass of water?' Lacy rasped.

Officer Johnson couldn't hide her irritation. Maybe she'd thought they were finally getting somewhere. She stood with a sigh. 'I'll get this one.'

She left the room, and Lacy craned her neck to see if there was anyone outside, but the door closed quickly behind her.

'Thirsty, huh?' asked the kind officer. *Officer Singh,* Lacy hazily remembered.

'Hmm,' Lacy agreed, counting the empty plastic cups on the table. She felt like she could drain the swimming pool and still feel thirsty. She promised herself, yet again, that she would never touch alcohol as long as she lived.

Apart from the horrendous dry mouth it had caused, the fact she had been drinking was making the police question everything she told them.

She couldn't blame them – she wasn't exactly a reliable witness.

All she'd been able to share with them was that she'd spent the evening drinking in her room with Chan and Marc, then had somehow found herself outside and alone. They'd seemed very interested when she told them about the person she'd seen inside the abandoned dorm, but Lacy had admitted that she wasn't certain there had really been anyone in there. And the more time that passed, the fuzzier her memories became.

Officer Singh smiled reassuringly at her as he lowered himself onto the chair Officer Johnson had just left. He fiddled with one of the empty plastic cups. 'I just… I'm struggling to see how your memory of the night can really be that patchy. I mean, people have blackouts like that after excessive quantities of alcohol, not the quarter that was missing from your bottle of wine.'

Lacy swallowed. She wished she could tell him what he needed to know. But she'd told them everything, even the bits that made no sense whatsoever.

She stared at her reflection in the undrunk tea. Her face looked warped and featureless, and she was reminded of the figure in the window of the abandoned dorm, the one she had seen standing behind her. Just before she'd found Rachel.

'Maybe I'm just a lightweight,' she mumbled, flinching as the image of Rachel's body rushed back to her yet again.

'Maybe,' Officer Singh reasoned. He rubbed his smooth chin. 'God knows I've been there myself – a few sips and my legs would wobble around like a baby giraffe.'

He chortled, but Lacy didn't have the energy to fake a smile in response.

'But I really believe, Lacy,' he continued, his voice more serious now, 'that if you tried, you could remember more than you've told us.'

Lacy shivered. The air conditioning was blasting an icy draft into the room, despite the fact it could only be twenty degrees outside. Couldn't the police see that she was more disturbed by the multiple blackouts she had suffered than they were? If only she could speak to Chan and Marc, then maybe they could start to piece the events of the evening together.

But they'd been kept separate. Lacy hadn't seen anyone since she'd run screaming from the abandoned dorm block and hammered on the first window she had come across. Lee had snatched his curtains back, astonished to find Lacy shrieking incoherently outside in the middle of the night.

She closed her eyes, swaying slightly in her seat. She remembered the bodies of the other staff pressing around her, asking what had happened. When she'd managed to spit out the horrible truth, Lee had surprised her by being the first to dash into the abandoned dorm to check on Rachel.

He'd returned to the group and slumped to the ground, hunching over and wrapping his trembling arms around his stomach. His haunted expression had confirmed that Lacy was telling the truth.

The police had arrived, taking a concerningly long time. The park was far away from civilisation, but there was nothing that emphasised the reality of their isolation quite like needing the emergency services at four in the morning. Dylan wasn't there – he must have gone home after Lacy and Rachel's fight. Chan and Marc had linked their arms through hers, and she'd sagged against them gratefully. She should have quizzed them then and tried to piece together the missing parts of the evening, but she couldn't even open her mouth without noisy tears escaping.

Not long after the police cars, an ambulance had come too, triggering a fresh wave of hysterical sobbing. It wouldn't be needed.

'Unless, of course, there was something more than alcohol involved at last night's party?' Officer Singh pressed, and Lacy blinked as she tried to understand what he was implying.

'Drugs, Lacy,' he elaborated. 'Did you take anything? Did any of the others? Look, no one will get in trouble. It's hardly going to be the focus of the investigation now. We just want to find out what happened to—'

'No,' Lacy cut him off. 'There were no drugs. Not that I saw, anyway.'

She closed her eyes. She'd never seen evidence of any drug taking at the staff parties, and there certainly hadn't been anything going on in her room last night, unless Marc and Chan had managed to hide it from her.

'We're testing the wine to make sure,' Officer Singh said, and Lacy widened her eyes. Did they think someone might have put something in her drink? Surely she'd just been drunk, that was all. She'd seen the others staggering around before, barely able to function after one of Rachel's parties. Was it really that hard to believe it had had such a strong effect on her?

The memory of Dylan, so out of his mind that he'd stumbled over a cliff, rushed back to her. He'd been confused about how he'd got in such a state, insisting he'd only had a couple of beers. What if...?

Officer Singh exhaled softly, and Lacy suspected he would soon be as fed up with her as his colleague was.

She wished she could help, she really did. She wasn't being intentionally difficult – she just *couldn't remember*.

Yet again, she tried to drag the memories into focus. She'd been with Chan and Marc, laughing, dancing, *happy*. Then she had been staggering around outside, in the dark, with no memory of how she'd got there. And then she'd woken up in bed...

She swallowed, the horror of the realisation that she hadn't in fact been in her own room returning to her.

There was something though...something nagging at the edge of her brain. Something important.

Lacy gasped and her eyes snapped open.

Officer Singh leaned back, startled by Lacy's sudden animation. When he saw the expression on her face, his own filled with hope.

'Do you remember something?' he whispered, as though afraid he would scare the memory away if he spoke too loudly.

Lacy nodded, her heart hammering against her breastbone. How had she forgotten? When she'd been outside the abandoned dorm, there had been a noise. Something that had stopped her slumping to the ground to let sleep claim her.

'I saw someone,' she said. 'I saw someone just before I passed out. Just before I woke up in the abandoned dorm.'

CHAPTER 26

'Who?' Officer Singh leaned forwards across the table, his eyes locked on hers. 'Who did you see, Lacy?'

Lacy squeezed her eyes shut and drummed her fingers against her forehead as she fought to remember the face she'd glimpsed just before she'd passed out. She had been outside, it had been dark, she could barely stand up or walk.

She could feel the anticipation coming off Officer Singh and frowned as she tried to block him out and concentrate.

Who *was* it?

Lacy remembered them looming over her, much too close for comfort. An ugly expression had twisted the features of their face. She had felt threatened, scared.

'It was that man,' Lacy said as the face solidified behind her closed eyes. 'A guest who stays in the empty part of the park. Gary Evans.'

Officer Singh scribbled frantically on his pad just as the door opened and Officer Johnson returned, two plastic cups of water in her hands.

'I have a name,' Officer Singh said, leaping up from his seat.

Lacy suspected his tail would be wagging frantically if he'd had one.

'Who?'

'Gary Evans. A guest, apparently.'

Water sloshed over the side of the cups as Officer Johnson lowered them to the table.

'I saw him just before I blacked out,' Lacy explained, her thirst forgotten as the horrible memory rushed back to her. 'I can't remember anything else, just that he was there, and he seemed angry.'

He *always* seemed angry, especially when it came to the staff. Lacy shuddered so violently the table wobbled, and spilt tea joined the puddles of water on its surface.

Had Gary dragged her into the abandoned dorm, tucked her into bed and then…?

She brought her fingers to her lips, nausea threatening.

'Ah, yes,' Officer Johnson was saying, sitting back down and rifling through more papers. 'This isn't the first time Mr Evans has been brought to our attention.'

Lacy swallowed in surprise. 'It isn't?'

Officer Johnson's eyes darted from side to side as she skim-read.

'Multiple complaints of harassment, both *from* him and *against* him,' Johnson listed. 'A couple of common assault charges raised and then dropped. He seems to make allegations against other people more than they do against him, though.'

Lacy nodded slowly. From what she'd seen of Gary, that made sense. He certainly seemed to believe that the park employees' sole purpose on earth was to make his life a misery.

But to do this…to *kill* Rachel?

'Had you had any interaction with him before last night?' Officer Johnson asked with renewed vigour now they were finally getting somewhere.

'No,' Lacy replied, before shaking her head. 'I mean, yes, I suppose you could call them interactions. It was just him shouting at me, really.'

Officer Johnson sat up straighter, her pen poised over the paper. 'Shouting? Did he threaten you?'

Lacy's head pounded as she tried to remember. 'Kind of. But it wasn't, like, that serious, you know?'

Officer Johnson frowned in a way that showed that she clearly did not know.

'I mean,' Lacy tried again, wishing her brain would start working at more than half power. 'He used to get annoyed with the staff for having parties and stuff. He'd shout at us to turn the music down. I guess he just didn't like teenagers.'

The police officers nodded knowingly at each other, and Lacy squirmed in discomfort.

'He never seemed that much of a threat, though,' she continued, remembering how Chan had calmly dealt with him and sent him on his way. 'He just seemed a bit grumpy…a bit sad.'

A bit lonely, according to Dylan. He stayed here because he missed his wife, and this was the last place they were happy together.

Was he really capable of slaughtering a girl in the most gruesome way imaginable?

'But has he threatened you, on more than one occasion?' Officer Johnson pressed.

Lacy could do nothing but nod, despite the increasing

feeling of something not being right. She just couldn't believe that it had been Gary reflected in the window, breathing softly in the dark when she had woken in the abandoned dorm block.

But who else could it have been?

Weariness crept up on her and the table suddenly looked almost too tempting to resist. She had to fight the desire to lower her head onto it and close her eyes. The last time she had fallen asleep, she had woken in the middle of a nightmare she was still unable to escape.

'Lacy?' Officer Johnson said, and Lacy blinked slowly as she tried to focus on her face. The policewoman's voice was softer now. 'Technically, as you turned eighteen –' she rifled through her papers and her eyebrows shot up as she clocked Lacy's birthday '– yesterday, we don't need to contact your parents. But I assume you'd like us to?'

'No,' Lacy said quickly. She darted her eyes to the side, not wanting to explain the myriad reasons why she didn't want to speak to them.

She'd barely checked in with them since leaving for this job, and guilt punched her in the chest as she pictured their faces. She'd abandoned them only months after Winter had left.

The last thing she wanted was for them to have to worry about her too.

'You shouldn't be alone right now,' Officer Johnson said. Lacy wished she could throw herself into her arms and sob against her sturdy shoulder.

'I'll be fine,' Lacy rasped.

It was a lie and everyone in the room knew it.

'We'll be in touch,' Officer Johnson said reluctantly, obviously hating the idea of letting Lacy leave but also keen to get on with her investigation. 'We might have further questions, and someone will sort out victim counselling for you. You shouldn't keep this in, Lacy. You've been through something terrible.'

Lacy thought of the bedroom and the smell of mould and rot and blood.

She stood abruptly, wanting to get out of the stuffy office as fast as possible. Her chair tipped to the floor with a bang. She felt Officer Singh's hand grip her elbow as she swayed, and she leaned gratefully against him, terrified she would black out again.

'Have you got a friend here?' he asked softly.

Lacy nodded. She wanted Chan and Marc to tell her that everything was all right, that there hadn't been a murder, that Chan had made it up to mess with her.

She gasped. Chan's story about the two decapitated employees had been a joke. But now…now it was real. And Catrin Roberts – she'd died the same horrendous way as Chan's made-up murdered teenagers. The same way as Rachel's very real murder.

A terrified squeak escaped Lacy's lips, and she put her fingers to her mouth to stop any further sounds escaping.

'I'll walk you back to your accommodation,' Officer Singh offered, eyeing her nervously.

Johnson nodded smartly at the suggestion. 'Yes. In fact, Officer Singh will stay nearby. If you remember anything else, anything at all, speak to him immediately, OK?'

Lacy nodded, her hands still over her mouth. She was sure that there was more she could be telling them to help solve Rachel's murder. But would the police seriously be interested in her crazed imaginings and a two-hundred-year-old ghost story?

She was exhausted, traumatised, and really, really needed to sleep. Maybe once she got some rest, things would make more sense.

'And, Lacy,' Officer Johnson called as Officer Singh guided her out of the office. 'We'll pick Mr Evans up now, but...' She paused and Lacy saw another flicker of gentleness behind the stern exterior. 'If you feel scared or unsafe, you come to us, right?'

Lacy swallowed and wished she could ignore the feeling that this nightmare was far from over.

CHAPTER 27

There was a gentle knock on Lacy's bedroom door and she leaped to her feet.

'Come in!' she shouted, her voice edged with desperation. She'd been left alone in her room all day. The only contact with the outside world had been Officer Singh bringing her a pack of soggy sandwiches and reassuring her that he was right outside if she needed anything. Lacy hadn't even got close enough to the food to see what the filling was. Just the thought of eating made her stomach clench.

The abandoned dorm had been wrapped in police tape. Lacy had spent hours perched on her windowsill, her forehead pressed against the cold glass as rain tapped incessantly against it. She'd watched police in white forensic suits scurrying back and forth through the pouring rain, leaving the abandoned dorm with bags of evidence. Was the weapon that had taken Rachel's head from her shoulders in one of those bags?

The door creaked open slowly and Lacy drummed her fingers against her thighs, hoping for a friendly face.

It was Andy, and Lacy tried to hide her disappointment.

He looked the same as he always did – placid, kindly,

slightly vacant. 'Hey, you,' he said softly as he closed the door behind him. 'How are you holding up?'

Lacy sighed. She felt terrible in every sense of the word. Her head throbbed, she was still nauseous and woozy, and every time she closed her eyes, she saw Rachel's body lying limply on the grotty mattress.

But worst of all was the sickening feeling of guilt that she couldn't shake, despite not understanding where it was coming from.

She just wanted to remember.

'I'm fine,' she told Andy, almost laughing at how ridiculous her flippant shrug of one shoulder must look. The only way she could be fine was if she were a complete psychopath.

'No, you're not,' Andy said, his face puckered with sympathy that made Lacy unreasonably irritated. 'You've been through something awful. I can't even imagine…'

His eyes grew moist and he wrapped his arms around himself.

Lacy suddenly ached with pity for him. He and Rachel had seemed close, in a weird kind of way. And this was practically his home – he'd worked here since he was sixteen. Andy must be feeling… She couldn't imagine how he was feeling.

'How are *you* holding up?' she asked.

Andy smiled gratefully at her. 'I've been better,' he admitted.

They stood in silence, the awkwardness of Andy's unwavering eye contact making Lacy squirm. What must he be thinking as he stared at her, unblinking? Did he suspect her of something? She wouldn't blame him if he did. She and Rachel did have a pretty explosive fight right before she was…

'What's been going on?' Lacy said quickly as another wave

of nausea hit her empty stomach. 'Where is everyone?'

'How much do you know?' Andy said slowly, as though weighing up what he could tell her.

Lacy frowned, suddenly reluctant to share her own intel with him. Shouldn't this stuff be confidential while the investigation was ongoing? But Officer Singh must have let Andy in to see her, she supposed. And he was technically their manager, so presumably it was OK to talk to him.

'I can't remember much of last night,' she admitted. 'But I saw Gary Evans just before I passed out.'

Andy nodded thoughtfully. 'That explains it then. He was arrested shortly after you finished speaking to the police.'

Lacy's eyebrows shot up. 'They got him?'

'Yes,' Andy confirmed. 'It's over.'

Lacy frowned and wished the news could have brought her a feeling of peace. But she felt wired and on edge, her instincts insisting that she should still be running.

'So, what's been happening all day?' she asked again, sweeping her frazzled hair away from her face. 'Where is everyone?'

'At work,' Andy said mildly.

Lacy gawped at him, waiting for him to crack a smile. But Andy's round face remained as benign as ever.

'I'm sorry, what?'

'Well, some of us were questioned first,' he explained. 'I told them everything I knew, which wasn't much at all. I think they took Chan and Marc in. And Lee, because he was the first to see you…afterwards. But I suppose nothing anyone said cast suspicion on anyone else, so they've taken Gary away and I assume that's the end of it.'

Lacy shook her head. *The end of it?* Rachel was dead – murdered in a place that should have been safe. How could everyone be carrying on as though nothing had happened?

'They can't,' she spluttered. 'They can't just—'

'Oh, the park has been closed,' Andy said briskly, and Lacy scowled at him. He could have led with that important piece of information. 'We've been getting the guests organised all day. Making sure they have what they need and understand the situation. Good customer service until the end!' he said cheerily, although he looked as though his heart might be breaking at the prospect of having to close the park gates.

'Are you telling me,' Lacy said slowly, 'that Chan has been forced to serve lager to guests after one of our colleagues was murdered? Has Marc been in the fucking bear suit, waving the kids off?'

Andy flinched and Lacy instantly regretted directing her anger at him. He just did what he was told – it was the park owners who were to blame.

'I-I-I…' Andy stuttered, making Lacy feel as though she'd just shouted at a small child.

'Shit, I'm sorry, Andy,' she sighed. 'It's just…it's been a day, you know?'

She should have seen it coming after last night, but before she realised what he was doing, Andy had closed the gap between them and pulled her into a tight hug.

'Let it out,' he breathed as he coaxed her head down towards his shoulder.

Not again.

Lacy tensed. Every instinct in her body told her to fight her way free, but she tried to relax. Andy was a nice guy, and even if she really, *really* didn't want this hug, maybe *he* needed it.

She tried not to grimace as she caught a whiff of his stale body odour and wondered whether he ever washed his polo shirt. She'd never seen him wear anything other than his uniform. He was still hushing her, his hand repeatedly passing heavily over her hair.

She felt like a cat being stroked by its adoring owner.

But then Andy's other hand started roaming lower, lingering over her bra strap, before moving to her waist and towards the belt of her trousers.

The bedroom door flew open and Lacy was flooded with relief as Andy released her.

Dylan's large frame filled the doorway. He was flushed and his bronzed skin shone with sweat, as though he'd run here. There was a dark, painful-looking bruise on his jawline.

'Lacy,' he said, his eyes darting between her and Andy, his forehead wrinkled in confusion. What did he think he'd just walked in on? Lacy opened her mouth to explain, then closed it, remembering that what she did was none of his business.

'What is it?' Lacy asked.

Dylan didn't answer, his chest heaving as he caught his breath. He was scowling at Andy in a way that Lacy thought he probably deserved, given the way his hands had just been roaming to a place they certainly hadn't been invited.

'I just wanted to check,' Dylan panted, 'that you were safe.'

Dylan is such a sweetheart – he never could resist a damsel in distress. Lacy shuddered. Those words had come from Rachel and now she'd never speak again.

'Is there anything else?' Andy asked Dylan, a harshness in his voice that Lacy had never heard before.

Dylan turned his attention to him, and his sparkling eyes became cold and hostile. 'The train is ready,' he said flatly, but Lacy noticed his jaw and fingers twitching in unison, as though he was struggling to contain his true emotions.

'Train?' Lacy asked.

Dylan's eyes returned to their usual warm ocean-blue when he looked at her. 'All the guests have gone now, and the staff with cars have left too. They've put a train on especially for the remaining employees.'

Lacy felt her knees weaken. They were getting out of there. She would never have to see this place again.

CHAPTER 28

It was raining, just as it had been when Lacy arrived at the park a month ago. The tiny train station felt even smaller now, with ten or so of the remaining staff clustered on the platform, their heads bowed against the worsening weather.

She wished she could go back and warn the Lacy of four weeks ago to stay on the train. To keep riding it until it retraced its tracks all the way back to her hometown, far from Peril Bay.

She hunched forwards, staring at the concrete below her feet, somehow feeling like she deserved the bitter cold biting at her bones.

'Come *onnnn*,' Marc groaned as he jiggled up and down on the balls of his feet, his arms wrapped tightly around his slender frame.

Lacy flinched at his use of Rachel's trademark phrase.

'What time will you get home?' Chan asked him, their hood obscuring their eyes.

Lacy had given up trying to take shelter from the rain, allowing the water to run down her face. Frizzy hair hardly seemed important anymore.

'Eugh, like, maybe eleven tonight, if I'm lucky,' Marc groaned. 'I have to change three times. Absolute nightmare.'

Lacy continued to stare blankly down the track while Marc and Chan's chat washed over her. They had kept her cocooned between them since they had finally been reunited just before setting off for the train station. Lacy appreciated the way they were trying to keep up the pretence of normality, even though she suspected she would never feel normal again.

Officer Singh was less subtle with his concern and hadn't stopped watching Lacy since they'd all trudged up to the platform. Every time she caught his eye, he gave her an awkward smile and stuck his thumbs up like a kids' TV presenter. She snorted – he and Andy could start a show together.

'You OK, Lacy?' Chan asked gently.

Lacy looked up slowly. 'Yeah, I'm grand. Why?'

'You're, um…laughing.'

Lacy quickly rearranged her face into a more suitable expression, alarmed at how little control she seemed to have over herself. Maybe she would feel better after getting some sleep.

The worst thing about last night, aside from the headless corpse, was the memory loss. She felt violated, like someone had stolen her body and done something with it without her approval or knowledge. And the prospect of never getting that time back, of never knowing what really happened, made her want to scream.

And she couldn't stop thinking about Rachel. The fight they'd had. How scared she must have been. Her family finding out that—

'Lacy?'

Dylan's voice was startlingly close to her ear, but she was too tired to jump. She turned to look at him, noticing the scowls on Chan and Marc's faces.

'What are you doing here?' Chan demanded. 'You only live over the hill. You're not going to get the train, are you?'

Dylan shook his head. He looked as pale and shaken as Lacy felt. 'No, I'll walk home.'

Lacy wondered how long that would take him. The little farmhouse he'd pointed out in the next bay had looked miles away.

'I just…' he said, awkwardly shifting his weight. 'I just wanted to say goodbye to Lacy.'

Lacy studied him. She wished she could understand how she felt about him. The attraction towards him had never gone away, no matter how hard she'd tried to convince herself that she was over their brief flirtation. But there was something about his dogged protectiveness that confused her. Was he really just a gentleman who happened to pop up whenever she was feeling particularly low?

Or was there something more sinister about the way he continued to hang around?

She sighed. It didn't matter now anyway. She was leaving.

She nodded at Chan and Marc to let them know she was OK with it, and then let Dylan lead her away from the other employees. As they dodged suitcases and potholes filled with rainwater, Lacy almost lost herself to inappropriate laughter again, remembering how pissed off she had been that first day when her favourite shoes had got wet.

'Do you want my jacket?' Dylan asked in his thick Welsh accent, already fiddling with the zip to take it off.

'No,' Lacy said, holding out a hand to stop him. It wasn't

like she could get much wetter. And she'd be on the train soon, dry and heading towards home. Dylan had an unpleasant trek on his own ahead of him. The least she could do was insist he keep his coat.

A wrinkle appeared over Dylan's left eye as he looked over Lacy's head. She turned to follow his gaze and saw that, although he was attempting to lurk casually, Officer Singh had clearly followed them.

'He's keeping a close eye on me,' Lacy explained.

'Or me,' Dylan replied darkly.

Lacy frowned quizzically and Dylan sighed.

'They questioned me for hours,' he explained, running his hand through his hair and flicking droplets of rain onto his shoulders. 'I think, for a while at least, they thought I might have had something to do with it.'

'What?' Lacy breathed. How could anyone suspect Dylan of being involved? He might look physically capable of crushing a skull with one hand, but they'd have realised after five minutes of talking to him that he would never hurt a fly.

But then, hadn't she herself briefly entertained the prospect of him hurling Ceri off the edge of a cliff?

She shivered, realising she'd never pushed to find out whether Ceri had made it home. Ceri, who had consumed her thoughts for a while, had been forgotten.

'They were interested in my, um, involvement with you,' Dylan said, dropping his gaze to the ground. 'And I don't think this helped,' he laughed dryly, pointing at the bruise on his jaw, which was even darker than it had been when he'd come into her room earlier.

'Huh?' Lacy asked, not understanding the relevance.

He closed his eyes for a moment. 'They asked me if Rachel had done this to me out of self-defence.'

'*What?*' Lacy gasped, bringing her hand to her mouth in horror. She seemed incapable of saying anything else, but how else could she possibly respond to this information?

He shrugged. 'They were just testing me, seeing how I would react…I think.' He frowned. 'I hope, anyway.'

Lacy longed to reach out to him, to tell him that she didn't believe him capable of causing upset, let alone injury. But she remembered Ceri's wide, scared eyes when she'd been sobbing on the beach. Hadn't Dylan been the last person to see her before she'd supposedly gone home?

'What *did* happen?' she asked, folding her arms around herself and nodding at the bruise.

The train had arrived, its brakes squealing as it came to a stop at the platform. It appeared to be the same rusting two-carriage tin can that she had arrived on. The staff suddenly came to life, straightening and surging forwards towards the train. They seemed as eager to get away as Lacy was.

Dylan sighed and looked warily at her. 'I don't suppose there's much point in telling you, not now.'

Lacy frowned. What was *that* supposed to mean?

She hesitated, trying to decide if she wanted to know, or if she should just step onto the train and start trying to forget this place and everything that had come with it.

But the memory loss from the previous night was still plaguing her. Could she really handle yet another mystery?

'I want to know,' she said firmly.

Dylan nodded slowly and glanced over her head to where

the others were picking up their suitcases and preparing to board the train. 'It was—' he began.

But his words were cut short by a high-pitched shriek of pain.

CHAPTER 29

Lacy's first thought was that someone had been hit by the train before she remembered it had already come to a stop. The alarmed shouts and cries of the other employees sounded muffled and distant as they crowded around the front carriage.

Lacy suppressed another inappropriate laugh. Surely nothing else could happen. Surely that was enough now.

Dread surged into her chest, making her knees weaken. Her instincts screamed at her to run in the opposite direction of the drama, but Dylan sprinted straight towards the distressed noises coming from the train.

'Dylan,' she said feebly, her voice lost to the hammering rain. She didn't want to be left alone.

But Dylan was gone, running to the rescue, as always. 'Someone help me with this!' he shouted as he was swallowed by the crowd.

Lacy warily crept closer to see what had happened, navigating through abandoned suitcases and panicked bodies, which were all angled towards the first door of the front carriage. She could see Marc's head floating above the crowd, his face twisted in a grimace.

What could he see?

'Out of the way!' Officer Singh shouted, his voice squeaking as though it had only recently broken. 'Step back and let me through, please.'

The staff parted to allow him past, and Lacy finally saw where the scream had come from.

Andy stood next to the train doors, his lips pulled back, exposing his teeth. His face was glistening with a mix of sweat and rainwater, and his eyes were clamped firmly shut. His left arm was trapped between the sliding doors.

Lacy's eyes widened as she took in the scene.

'Help me get them open!' Dylan instructed as Officer Singh joined him.

The two of them hooked their fingers through the gap above Andy's forearm, braced themselves and heaved. Dylan's muscles strained beneath his T-shirt, and a vein bulged alarmingly in Officer Singh's forehead.

Finally, they managed to open the doors wide enough for Andy to slip his arm free and stagger backwards, away from the train. The doors snapped shut.

The others gathered round Andy, who was bent double at the waist, his back heaving up and down as he breathed.

'What happened?' Officer Singh said.

Lacy noticed the train driver lurking awkwardly at the back of the group.

'I dunno.' The driver gestured helplessly at the doors. 'Never happened before.'

Andy slowly straightened, but kept his arm cradled against his green chest. His face was turning a similar shade. Dylan reached out to touch his injured limb, but Andy flinched away.

'I'm fine!' he snapped.

'Let me check your arm,' Dylan pressed. 'You could—'

'I said I'm fine!'

Andy stared at Dylan with a ferociousness that made Lacy wonder what had happened between the two of them. She couldn't shake the feeling that it somehow involved her.

'Could you please get the doors open?' Officer Singh asked the train driver, unable to keep the irritation out of his usually mild voice.

The driver shuffled forwards and reached a finger out to press the button. Nothing happened. He pressed it five more times, just in case, and Lacy tried not to groan with exasperation.

The driver turned to Officer Singh and shrugged.

'Isn't there a master switch or something?' Chan asked from beneath their hood.

The driver twitched. 'Oh yeah.'

He lumbered towards the door to the driver's cabin and pressed the button. Again, nothing happened.

'Can't get in,' he said, pointing uselessly at the door.

'Jesus Christ,' Marc breathed.

Officer Singh pinched the bridge of his nose. His uniform was soaked through and clung to him like an oversized seal skin. Lacy wondered how long he had been a police officer and how this compared to his average working day. 'Right, so what happens now?' he asked.

The train driver scratched his head and stared thoughtfully at the train. 'I dunno,' he repeated. 'This has never happened before.'

'Is there someone you can call?' Officer Singh said, tapping his heel impatiently.

'My phone is in there.' The driver gestured at the train.

'There's no pissing signal here anyway,' Marc groaned, his teeth chattering furiously. 'Can't we prise the doors open or something? Seriously, I'm freezing my tits off out here.'

'I'm not going near those doors,' Lee grunted. 'They nearly chopped Andy's arm off.'

Lacy flinched at Lee's choice of words and peered at Andy's arm. He still held it close to his body with his other hand, so Lacy couldn't see much, but it seemed to be intact. Though she suspected he was in a lot of pain, if the ashy pallor of his face was anything to go by.

'Must have been some kind of malfunction,' the driver said sagely, as though he'd just diagnosed a complicated technical issue.

'No shit, Sherlock,' Marc muttered.

Officer Singh had his eyes shut, and Lacy felt bad for him drawing the short straw and being left to look after them. It would have been easier to be the officer in charge of Gary Evans.

'Right,' he said finally. 'Let's head back to your accommodation.'

'No!' Lacy blurted. She shrunk under the curious stares of the others as they turned towards her. 'We can't go back there.'

She blinked furiously as she tried to keep her emotions in check. They were supposed to be *leaving,* not going back to the murder scene.

'Lacy,' Chan said softly, stepping towards her. 'It won't be for long, just until the train is fixed. And then—'

'I'll wait here,' Lacy said firmly. 'You can all go back and keep dry.'

She folded her arms and stared resolutely at the train. She knew she was being stupid, that the danger was gone. But she would rather get hypothermia than go back there.

'I'll stay,' Dylan said, stepping towards her. 'I'll wait with her – you lot go back.'

'We'll stay too, then,' Chan nodded. Marc opened his mouth to protest, but Chan whacked him smartly on the chest and he reluctantly nodded.

'No one is staying,' Officer Singh sighed. He turned to Lacy, his eyes pleading. 'It's safe now, and—'

'He's right,' Andy interrupted, straightening as he stepped towards Lacy. His bottom lip trembled as he stared earnestly into her eyes. 'I won't let anything else happen to you, Lacy. I promise.'

Lacy squirmed. What was it with everyone wanting to protect her? She tried so hard to come across as fearless and independent, but clearly people still saw her as the useless, timid girl she'd tried to leave behind. Winter would be ashamed of her.

She closed her eyes and listened to the drumming of rainwater on her skull. If she stayed here, she really might die from exposure. But if she went back…

She gasped as images of dark corridors and looming shadows filled her head. Rachel's body. Rachel's *neck*.

The train platform seemed to tip just enough to send her teetering to one side. She didn't fight the feeling – it would be quite nice to be unconscious, she foggily reasoned. Then she wouldn't have to deal with any of this.

Gentle hands gripped her elbows. She was being led back to the dorms, she realised. She didn't have the strength to fight it anymore. She could barely keep herself awake, let alone convince a group of teenagers and a police officer that she would be fine on her own in the pouring rain as they waited for the world's most incompetent driver to figure out how to get back inside his train.

Lacy leaned gratefully on Chan and Marc's arms as they linked hers. She wasn't sure she'd manage the walk again without them.

'Don't worry,' Chan said firmly. 'We won't let you out of our sight this time.'

Lacy frowned. She'd been so desperate to get away from Peril Bay that she'd forgotten to ask Chan and Marc about their version of last night.

'What happened?' she asked, glancing quickly over her shoulder to make sure the rest of the group were out of earshot. 'What happened last night?'

Chan threw an unreadable glance at Marc.

'You know what happened,' Chan said slowly.

'No,' Lacy insisted. 'No, I really don't. We had a bit of wine, then I woke up outside. What I don't understand is how I got there.'

Chan shrugged helplessly. 'You're not used to drinking, that's all. I remember how wasted I was after my first beer. I could hardly stand up.'

'And we were the only ones with you all evening until we all went to bed,' Marc added earnestly. 'So it's not like you could have been spiked or anything.'

Lacy nodded, flicking rainwater out of her sodden hair. They were right. The police would test her wine and confirm that it really was just wine. She was a lightweight who had been unlucky enough to have a hellish experience the first time she'd really drunk.

She watched her feet trudge over the wet tarmac and wished she could believe that it was as simple as that.

CHAPTER 30

'Did they find her head?'

Lacy looked up from the patch of grimy kitchen floor she'd been staring at for the last hour, her mouth falling open in horror.

She wasn't the only one looking at Lee in that way.

'What?' he asked, before ducking his head to hide his face behind his baseball cap. 'I know I can't be the only one thinking it.'

Lee's eyes were bloodshot, and Lacy noticed he had to clasp his hands together to stop them from shaking. Out of everyone here, he was probably closest to Rachel. He'd certainly seemed to dote on her, even though his adoration hadn't exactly been returned.

She couldn't blame him for asking the question everyone else was too scared to voice.

Her skin prickled in the silence, and she looked up to see that the attention of the entire room was on her. She could feel Andy's breath on her cheek from where he sat beside her, uncomfortably close. Dylan stood stiffly by the door as though on guard duty, the only one not sitting or leaning against something.

Lacy braced her hands on the kitchen counter she was sitting on. 'I didn't see it,' she murmured.

She wasn't sure what disturbed her the most – the fact Rachel's head had been absent from the murder scene, or the prospect of discovering it as well as her lifeless body.

Lee nodded and drummed his heels against the cupboard beneath him. Lacy wanted to tell him to shut up, that she felt anxious enough without his restless legs hammering a beat that vibrated up through the seat of her jeans. But she bit her words back. It couldn't be much longer now.

'Bad news,' Officer Singh announced as he stepped into the kitchen, shaking the rainwater off his uniform.

'What?' Marc said sharply.

'The doors still won't shift. The driver managed to get hold of headquarters through the phone at the park's reception,' Officer Singh explained, his hat clasped in his hands. 'But there's been an issue further down the line – something about the tracks being underwater. Anyway, long story short, there are no replacement buses available until tomorrow.'

A groan rippled around the group.

No. No, this can't be happening. We can't be trapped here.

'Taxis,' Lacy said, her knuckles whitening as they gripped the countertop. 'Or police cars. *Horses*, for god's sake. There must be some way to get us out of here?'

Officer Singh shifted awkwardly. 'I've been told to wait it out until morning. The weather is terrible and what with there not being a threat anymore—'

'Someone died!' Lacy shouted and lurched forwards so she could stand. She still felt drunk, or maybe it was the sleep deprivation, or the reaction to trauma. Whatever it was, she wanted to get out of there, *now*. 'She was murdered just metres away from here.' She jabbed her finger towards the kitchen wall in the vague direction of the abandoned dorm block.

'I kno—' Officer Singh began, but Lacy cut him off. She didn't want to hear him tell her, yet again, that it was safe now that Gary was gone.

She didn't *feel* safe.

'She was one of us,' she elaborated, hoping no one decided now was the time to comment on how much she and Rachel had disliked each other.

'You're right,' Officer Singh said finally. 'You're absolutely right. It's not fair to expect you to spend the night here, especially…' He looked apologetically at Lacy, as though the fact she'd discovered a corpse less than twenty-four hours ago had only just dawned on him.

Lacy dug her fingernails into her already scarred palms until it hurt.

'I'll try again,' he said, nodding vigorously to psych himself up. 'I'll see if there's anything else they can do.'

He scurried from the kitchen and back into the gale outside. Lacy tried to believe that he would be able to convince his superiors to prioritise their rescue over the many others that would be needing help on a stormy evening like this.

The morbid silence resumed, and Lacy wearily clambered back onto the kitchen counter.

'Are you OK?' Andy whispered softly.

She stifled the sharp retort forming on her lips, reminding herself that he was asking because he cared and that he must be in a lot of pain. His arm wasn't broken, but a dark bruise was already forming where the doors had slammed shut on it.

And he'd lost Rachel.

She offered him a smile.

'I was thinking,' he said, pressing his face closer despite her attempts to withdraw to a more acceptable distance. 'We should have a drink, to pass the time, you know?'

Lacy's mouth dropped open in disbelief.

'That's not such a bad idea, you know,' Chan said, overhearing despite Andy's attempts to whisper the suggestion to Lacy. 'It might help a bit, Lacy, especially as you'll probably find it hard to sleep.'

'Yeah,' Marc agreed. 'If we're going to be stuck here, we may as well—'

'What?' Lacy snapped, unable to believe what she was hearing. 'Make the *most* of it?'

Marc squirmed under her glare. 'Well…when you put it like that.'

'I'll put the tunes on,' Lee grunted, fishing in his rucksack for his portable speakers. The usual monotonous pounding beat started, the bass distorted by the cheap sound system. 'This one was Rachel's favourite,' he said, his voice thick with emotion.

Bottles clinked as someone stooped to dig around in a corner cupboard, producing two half-full bottles of vodka. The idea of one last party seemed to be gaining traction and Lacy watched the scene unfold in horror. What was *wrong* with these people?

Andy tried to pass the bottle to her with his good arm, then recoiled from Lacy's poisonous stare.

'Obviously *not*,' she hissed.

It came out louder than she'd intended, and, once again, the attention of everyone in the room was on her.

This time, she didn't care.

'I can't believe you think this is appropriate,' she said in a low voice.

'Lacy,' Marc began. 'It's what Rachel—'

Lacy abruptly slid off the kitchen counter, unable to bear being sandwiched between these people any longer. It was Lacy against all of them, but again she didn't care. That's how it had been when she'd first arrived at Peril Bay, and that's how it would be when she left.

'You don't know what she would have wanted!' Lacy shouted at him, gesturing towards the abandoned dorm. 'She's dead!'

'We know that,' Chan replied, their voice hardening in a way that would have once made Lacy nervous.

But not anymore.

'Can't you see how messed up this is?' Lacy asked the group, tapping her head furiously to remind them where their brains should be. 'Can't you lot do anything apart from drink, listen to shit music and have moronic conversations?'

'Oh, give it a rest,' Chan barked suddenly. Their knuckles were curled around the kitchen counter, and the tendons in their neck were tight as they glared at Lacy.

Lacy snapped her mouth shut, stunned by the potency of Chan's anger. Lacy had always suspected there was a side of Chan not to be messed with, and it seemed that, by having a go at Marc, she had finally provoked it into making an appearance.

Chan leaped off the kitchen counter and took an aggressive step towards Lacy. 'You need to pull that stick out of your arse before you end up as alone as your sister!'

CHAPTER 31

'What?' Lacy breathed, her rage extinguished in an instant. 'What did you say?'

Chan looked as surprised by their own words as Lacy was, dropping their gaze to the floor and taking a step backwards.

'Nothing.' Chan shrugged. 'I'm sorry, I just…I don't know where that came from. Forget it, OK?'

Forget it?

Chan went to climb back onto the kitchen counter beside Marc, but Lacy's hand darted out of its own accord and gripped their upper arm.

'What did you mean?' she demanded. 'What did you mean when you said I'll end up as alone as my sister?'

Chan stared at Lacy's hand, but Lacy held firm – she wasn't going to let go until she got an explanation. The way Chan had said it…it sounded as though they *knew* Winter.

'Lacy, Chan,' Andy said nervously. He lowered himself gingerly to the kitchen floor and held up his good hand soothingly. 'Can we talk about this?'

'That's what we're doing, Andy,' Lacy snapped without

taking her eyes, or her hand, off Chan. She was past caring about hurting Andy's delicate feelings.

She felt Chan attempt to twist free, and she tightened her fingers. Chan didn't look intimidating anymore. They looked like they wanted to be swallowed by a hole in the ground.

'Lacy,' Marc said, sliding gracefully down from the countertop. 'It was just words. We're all upset, that's all. They didn't actually mean anything by it. Right, Chan?'

Lacy's anger bubbled and churned inside her stomach. She'd been stupid to trust either of them.

'Chan lies,' Lacy hissed. 'They lied about the murders in the abandoned dorm. Who knows what other bullshit they've been feeding me.'

'I haven't been *lying* to you,' Chan insisted. 'I swear – we just wanted to be your friends, right, Marc?' She widened her eyes at Marc, who nodded vigorously.

Lacy frowned at her fingers, which were still pressed into Chan's upper arm.

What was she doing? Chan was her *friend*.

She stared slowly around the room at the other staff, who were all watching her with wide eyes. They weren't entertained by this, she realised. They were traumatised by Rachel's death and now her erratic behaviour was freaking them out even more.

'I did know her,' Chan blurted, just as Lacy loosened her grip.

'What?' Lacy breathed.

'*What?*' Marc parroted, looking down at Chan in surprise.

Chan squirmed and rubbed their arm, but Lacy was too

stunned to feel guilty. Chan had known Winter? How was that possible?

Chan sighed. 'I didn't really *know* her, know her. But I did...'

'Know her?' Marc suggested helpfully, and Chan rolled their eyes at him.

'I worked with her.'

Lacy shook her head and tried to jostle her thoughts into some kind of logical order. Chan and Winter had worked together? *When?* Winter had never held down a job for more than a few days, as far as Lacy knew. She always left for some dramatic reason – the pollution on the commute to town had been at dangerous levels, the parent company had been against her anti-capitalist values, the uniform had been 98% polyester.

'At Christmas,' Chan explained.

'Which Christmas?' Lacy snapped, her voice harsher than she'd intended.

'The one eight months ago?' Chan said slowly.

Lacy was still shaking her head. 'You're lying,' she insisted. 'Winter left for Paris at Christmas.'

Chan shrugged and dropped their eyes to the grimy kitchen floor. 'I dunno. Maybe there's more than one twenty-year-old calling themselves Winter. But I worked with one of them last Christmas – in Blackpool, not Paris.'

Lacy let out a sharp laugh of relief. Chan had got it wrong. There was no way her sister would be caught dead in a tacky seaside resort town like *Blackpool*.

'That wasn't my sister,' she informed Chan, feeling her shoulders relax. This was all a mistake.

Chan shrugged again. 'Pretty weird coincidence if it wasn't.

She kept banging on about Paris and living on the Champs-Élysées,' Chan said, sounding the unfamiliar name out slowly. 'Said she was gonna be a fashion designer or something.'

Tension rushed back into Lacy's chest, crushing her lungs and making it difficult to breathe. That was where they'd talked about living. How could Chan know that unless…?

'What did she look like?' Lacy asked quietly, dreading the answer.

'Tall,' Chan said. 'Dark hair, pale skin. Kind of like you but with harsher lines.'

Lacy closed her eyes. That was exactly how she would have described Winter.

'We worked at a bar together,' Chan continued to the rapt attention of the room. 'There were loads of us – all hired through the same agency, the same one most of us used to get this job.'

The hospitality agency. The card Winter had left for Lacy. Lacy had always assumed the message was the important bit – *See you in Paris*. But what if the card it was written on was actually the message? What if Winter had been telling her where she'd gone, in her own frustratingly mysterious way?

'It gets crazy with Christmas and New Year parties,' Chan said. 'So it was all hands on deck, every night of the week. Knackering work, but you can make a decent amount of money pretty quickly.'

Was that what Winter was doing? Trying to make fast cash so she could escape to France, just like Lacy was doing now?

Then why hadn't she told Lacy?

Lacy answered her own question before she'd finished asking it. There was no way Winter would admit to working in some tacky tourist bar. She would have kept it secret, then mysteriously appeared with a suitcase full of cash to bask in Lacy's awe. That was her style.

So why hadn't she returned home once her job was finished?

'She left before the season ended,' Chan said, predicting Lacy's next question. 'She'd always been a bit…rude, a bit snooty, laughing at people's clothes and taste in music and stuff.'

If Lacy had any lingering doubts that the person Chan was describing was her sister, they were now gone.

The room suddenly felt too hot, too small. She would have fled into the cool night outside, but desperation to learn more about her sister's whereabouts glued her to the sticky lino.

'It was New Year's Eve, and we had a staff party once the bar closed,' Chan went on. 'It got a bit heated. Winter got drunk and started ranting about being destined for bigger things, how we were all beneath her.'

Lacy winced, remembering how rude her sister could be.

'And then she wandered off.'

'What?' Lacy asked, sure that couldn't be the end of the story.

Chan shrugged again, and Lacy had to resist the urge to grab their shoulders.

'I saw her when I was walking home after the party. She was on the pier, just staring out to sea. I called over and asked if she was OK, but she told me to leave her alone, so I did.'

'And that was the last time you saw her?'

Chan nodded.

That meant Winter had only been working in Blackpool for two weeks.

'And no one questioned where she had gone, why she didn't turn up for work the next day?'

'Do I look like I work in HR?' Chan snapped, then grimaced apologetically. 'Sorry. Like I said, she hadn't exactly made herself popular. She kept talking about buggering off to Paris, so we all just assumed that's what she'd done.'

Pressure suddenly built behind Lacy's eyes, and she scowled, willing the tears to stay put. She wouldn't cry, not here, not with everyone staring at her. But her chest ached with the thought of her sister.

Lacy had been so sure that Winter was in Paris, living the life they'd dreamed of together. Yes, she'd been hurt that Winter had gone on ahead without her and then failed to get in touch. But she'd tried to focus on what was important – joining her. To find out that she had ditched Lacy for *Blackpool*...

Somehow it stung even more.

And then there was the fact that Chan had seen her more recently than she had, which made her want to scream.

But worst of all was that no one knew, or even cared, where she had gone when she had failed to turn up for work one day.

Would the same have happened if Lacy had fled the caravan park in the middle of the night?

She blinked rapidly, shrinking under the stares of everyone in the room. Her eyes met Dylan's. He hadn't moved from the door but looked ready to dash towards her and save her the second she needed him.

'I'm sorry, Lacy,' Chan said gently. The concerned, kindly expression had returned, transforming them from someone Lacy had been ready to fight back into her friend. 'I shouldn't have said all that about your sister. I'm sure she's nice once you get to know her.'

Lacy sniffed and bowed her head. A single tear finally dropped from her eye and splashed onto the floor.

She'd spent her whole life trying to impress Winter. She did everything she was told, liked everything she was told to like, and hated everything, and everyone, she was told to hate. But since arriving at Peril Bay, it had become clear that the only thing her efforts had achieved was to cut herself off from everyone other than her sister, who had ultimately abandoned her.

She couldn't deny it anymore.

'No,' she sighed. 'She isn't.'

Before more tears could fall, Lacy darted from the kitchen. She brushed Dylan's comforting hand away as he reached for her and ran down the corridor, away from all the staring, curious eyes.

CHAPTER 32

Lacy could feel her heart vibrating in her throat as she fled from the kitchen, memories of last night swamping her already scrambled thoughts.

Where was she even going? Her room wasn't her own anymore – her stuff was all packed up. And she wasn't about to wander around outside in the storm until Officer Singh returned. The park may be empty now, but it still didn't feel safe.

She arrived at the room that was once hers and slid hopelessly down the closed door.

She wanted to go home.

She'd never been homesick in her life. She'd assumed you actually had to like your home to feel sad about being away from it. But right now she regretted ever leaving the tiny terrace house that was full to the brim of her mother's bric-a-brac – items Lacy had always seen as rubbish but now wondered if they might be treasures after all. She missed the sharp smell of her father's cleaning products and being woken up at five in the morning because he was scrubbing the bathroom before starting his shift at the hospital. She missed their stories. She used to listen with amazement when they spoke of the people they had encountered and situations they'd dealt with. When had she decided to start copying Winter's snort of disdain whenever either of her parents so much as opened their mouths?

Lacy drew her arms closer over her stomach and clenched her fists beneath her armpits.

What were her parents doing right now? They had left endless messages on her phone when she'd first left, begging for an address so they could send care packages, like she was off on some kind of boarding school adventure. She'd ignored their requests. What was she going to do with a box full of chocolate Hobnobs and Parma Violets, treats she was obsessed with as a child and her mother still bought for her even though she'd stopped eating refined sugar a year ago?

She squeezed her eyes shut and let her head fall heavily against the door. She'd been a terrible daughter.

She'd witnessed Winter making her parents' lives difficult. She'd resisted every single thing they'd suggested, even activities that should have been nice, like family dinners, family holidays…anything with the word 'family' in it, really.

Lacy had been the good child, the easy one. But now, looking back on it, she wasn't sure she had been so easy after all.

'Hey.'

Lacy snapped her eyes open to find Dylan standing a few metres away. The dim light of the corridor cast shadows over his face that made him look like he had lost his solid form.

'Hi,' Lacy replied wearily.

'I don't think you have a stick up your arse,' he said solemnly, and Lacy snorted humourlessly.

But Dylan wasn't put off. 'From what I've seen of you, you're friendly and—'

'You're sweet,' she cut in, not wanting to hear more compliments she didn't feel she deserved. 'But I think you've got the wrong impression of me. The truth is…'

Lacy closed her eyes and tried to ignore the echo of Winter's scornful voice in her head, telling her to stand up and handle herself with dignity.

'The truth is, I don't even know who I am myself, so I don't see how you can.'

'I see more than you think,' Dylan said softly.

Lacy opened her eyes to look at him, hit by the feeling that there was some kind of deeper meaning behind his words. But she was tired. And she was done with riddles, and hints, and people hiding things from her.

She just wanted to go home.

Why hadn't *Dylan* gone home? If Lacy had a cosy farmhouse to flee to, she'd have been sprinting across the hills towards it the second the police let her go.

Did he *ever* go home? He was always at the evening parties, and then what? Did he really walk home in the dark every night?

'Why haven't you gone home?' she asked. 'Why are you still here when you could leave and never come back?'

A puzzled frown appeared on Dylan's forehead, as though he couldn't believe Lacy didn't know the answer. 'For you,' he said. 'I stayed for you.'

Lacy stared back at him. Did he really like her that much? Or would he have stayed for anyone he sensed was in trouble?

She allowed her head to slump forwards onto her knees,

exhausted by it all. She didn't know how she felt about Dylan, or how she felt about anything anymore.

She sensed rather than heard Dylan drawing closer to her, and decided that this time, if he reached out to her, she wouldn't flinch away.

The front door of the dorm block flew open with a bang, and Lacy looked up sharply to see a dark figure standing at the end of the corridor. The rain hammered down behind them, and, for a moment, Lacy's heart threatened to burst out of her chest as she remembered stumbling down the hallway in the abandoned dorm.

But as her eyes adjusted, she realised it was just Officer Singh, looking even wetter than the last time she'd seen him.

He closed the door behind him and his feet slapped on the threadbare carpet as he approached them. He removed his hat and flicked the water off it.

Lacy could tell from his face that he didn't come bearing good news.

He sucked air through his teeth. 'I'm afraid—'

'We're stuck here until morning,' Lacy finished for him.

Officer Singh nodded regretfully.

Lacy's head thumped painfully back against the door and she breathed heavily through her nose. She considered asking Dylan if she could come home with him to his farmhouse. She pictured his parents – his mother would be a rosy-cheeked woman who baked delicious, comforting treats between dealing with the livestock on their farm. And his father must be a giant, but as gentle as Dylan.

That fantasy couldn't be entertained for more than a moment though, not least because she was too exhausted to make it out of the park, let alone over the hills to his house.

'I'm going to bed,' she announced, not bothering to open her eyes.

'I can get your bag,' Dylan said.

Lacy shook her head as she clambered ungracefully to her feet. She didn't need it. She was going to collapse onto her unmade bed, pull the tatty duvet over her head and finally allow oblivion to claim her. She didn't even have her camera, she realised dully. Usually, its absence would have felt wrong, like she'd lost a limb. But right now, she wasn't sure she'd ever feel like taking photos again.

She pressed the door handle down and hesitated, realising that this was the last time she would ever see Dylan.

How she wished her summer could have continued in the same way it had started, filled with poolside flirting and the promise of sunset walks.

She slid into her room and closed the door behind her without saying goodbye.

CHAPTER 33

Icy terror paralysed Lacy and pressed her into the mattress. She lay on her back, her heart racing in her heaving chest. The darkness was absolute.

Not again.

She tried to calm her panicked thoughts, but her entire being screamed that she was back there again. She could sense the black mould on the walls, the rotting mattress pressing into her back. She could smell the fetid stench that had hit her the second she'd stepped off the train.

But she couldn't be in the abandoned dorm. She'd fallen asleep in her own room, in the staff block. There was no way she could be reliving the horror for the second night running.

It was impossible.

She just wished her mind could convince her body of that fact so adrenaline would stop rushing through her veins and telling her that she was about to die.

Breathe, Lacy.

But the more she tried to slow the movement of her lungs, the tighter her airway felt. She brought her hands to her throat, suddenly convinced there was something wrapped around her neck, choking her.

The feeling of her pulse trembling beneath her fingers intensified the panic even more. She needed something to focus on, something real.

She wanted the bracelet Winter had given her, but it lay at the bottom of the ocean, its bright metal turning to rust.

The rain tapped at her bedroom window, and she released some of her fear – the window was on the right side. She wasn't back in the abandoned dorm.

She let out a long, noisy breath and wished it could be morning. But dawn must be hours off. The rush of fear had jolted her awake so violently that she was sure she wouldn't be getting any more sleep tonight.

She was just going to have to wait it out, staring blankly at a ceiling she couldn't see.

How would her parents react to her return? She should call ahead and let them know she was on her way, she realised. That's what any normal, loving daughter would do. They might even be able to pick her up from the train station if her arrival didn't clash with their shifts. Maybe she could suggest they eat dinner together.

She couldn't remember the last time they'd shared a meal. Winter had been so disgusted by the microwave lasagne and frozen pizzas, that she'd insisted on her own cupboard and shelf in the fridge. And of course Lacy had followed suit.

Why had it taken finding a dead body for Lacy to realise how unfairly she'd treated her parents? They were trying their hardest – both of them worked long, exhausting hours. No wonder they didn't cook healthy meals from scratch.

She pressed her lips together as she imagined their reactions when she tucked into a plate of food with them and said thank you.

She was never going to take them for granted again.

The tension went from her body and she felt herself sink into the lumpy mattress. Maybe some good could come of her summer at Peril Bay after all.

She winced as she thought of Rachel and how her family must be feeling right now.

Lacy tried to push the guilt away. Rachel's death had been a random event, completely unrelated to the argument they'd had just hours before she was murdered. It had been a coincidence that she'd drunkenly decided to go wandering in the exact same place Rachel had been killed…

What had Rachel been doing out there anyway?

Lacy frowned into the dark. As the chaos of last night ebbed, huge questions were left behind in its wake.

Lacy squeezed her eyes shut. There was no point obsessing. It was an awful act of mindless violence. But in just a few hours, she would be chugging away from Peril Bay on the train, never to return. She tugged the covers up to her chin and nestled her head down into the scratchy pillow.

And then she heard it.

A breath.

Lacy's own breathing stalled in response. She lay frozen, straining to hear, praying she'd imagined it. But it came again – soft and snuffly from the corner of her room, by the door.

She clamped her molars together to contain her terrified whimper.

Another sound. This time a shifting of fabric, like clothes rustling.

Lacy's mind whirred as her body lay paralysed. Had Gary escaped? Had they let him go due to a lack of evidence?

Or had they arrested the wrong person entirely?

Officer Singh was here, keeping them safe. He wouldn't have left the dorm block unguarded, would he? But the police were convinced the danger had passed. Maybe Officer Singh was fast asleep.

Maybe Officer Singh was dead.

Lacy clenched her fists under the duvet and wished she could disappear.

Whoever was breathing softly in the corner of her room was in no hurry to – Lacy swallowed painfully, thoughts of Rachel swamping her head – to do whatever it was they were planning on doing.

She should do something to scare them off. Sit up and scream, shout for help. Throw something at them. They wouldn't be expecting that.

But what if that made them finish her off quicker, just to shut her up?

Footsteps crept across the floor, getting closer to the foot of her bed.

She felt her duvet slide ever so slightly down her body. Her heart pounded like it was going to explode as her eyes flew open and stared blindly at the ceiling.

Inch by inch, the blanket slid lower. Lacy lay as still as a corpse, her face contorted into a silent scream. When it was just the breathing, she could have convinced herself that it was all in her head.

But this…this was real.

She considered gripping her duvet and fighting the person tugging it from the end of the bed. But then they would know she was awake.

And then what would they do?

The duvet reached her knees, and Lacy tried not to shiver as the cool night air found her body. She was dressed, thank god – though her trousers and top were still damp from the rain, which continued to tap against the window.

With a soft thud, the blanket reached the end of the bed and fell to the floor.

Lacy wanted to curl into a ball, cower beneath her arms and protect herself from whatever was about to come. But her body seemed to have shut down. Tears leaked from her eyes as she waited.

Her mattress shifted as a weight lowered slowly onto it, just by her knees.

Something landed tentatively on the other side, by her hip.

The darkness was so complete that she couldn't see a thing, but she knew there was someone crouching over her, their face just inches away from hers.

She felt their breath on her cheek.

CHAPTER 34

Lacy wondered whether it was possible to die from terror.

She wondered if that would be preferable to having to live through it.

Her heart felt like it was being repeatedly stabbed as it lurched against her ribs. Was this what a heart attack felt like? Maybe it would be the better way to go, compared to...

The weight above her shifted. Whoever was on top of her must be as close as possible without actually touching her.

They must know she was awake by now. She was having to clamp her jaw shut to stop her teeth from chattering together.

But they weren't moving. What were they waiting for?

What were they going to do?

The mattress shifted and she felt them inhale as they lowered their face towards hers. She could feel the warmth radiating off their skin. She could smell them – a stale, sour smell. A smell like...

'No,' Lacy gasped, her voice piercing the silence. 'NO!'

The sudden bang of the door joined her shout, and the overhead light came on. Lacy screwed up her eyes, blinking as the light dazzled her. The image above her came fuzzily into focus.

'*You*,' Lacy whispered, confirming her suspicions.

Andy was straddling her, blinking stupidly in the light, looking as traumatised by the situation as Lacy felt. Her fear had evaporated, replaced by shock so intense that she wanted to scream.

'You!' came a cry from the doorway.

Lacy peered around Andy's lime-green body to see Chan and Marc in the doorway, tensed like superheroes in a comic book who had arrived to save the day. Marc was wearing nothing but a pair of skimpy boxers. He held a saucepan in his hand and was pointing it at Andy.

'Get the hell off her,' Chan snarled, their face contorted with rage as they raised a huge kitchen knife.

How had they got here so quickly, and with *weapons*?

Andy scrabbled away from Lacy, freeing her from the reek of his stale breath and crushing her beneath his sweaty weight in the process.

'What...the...*fuck*?' Lacy panted. Her entire body rippled with repulsion. She swatted at her clothes, trying to rid herself of the sensation that spiders were swarming over her flesh.

'Yeah, Andy. What the fuck?' Marc yelped, waving the pan in the air. His usually perfectly styled hair was stuck up in all directions.

Andy cowered on the floor, cradling his bad arm to his chest. His round face was even more mottled than usual. He looked close to tears.

'P-p-please,' he spluttered. 'Please. I can explain.'

'Go on, then,' Chan snapped, jabbing the knife towards him.

Andy blinked in surprise, as though he hadn't actually expected to be given the chance to tell his side of the story.

Lacy stared at him from her bed, willing him to come out with something good. The alternative was too horrible to think about.

'I...' he said slowly, looking around the room as though searching for inspiration. 'I, um. I was just checking on Lacy.'

'Checking on what?' Marc asked sharply. 'Her breasts?'

Lacy shuddered and wrapped her arms around her chest.

Andy let out a chuckle, but his eyes were wild and desperate. 'No, no, of course not. What do you take me for?'

'Er, a massive perv,' Chan spat, a fleck of spit landing on the knife.

Andy laughed again as he seemed to regain his composure. 'You've got it all wrong. I was just checking on her. She left in such a state last night. I wanted to make sure she was OK, that's all.'

He smiled tenderly at Lacy as he caught her eye. But there was something off in his expression – a coldness. He clearly wasn't the lovable buffoon she'd thought he was.

'Why were you *on top* of me, Andy?' she hissed.

Andy ran his fingers through his hair. 'Silly, really. I'm ever so embarrassed now, of course. But I thought for a moment...I thought you weren't breathing, so I just wanted to check. That's all.'

Lacy remembered the excruciating slowness of the duvet being tugged down her body and shook her head. 'Why didn't you just say my name?'

Andy's cheeks reddened as his eyes resumed their desperate dance around the room. 'I, um, I...'

'He's full of shit!' Chan snapped, and Marc jumped so theatrically that he flung the saucepan into the air and had to catch it again. 'He's been creeping around, perving on you ever since you arrived here!'

Lacy gawped at Andy. '*What?*'

'Well,' Marc said. 'To be fair, we didn't actually know it was him. Until now, that is.'

Lacy closed her eyes. *More* secrets?

She turned her attention to Marc and Chan. 'You need to tell me what's going on.' She was amazed by how steady her voice was. 'The truth this time. All of it.'

Chan nodded, and Lacy noticed the hand that held the kitchen knife was trembling.

'Someone has been spying on you,' Chan explained. 'We've seen them a few times. Someone lurking outside your window, trying to peer in through the curtains. But we never managed to catch who it was. It was always dark when we saw them and they would scarper before we could catch them.'

Lacy's skin crept with repulsion. That sensation of never being alone that she'd experienced since arriving here…that had been *Andy*?

'We assumed it was Dylan,' Marc chipped in. 'We even saw him coming out of the empty room next to yours.'

He pointed at the hole in the wall where Lacy had imagined an eye staring through at her.

At least, she'd *assumed* she'd imagined it.

'And Marc caught him trying to peer through your door that time too, remember?' Chan nodded angrily. 'We thought he was obsessed with you or something.'

'And when we found him sitting outside your door tonight, we suspected he was going to try something, what with this being your last night,' Marc added, gesturing with his pan.

Lacy was struggling to keep up. Dylan had stayed outside her room after she'd gone to bed?

'So we kept an eye out,' Chan continued. 'We armed ourselves and took it in turns to check he was still sitting there. Then the last time we checked, he was gone.'

Marc picked up the story. Lacy's neck was beginning to ache from switching her focus between the pair of them. 'We waited outside, listening—'

'Yeah, we didn't want to burst in on you and scare you to death if Dylan wasn't actually in here and had just decided to go home,' Chan interrupted.

'But we heard you shout "NOOO!", so we burst in.'

Lacy narrowed her eyes at Marc's exaggerated girly impression of her.

'We weren't expecting to find *him*,' Chan said, pointing at Andy with the knife.

Lacy's head ached. 'Is this why you made friends with me?' she asked quietly, realising how stupid it was that this should somehow be her biggest concern right now. 'Because you were trying to protect me from a perv?'

'Yes,' Marc said, at the same time Chan said, 'No, of course not.'

Chan glared at him furiously, before admitting, 'OK, there was an element of wanting to keep an eye out. And I felt bad about how much my stupid murder story seemed to have messed with your head. But once we got to know you, we realised you were all right. Right, Marc?'

'Oh, um, yes,' Marc agreed, but Lacy didn't miss the elbow to the ribs he'd received.

Lacy sighed sadly. She'd been wondering why they'd chosen

to befriend her. At least now, she understood.

What she didn't understand was why their manager was on her bedroom floor in the middle of the night. Or how Dylan was involved.

'Tell me the truth, Andy,' she said, her voice low. 'Why did you come into my room?'

Andy looked up at her imploringly. It was impossible to feel angry with him. He was too pathetic. Even now, she pitied him – poor, nice Andy who just wanted everyone to like him.

But even though he still couldn't meet her eye and addressed his next words into the threadbare carpet beneath him, they still chilled Lacy to the core.

'You like it,' he mumbled petulantly. 'You like being watched.'

CHAPTER 35

Lacy, Chan and Marc stared dumbly at Andy, who remained sat on the floor, arms curled around his knees like a child who'd been put in time out.

'You've been spying on me?' Lacy choked out.

Andy's eyes flicked towards her for a brief moment, before returning to focus on the carpet. 'Not *spying*,' he insisted. His jaw moved from side to side as though he were searching for a more palatable word somewhere inside his mouth. 'Observing,' he finally settled on.

'Perving on her, you mean!' Marc spat, his face contorted with disgust.

Andy's head twitched and a troubled frown appeared on his face. 'No. No – *admiring*.'

'Oh my god, stop coming up with less creepy ways to say that you've been watching Lacy get undressed without her knowing!' Chan spluttered, the kitchen knife waving dangerously in the air.

'Is that really what you've been doing?' Lacy asked, revulsion crawling over her entire body as reality finally dawned on her.

She was still trying to give him a chance to explain himself, she realised, desperate for there to be a reason for his bizarre behaviour.

Andy's tongue darted out to moisten his thin lips. The way his eyes repeatedly snatched glances at her was making Lacy feel sick. When he finally spoke, he couldn't find the courage to look her in the eye.

'I knew you were special,' he breathed. 'From the first night, I knew.'

His ever-roaming eyes flicked involuntarily towards the peephole in the bedroom wall. Lacy followed his gaze, horrified to learn that she *had* seen someone staring through the gap. That had been the beginning, she realised. The beginning of her convincing herself that her imagination was conjuring up things that simply weren't there.

What else had she dismissed as a figment of her imagination when it had in fact been very, very real?

A light, fluttering touch on her ankle pulled her attention away from the peephole. Andy had brushed her leg as his hands turned upwards, pleading and pathetic. 'Lacy, please…'

The feel of his fingers on her bare skin triggered such a strong reaction in her that Lacy's leg seemed to swing upwards of its own accord, booting Andy in the face, hard.

She felt the cartilage in his nose shift beneath her bare foot. Andy bellowed and covered his face with his hands.

Lacy flinched, fighting the urge to apologise.

Andy did not deserve her pity. He never had. She thought of the lingering hugs, the hands that had roamed too freely. When else had he watched her without her knowledge?

'What the hell is wrong with you?' Lacy cried, pulling her feet up onto the bed and tucking them underneath her, the idea of Andy touching her again making bile rush up her throat.

'I thought you liked me too,' Andy whined. He tentatively brought his hands away from his face and studied them, checking for blood.

There wasn't any and Lacy wished she'd kicked him harder.

'Mate, you're deranged,' Chan said matter-of-factly from the doorway.

Andy ignored Chan and turned his watery eyes to gaze imploringly up at Lacy. 'You were different from the others!' he wheedled. 'You were classy, *special*.'

Once, Lacy would have been flattered by someone seeing her as classy. But right now, the compliment made her want to vomit.

'Wait a minute,' she said, after she'd recovered. 'What do you mean, the others? What others?'

But Lacy didn't need Andy to explain, as realisation hit her, turning her blood to ice. There had been others. Before her, and even at the same time as her.

Ceri's words the day of the beach party. *Something happened to me.*

In Lacy's memory, Ceri's dark eyes morphed into Winter's, aged sixteen and sobbing on the bathroom floor after returning home from a house party.

'Did you do something to Ceri?' she breathed, still wishing she'd somehow got this wrong and that Ceri had left because of some petty drama between her and Rachel. Not because Andy…

But the way Andy's pupils darted from side to side, urgently searching for a way out of this line of questioning, told Lacy everything she needed to know.

'You sick piece of shit!' Chan spat, darting towards him, brandishing the knife.

Marc grabbed Chan around the shoulders. 'Don't – he's not worth it!'

Lacy wondered if he might actually be worth it. She had clamped her shaking hands beneath her knees, barely containing her own rage.

Her heart ached for Ceri. She'd been sobbing, trying to tell Rachel what had happened to her. Had Rachel brushed her friend off before hearing what she had to say? Would she even have cared if she had given Ceri a chance to speak?

The way Andy sat, hunched and exposed on the floor, made Lacy think of some kind of maggoty creature revealed when the rock they'd been hiding under was turned over. How had Andy managed to conceal who he really was so effectively when there was this much poison brimming beneath the surface?

'How long have you been doing this sick shit?' Marc asked, his hands still clamped around Chan's shoulders. 'You've worked here for years, and you've always been a sneaky little weirdo lurking outside… Oh god.'

'What?' Lacy demanded. 'What is it, Marc?'

Marc was staring into the mid-distance, a troubled expression on his face. 'I saw you,' he said, frowning as he looked at Andy. 'I saw you that night – when I went to meet Chan after work. I saw you outside the caravan, creeping around like you were trying to look into the windows or something.' He shook his head, and Lacy struggled to understand which night he was referring to.

'You were outside *the* caravan,' Marc finally breathed, his eyes wide. 'Carl Jones's caravan. Holy shit, Andy. Did you kill him? Was it you?'

Andy's lizard tongue was doing overtime now, frantically darting in and out of his mouth as his beady eyes searched for an escape route. Lacy tried to picture him killing a man. He was a creep – a nasty, slimy little creep. But a murderer?

'He attacked me,' Andy rasped, extinguishing Lacy's assumption of innocence. 'He saw me outside and he attacked me. I hit him with a rock, but it was self-defence… I had no choice!'

Lacy's eyes widened. Andy had *killed* a man. He'd been caught spying through the window of the couple's caravan and bashed the guy's head in with a rock before stashing the body beneath the wooden stilts.

She had been so sure he was harmless. But had *anyone* seen Andy for who he really was?

Dylan. Dylan had tried to warn her about something. What if he hadn't been spying on Lacy, as Chan and Marc had thought?

'And Dylan?' she asked. 'Did he catch you too? Did you think about bashing *his* head in with a rock?'

A dark, sneering expression passed over Andy's face then disappeared, and Lacy remembered the weird tension between the two of them, and the bruise on Dylan's jaw. Had Andy already reacted to being caught by Dylan?

Andy opened his mouth to reply but was cut off by Marc's appalled gasp. 'Wait, did you kill Rachel too?'

The temperature in the room felt like it had plummeted.

But Andy shook his head, his eyes wide as though appalled at the idea. 'No, no! Why would I kill Rachel?' He blinked rapidly, his bottom lip wavering. 'She was my friend.'

Lacy scrutinised him, searching for the lie. But no – Andy and Rachel *had* been friends, in a weird, mismatched kind of way. And, she realised with a sickening swoop, she'd always thought Rachel was using Andy for his access to alcohol. Was it possible that Andy had been using her too?

Lacy again thought of Ceri that day on the beach. Her haunted eyes as she tried to process what had happened to her.

She thought of Winter, and the way she'd struggled to breathe as vomit and tears hurtled violently out of her body.

And even though it was two hundred years ago, she thought of Catrin Roberts. The innocent woman who had just tried to help and been murdered for it.

Lacy had thought it was impossible for her to feel any more repulsed. Andy had designed this. He'd created the perfect setting for his predatory plans, supplying alcohol to minors so he could get to them when they were at their most vulnerable. Who else had he targeted? Who else had been put in a position where they couldn't control what was happening?

'The wine,' she gasped, the lurching, sickening memory of her own vulnerability returning to her. 'You passed me my bottle, and then I…I can't remember anything after that.'

That was a lie. She could remember snatches of time, horrible, awful moments that she wished she couldn't remember. She'd been so lost, so helpless, so…

Lacy frowned. That was just how Dylan had been when he'd stumbled off the cliff. Had that been Andy's doing too? Had Andy spiked Dylan when he'd noticed how close Lacy was getting to him?

Andy slid his eyes away from the wall and onto her face, still earnestly searching for a hint of connection between them.

'I just wanted to get you to relax,' he whispered. 'You were so uptight, so on edge. But when I came to check on you, your room was empty. You'd wandered off somewhere.'

The long, dark corridor inside the abandoned dorm stretched endlessly in Lacy's memory. It had been horrible, terrifying. But would something worse have awaited her if she'd stayed in her room?

She felt dirty.

She glared down at Andy. He'd made her feel *dirty*.

She thought she might actually be sick this time, but the shock of Chan lunging wildly across the room pushed the threat of vomit back down into her stomach.

Marc grabbed the empty air too late. Chan had flattened Andy against the floor and he grunted with surprise. Lacy's eyes widened at the thought of Chan's kitchen knife. Surely they hadn't…?

'Get him, Chan!' Marc cheered, and Lacy turned to see him thrusting his saucepan encouragingly in the air. In his other hand was Chan's knife.

Relief rushed through Lacy, but even without the weapon, Chan was doing some damage. Andy was pinned to the floor, crushed beneath Chan's knees and flinching as blows landed on his blotchy face.

'See…how…you…like …it,' Chan panted with each strike.

Lacy nodded furiously. Yes, see how he liked feeling powerless and vulnerable.

But her anger ebbed away as she noticed Andy's face deepen from red to dark purple. His eyes were bulging, the whites turning bloodshot as his tongue protruded helplessly from his mouth. He croaked as he gasped for air.

'Jesus, Chan, don't actually murder him,' Marc said, lowering his weapons.

'I'm not!' Chan insisted, raising their hands in surrender before scrambling away from Andy.

Andy continued to splutter on the floor.

'Is he having an allergic reaction or something?' Lacy said. She had no idea what to do. Even if she could bring herself to touch him, she wouldn't know how to administer the first aid he needed.

But as she stared at him, she realised this was far beyond her – or anyone else's – help.

The image came hazily at first, like the scratchy shadow caused by getting dust in your eye. But the more that Lacy focused, the stronger the outline became.

The outline of a person straddling Andy, just as Chan had moments before, their hands tight around his throat.

CHAPTER 36

Dark hair hung over their face like a tangled, filthy curtain. The skin on their hands was deathly white as they gripped around Andy's throat. The fingernails looked black, rotten. The long, floaty dress also looked black at first glance, but it was actually a deep, bruised purple.

The smell was back. The fetid, damp smell that Lacy had thought was something to do with Peril Bay. How wrong she'd been. The smell of lavender was stronger now – lavender perfume mingled with rotten leaves and stagnant water.

Winter slowly swivelled her head towards Lacy.

It was Lacy's sister…but also, it wasn't.

She had the same pale face and thick black hair as Winter. She was wearing the purple velvet dress she'd always cherished, but the material looked heavy. Water was dripping from the tattered pleats, collecting in a grimy puddle on the floor.

Her hands were puffy and swollen, and the skin around her joints looked cracked and sore. There were crevices on her cheeks too – bloodless, open wounds. Her skin was puckered and ridged, like fingers that had been in the bath for too long.

And her eyes…

Her eyes rooted Lacy to the spot, making her feel as though she would never breathe again. The sockets looked too big, the lower lids sagging and exposing the anaemic pink beneath.

Winter's lips retracted, revealing black, rotting gums. She chattered her teeth together. The noise sent a jolt of horror through Lacy's heart.

Chan and Marc were pressed against the wall of Lacy's bedroom, their eyes wide with terror. Winter seemed to lose interest in Lacy and turned her attention back to Andy, who was gasping shallowly beneath her hands, like a fish taking its last pathetic breaths. Winter pressed her face closer to his… and sniffed.

Whatever she smelled – the stench of death, perhaps – seemed to excite her. Her teeth clacked together with increased enthusiasm.

Lacy knew she should be doing something. Shouting, pulling the thing that looked like her sister away from Andy. But she couldn't move. She'd been stuck in a nightmare ever since waking up in the abandoned dorm and finding Rachel's body, but this…this was something else.

Winter was moving her head with an inquisitive expression as she watched the life drain out of her victim. She brushed her nose against Andy's cheeks as she sniffed him again, and her lips stretched further than should have been possible.

She was smiling. She was squeezing the life out of Andy and *smiling*.

'Winter?' Lacy breathed.

Winter's head snapped towards Lacy, her singular focus now directed at her. Lacy cowered on her bed, her back pressed against the wall.

'Winter?' Lacy sobbed, her voice a tiny, terrified squeak.

Winter let Andy's lifeless body slump to the floor and lurched to her feet with staggering speed. In the time it took Lacy to blink, she'd somehow moved to the foot of her bed and clambered over the mattress.

Lacy could feel the coldness of Winter's skin next to hers. She tried to keep perfectly still as Winter scrutinised her but couldn't stop the whimper that escaped her mouth.

The noise seemed to aggravate Winter, and she bared her teeth, chattering them just millimetres from Lacy's face. Lacy clamped her eyes shut.

'Holy shit!'

Lacy opened them again to see Lee standing in the doorway behind Chan and Marc, who were still frozen with terror. He wore old-fashioned tartan pyjamas and the baseball hat that never left his head, even as he slept, it seemed. He must have come to investigate all the noise.

Winter snarled. A deep, guttural vibration that started in the pit of her stomach and escaped through her broken lips. Lacy gagged as her sister's foul breath hit her nose. Winter's attention, and fury, now turned towards the three teenagers standing in the doorway.

Lee's eyes bulged as he backed slowly out of Lacy's room before turning to sprint off down the corridor.

Lacy opened her mouth to scream at him to stay put, instinctively knowing that running would only make the Winter-creature chase him. But he was already gone.

Winter launched forwards, past Andy's limp body, bowling through Chan and Marc as though they weren't even there.

The paralysis that had gripped Lacy disappeared the second

she was released from Winter's hypnotic glare, and she sprang to her feet. Trying not to look at Andy's blotchy corpse, she jumped over Marc and Chan, who lay groaning on the floor, and followed the thing that was wearing her sister's body.

Winter was flickering in and out of sight as she pursued Lee down the corridor, like a film struggling to buffer. At times, she was barely there at all, and if Lee hadn't been running for his life, Lacy might have been able to convince herself that this was yet another figment of her imagination.

The thin, scratchy carpet burned her bare feet as she followed, and her damp clothes made her feel sluggish. She had no idea what she would do if she caught up with them. But she had to try.

Towards the end of the corridor a door opened. Officer Singh emerged, dressed in a baggy vest and a pair of oversized boxers. 'What's going on?' he asked blearily as Lee came haring towards him.

His eyes widened when he spotted Winter, shifting in and out of focus as she ran. Lee barged past him, sending him flying back into his room, and his head hit the doorframe with a sickening crack. He slumped to the floor.

But Lacy didn't have time to check on him – because Lee and Winter were gone, into the night.

'Winter!' Lacy shouted as she pushed the swinging door away from her. 'Stop!'

The rain hit Lacy hard in the face and she narrowed her eyes as it lashed against her stinging cheeks. Winter was invisible once again, but the feeble light from the dorm block's fire exit sign showed the white of Lee's trainers as he sprinted towards the clifftop.

And then he was swallowed by the darkness.

'Winter!' Lacy screamed, but she could hardly hear her own voice above the gale.

She set off at a jog, terrified of running in the dark. But she couldn't just stay in the dorm doing nothing. That was her *sister*.

Or at least, it used to be.

'Winter!' Lacy pleaded as she spun round, realising she couldn't see the dorm block anymore. She was surrounded by darkness and had no idea which direction to run.

She staggered onwards, praying she could rely on her sense of direction. From the way the wind suddenly doubled in force, Lacy assumed she had arrived at the cliff. She stumbled to a halt and squinted through the darkness. The clouds shifted and the moonlight showed just how close to the edge she was.

The sea was an empty, black void.

A cold hand seized Lacy's forearm and she screamed, wrenching herself free and staggering backwards. Lee stood inches away from her.

'Run,' he said, his face leached of all colour. Then, following his own command, he set off sprinting again, back towards the dorms.

Lacy watched after him in astonishment. How had he got away from Winter? And more importantly, where was her sister now?

Lee's baseball cap had been scooped off his head by the wind, and Lacy watched it tumble towards the cliff. It paused for a second, before disappearing over the edge.

Watching it fall stood Winter, her toes touching the grassy rim of the cliff. As she stared silently out at the ocean, her purple dress flapped in the wind and her hair whipped around her face in wild, dark tendrils.

'Winter?' Lacy asked cautiously.

Winter stepped forwards and plummeted off the edge of the cliff.

CHAPTER 37

'No!' Lacy screamed.

Her legs propelled her forwards through rain that felt like it was slicing her flesh. She landed heavily on her knees by the edge of the cliff.

The clouds shifted and the moon appeared, full and bright enough to reveal the black water churning and foaming far below as it crashed against the jagged rocks. Her eyes darted from side to side, desperately searching, as she gripped the crumbling clifftop.

'Winter!' she cried, but her voice was stolen by the wind.

She found what she had been looking for – the ledge that had saved Dylan's life. She craned her neck, pressing her face closer, daring to hope.

But no. The shadow she had desperately convinced herself was Winter's purple dress was just that, a shadow. Her sister wasn't on the outcrop. She hadn't been saved.

Lacy slumped backwards, away from the cliff. She moaned and buried her head in her hands, gently rocking herself as she struggled to process what had happened. The rain seeped in through the cracks in Lacy's cocoon and ran down her cold cheeks.

Winter had been here. Her presence had been as real to Lacy as the icy rain that was chilling her to the bone. For the first time that summer, she was sure that what she had seen had been real. It wasn't in her head, it wasn't a symptom of stress, it wasn't someone playing tricks on her.

Winter had been here. But it hadn't been the Winter Lacy knew.

Lacy clenched her fists and pressed her forehead harder into her knees.

Winter had been *wrong*. Feral, broken, *wrong*. A deep shudder ran up Lacy's body, starting at her bare feet. She stared at her toes as they sunk into the wet moss. They were slick with mud.

'Lacy!' a voice shouted over the wind.

Lacy raised her head to see Marc and Chan standing in front of her, the torches on their phones shining through the darkness. Chan angled the beam at Lacy's legs so as not to dazzle her. There was blood on her feet as well as mud, she noted dully.

'We saw Lee running towards the park entrance,' Marc panted as he spun in circles, twitching his light in every direction.

Lacy pictured Lee sprinting as though the starter pistol had been fired at the Olympics and wondered whether he would ever stop running. He couldn't have chosen a worse time to be curious about the noises coming from her bedroom.

'You OK?' Chan asked, eyes wild and frantic as they scanned the cliffside. 'Where is…where is it?'

Lacy bristled, but she couldn't argue with Chan's choice of words. What they were dealing with wasn't human.

Lacy braced the heels of her hands on her thighs as she knelt in the grass. 'She went over,' she said stiffly, nodding towards the cliff edge.

She could feel the relief coming off Chan and Marc in waves and wished her emotions were as easy to categorise.

She knew she should be scared, horrified, glad that they were safe from whatever demonic force had possessed her sister.

But all she really felt was overwhelming grief.

'That wasn't your sister,' Chan said, drawing closer and putting a strong hand on Lacy's shoulder. 'I don't know what it was, but it wasn't her. It wasn't Winter.'

Lacy nodded, wishing she could believe it.

'That was your *sister*?' Marc gasped.

Lacy sighed, and suddenly the cold in her bones, the pain in her feet and the ache in her heart magnified.

'No,' she said, recalling the wretched thing that had pressed its face towards her. 'It wasn't my sister.'

That *thing* wearing Winter's body was gone, leaving them with nothing but questions, PTSD and a dead manager they were somehow going to have to explain to the Gwynedd police force.

'Lacy,' Marc breathed, and Lacy slowly looked up from the sodden ground.

His face was frozen in a grotesque mask of terror, which instantly sent Lacy's exhausted heart thundering in her chest. She followed the direction in which his eyes were unblinkingly staring.

The two torch beams followed suit and landed on something standing motionless on the clifftop.

She was back, her deep purple dress billowing in the wind. Her back was slightly hunched, as though she was fighting the urge to pitch herself back over the edge.

Winter cocked her head to one side, almost sweetly. 'Why would you tell them I'm not your sister, Lacy?'

CHAPTER 38

Winter's voice sounded painful, as if it were forcing its way out through a tunnel of barbed wire in her throat. Her deathly pale skin was even whiter in the moonlight, and her eyes looked like holes in her face.

'Winter?' Lacy whispered.

She slowly prised herself from the wet ground, her knees trembling as they took her weight. She'd been close to convincing herself that the monster was nothing to do with her sister, and its appearance was some sadistic coincidence. But now that she knew it could speak…

And it knew her *name*.

'I don't know why I keep coming here,' Winter rasped, turning to stare forlornly out to sea, as though forgetting Lacy was there. 'I keep losing time…and whenever I return, I'm here.'

The heavy folds of Winter's dress swayed in the wind and Lacy inched towards her. Chan reached out to stop her, but Lacy brushed their fingers aside. She needed to get closer, to see if it really was her sister she was speaking to.

Or if it was something else entirely.

Winter continued to look out across the bay. There was something so beautiful about the image that Lacy found herself wishing she'd brought her camera and almost laughed at the preposterous thought.

'And whenever I'm here,' Winter said dreamily, 'I get the urge to just…step off.'

She raised her foot to hover over the cliff edge and Lacy lurched forwards, her hands held out helplessly.

'Winter,' she breathed. 'Don't.'

She couldn't watch her sister fall, not again. Even if this Winter had the ability to return to the top of the cliff, apparently unscathed, Lacy wasn't sure her heart could take it.

Winter finally looked at her. 'Lacy,' she said, as if pleasantly surprised to see her there. 'What are you doing here?'

Lacy took a tentative step forwards. 'I followed you,' she said carefully.

Winter frowned, creasing the greyish skin above the puckered scar on her cheek. 'Are we in Paris?'

Lacy couldn't catch the sob before it escaped her mouth. This *was* her sister.

She'd found her.

And nothing else mattered. Whatever had happened to Winter, whatever she was now, Lacy knew they could make it work.

'I'm cold,' Winter said abruptly, a deep shiver running up her body. 'I'm cold all the time.'

Lacy took another step forwards, wishing she'd brought a jacket so she could wrap it around her sister's shoulders. She frowned as she stared at the heavy fabric of Winter's dress, which should have provided some warmth. She'd assumed it was billowing in the wind, but now she was closer, she saw that it was swirling and shifting in a pattern of its own, gently drifting in all directions, as though…

As though underwater.

'You fell,' Chan said from beside Lacy, making her jump. For a moment, she'd completely forgotten about the other two. It had been her and Winter, just like it was supposed to be. 'On New Year's Eve, I saw you walking by the pier and I thought you'd just left, but…you fell, didn't you?'

Lacy turned her attention to Chan, whose face was etched with sorrow.

Her thoughts raced, seeing the sense in Chan's words but hiding from their truth. After months of wanting to know where her sister had gone, the prospect of finally discovering what had happened to her filled her with dread.

Winter considered Chan's words, then nodded slowly.

'Yes. I…fell.' She looked back towards the ocean and Lacy saw her foot twitch as though her body wanted her to repeat the experience all over again. 'I remember…cold.'

Lacy squeezed her eyes shut, the horror of it overwhelming her. Chan had seen Winter walking on a Blackpool pier in the middle of a freezing night.

Winter had gone into the water.

Which meant that no matter how much Lacy had fought to believe the fantasy of Winter living in Paris, Winter was dead.

And yet, she was standing right there, wearing the same clothes she'd died in, *talking* to her.

'I'm sorry,' Chan gasped. 'I'm so sorry. I should have spoken to you that night. I should have made sure you got home safe. I'm so sorr—'

Winter snapped her head around to glare at Chan, her face twisted in disgust. Her hiss was somehow audible above the wind. 'I wouldn't have wanted your help anyway, you scruffy little loser.'

Both Lacy and Chan recoiled from the venom in Winter's voice. Lacy tensed, waiting for the feral creature they'd encountered in her bedroom to make a reappearance. But Winter remained motionless, unaffected by the weather that mercilessly hammered the rest of them.

There was no wildness in Winter's eyes now, only the cold, cruel sneer that Lacy knew so well. She hadn't changed, Lacy realised. Even in death, Winter was just as judgemental as she'd been in life.

'Why are you here?' Lacy asked.

The smirk on Winter's face shifted as she turned her attention to Lacy. But what replaced it wasn't much better. It was pity.

'Why am I here?' Winter asked, a lilt of surprise in her croaking voice.

Lacy nodded.

'I never left your side, little sister. I told you it would be you and me forever, didn't I?'

Lacy swallowed. Once, those words would have filled her with joy. Now, they felt threatening. The dark figure that had haunted her since she had arrived at Peril Bay hadn't felt protective or comforting. She remembered the outstretched hand, the finger pointing directly at her. Their presence had made Lacy feel, at best, like she was imagining things and, at worst, scared and vulnerable. And it had been Winter all along.

'But you left me,' she said. 'I had no idea where you'd gone.'

She shook her head, hoping Winter understood that she was upset by her leaving Lacy for Blackpool, not death.

'Well, I'm here now, keeping you safe,' Winter said, almost angrily. Lacy suspected she was perturbed by her tepid response – she was used to unconditional adoration from her little sister.

'There's something about this place,' she continued as she stared out across the ocean. 'Something that makes me stronger. I can do more things here than I could at home.'

Lacy thought of the ghost stories she'd absently scrolled past when researching Peril Bay, searching for evidence of Chan's bogus story. The most haunted place in North Wales. The dead sailors rotting beneath the waves, the terrible murder of Catrin Roberts... Had the turbulent history of this place made it somewhere Winter could thrive?

What else had Winter done with her new-found strength, other than appearing to her as a ghostly figure? Would Winter have had the power to slam the train doors on Andy's arm, keeping Lacy at Peril Bay, where she was at her strongest?

'This place is good for us,' Winter murmured, confirming Lacy's suspicions. She swivelled her head away from the sea and stared deep into Lacy's eyes. 'I can protect you here. I've already saved you more times than you can imagine.'

CHAPTER 39

'What do you mean, you've saved me?' Lacy said slowly.

'I stopped you getting your head chopped off by your idiot boyfriend,' Winter said. Lacy noticed her voice was becoming more pronounced the more she spoke, the rasp of her disused voice box fading.

'What?' Lacy breathed. 'Cal was going to *kill* me?'

Winter rolled her eyes in disgust. 'No, not him, you moron.'

Lacy winced. She'd been without Winter's insults for a while now and had become accustomed to being spoken to like she was an actual human with feelings.

She wrapped her arms around herself, feeling the chill of her skin beneath her fingers. 'Who then?'

'The *lifeguard*,' Winter sneered.

'*Dylan?*' Lacy gasped.

She wasn't sure what she was finding harder to comprehend, the fact Winter had called him her boyfriend or…

'He would never *chop my head off*!' Lacy insisted, appalled. Her chest swelled with panic. It couldn't be… Not Dylan. Could it?

'He would have,' Winter said. 'If I hadn't pulled you to safety.'

Lacy blinked at her sister through the rain, wishing she could keep up. She always felt so stupid around Winter. Stupid and small and like she'd never be good enough.

Winter sighed noisily and shook her head in despair at Lacy's slowness. 'The boat!' she snapped, gesturing angrily in the air. 'He was inches away from ploughing straight into you.'

And then Lacy saw it – around Winter's wrist was Lacy's bracelet. The bracelet she had lost in the sea.

Understanding hit Lacy like the relentless waves in the ocean that day. She'd been in the water, trying to save the little boy. She'd been struggling, and then…

A hand had grabbed her ankle and yanked her down towards the depths of the ocean.

'That was you?' Lacy cried.

What else had Lacy convinced herself was her imagination? The figure walking by the clifftop, the figure *falling* off the clifftop. The feeling of never being alone, always being watched. It must have been Winter – all of it.

Well, the parts that weren't Andy.

'If I hadn't pulled you to safety, he would have killed you,' Winter confirmed, nodding her head proudly.

Lacy's bottom lip trembled violently. She thought she'd been abandoned. She'd assumed Winter had escaped to Paris and was enjoying her new life so much that she hadn't even considered getting in touch.

But she'd been here the whole time. So close that she'd saved Lacy's *life*.

'Don't cry,' Winter snapped, wrinkling her nose in disgust.

Lacy nodded and pressed her teeth into her tongue until she regained control. Winter hated crying.

'You said "more times than you can imagine".' Marc's voice came from behind Lacy, and for the second time, she jumped. 'You're saying you saved her more than once.'

Winter's eyes roamed up Marc's long body, her lips twitching with suppressed laughter when her gaze fell on the tiny shorts he wore to bed. Lacy sidestepped slightly to shield Marc from her scrutiny.

'I saved her from that wormy little man,' Winter explained casually.

'Andy?' Chan asked over the wind. Lacy's breath caught in her throat as she remembered his eyes turning from white to red as Winter squeezed his neck.

Winter nodded.

'I'm pretty sure we had that under control,' Chan said, and Lacy was relieved to see their confidence was back – they'd need it when speaking to her sister. 'There was one of him and three of us. We were handling it.'

'Not *then*,' Winter scoffed. 'The previous night, when he spiked my little sister's drink. You were nowhere to be seen then, were you?'

Chan stiffened, and Lacy wanted to insist that it wasn't their fault, that it wasn't their job to look after her. No one could have known what Andy had been up to. He'd perfected the disgusting art of preying on vulnerable girls – a predator disguised behind citrus and smiles.

But she couldn't spare words for Chan, because her thoughts were racing ahead, demanding to know the truth. The truth of what had happened in the abandoned dorm.

'How did you…?' Lacy whispered, before coughing to clear her throat. 'How did you save me that night?'

'Andy was in your room. I'm sure he expected to find you blacked out in bed rather than gone for a midnight wander. But I knew you wouldn't be able to resist coming to see me – I've been appearing to you all summer. So I let you catch a glimpse of me outside your window and you came staggering after me, like you always do.'

Winter smirked and Lacy felt the rainwater on her cheeks warm from her blush. All those times she'd seen a figure lurking in the distance – could it have been her sister all along?

'But he would have found you eventually, so I appeared again, this time inside the abandoned dorm.'

Lacy squinted against the wet wind as she tried to remember. It made sense. If she had seen the figure that night, she would have gone to investigate, just as she had been doing all summer. But something wasn't adding up.

'What about Gary?' Lacy pressed. 'I saw him in the entrance of the dorm. I know I did.'

It had been pretty much the only thing she had been sure of that entire evening.

Winter shrugged flippantly. 'He spotted you struggling and came to help. But you freaked out and ran away from him, realising you were better off inside the abandoned dorm with me.'

Guilt twisted Lacy's stomach.

'Why did you kill Rachel?' Chan asked softly.

Lacy gasped. She'd been so absorbed in Winter's story, so focused on the fact that her sister hadn't left her side for the last eight months, that she somehow, stupidly, hadn't put those pieces of the puzzle together.

'The blonde girl.' Winter nodded thoughtfully. 'Yes, that was…unfortunate.'

Winter's words may have been regretful, but the corners of her mouth were twitching as she battled the grin that fought to stretch across her face.

'She didn't hurt Lacy,' Marc said, his voice thick. 'She didn't hurt anyone!'

Winter's eyes flashed with rage and Lacy shrank away from their ferocity. 'She was an enabler! Without her and her parties, Andy wouldn't have got away with half the stuff he did!'

Marc backed off, unable or unwilling to argue the point.

Winter turned her attention to Chan. 'You inspired me, actually, with your little story about the murdered staff in the abandoned dorm.'

Chan exhaled sharply and staggered slightly as a gust of wind pummelled them from across the sea.

This was too much. Lacy couldn't process it. Her sister was dead, but her sister was standing right here. And the things she was saying she'd done…

'No,' Lacy whispered, shaking her head. 'You can't have.'

'Oh, but I did,' Winter replied, her grin stretching her lips wide and showing the blackness of her gums.

'How? How did you even do it?' Lacy asked, swallowing the bile that seeped into her closed mouth. 'Her *head*?'

Chan's voice came down her ear, low and urgent. 'Lacy, this isn't your sister. Don't forget what she was like back in the dorm. She was strong, remember? She probably dragged Rachel in there and ripped—'

Lacy's sharp intake of breath spared her having to hear Chan finish the sentence. She did not need to imagine her sister killing Rachel with her bare hands.

Winter's dark gaze lost focus as she stared across the tumultuous ocean. 'Sometimes I feel a little…different. It's difficult to remember who I was when I was alive, and' – her voice grew distant and dreamy – 'it feels nice to give in to my instincts.'

'What did you do with her head?' Marc asked, his voice squeaking as though he wasn't sure he wanted to know the answer.

'It's mine,' she murmured, still staring out to sea. 'You can't have it, it's mi—'

'OK!' Lacy said placatingly. 'OK, Winter, no one is trying to take…*it*…from you.' She swallowed, trying not to think about where it might be. Winter had always been a hoarder, her room full of stolen treasures and random knick-knacks. Had Rachel's head been given the same prized status? 'But, please, this has to stop.'

'I told you,' Winter said, turning and flashing Lacy a rotten smile. 'I'm looking out for you. Rachel wasn't the first, and she won't be the last.'

CHAPTER 40

The rain drummed against Lacy's skull like fingers tapping over a keyboard. She stared numbly at Winter. Her sister – the walking corpse. Her sister – the murderer.

Any joy Lacy had felt since finding Winter again had been extinguished. This wasn't her sister. This was something else entirely, something that had clawed its way out from God knows where and attached itself to her sister's body.

Unless, Lacy thought with a horrible lurch, unless it really was Winter, and death had simply enabled her to become who she was meant to be. She was just embracing her instincts, after all.

'Rachel wasn't the first?' Chan said.

Lacy didn't need Winter to bring her up to speed this time. 'Cal,' she whispered.

Winter nodded.

Lacy closed her eyes, swaying as the wind rocked her body.

'He hurt you,' Winter growled. 'He hurt you, and he had to pay.'

Lacy kept her eyes clamped shut. She wanted to figure it out herself so she didn't have to hear the horrible truth spewing from Winter's lips. Nor did she wish to see the vicious smile that would surely be on her sister's face.

Cal *had* hurt her. She'd been vulnerable when they'd met, just after Winter had left. She'd opened herself up to him, revealing her insecurities and allowing him closer than she should ever have allowed a boy like Cal to get. And then the moment she hadn't given him what he wanted, he'd plunged his hand into her chest, ripped out her heart and given it to his pack of dog friends to savage like a chew toy.

It made sense now – the scratch on his face, the one she didn't remember making. It hadn't been her who had fought him off and stopped his greedy hands roaming her rigid body. It had been her sister.

Cal hadn't fallen from the balcony, he'd been pushed. For the thousandth time, she pictured him plummeting to his death, arms flailing…

She gasped and opened her eyes to see Winter still staring at her through a mane of wild dark hair. She recalled Dylan grappling with a dark-haired girl on the edge of the cliff. It hadn't been Ceri, it had been Winter. Trying to kill Dylan for…what? Nearly accidentally hitting Lacy with a boat? Or did Winter hate Dylan because he was getting close to Lacy and making her less dependent on her big sister?

The cold had found its way through Lacy's skin, and her teeth chattered together uncontrollably. She needed to get inside, to get warm.

She warily looked around at the others. Chan's hoodie was sodden and Marc was visibly trembling, his bare flesh mottled and goose bumped.

She braced herself, her eyelids drooping closed again,

dreading having to tell Winter that they needed to wrap this conversation up before the living people on the clifftop all died from exposure. Giving Winter orders had never gone down well before. She doubted dead-Winter would take them any better.

Lacy opened her eyes to find Winter standing an inch away from her. The decay of her face was even more apparent up close, and the smell of rot was overpowering. Lacy shrank backwards and tried not to gag.

'I'll never let anyone hurt you,' Winter growled.

Lacy's heart thudded in warning. The wildness in Winter's eyes was returning, and her jaw twitched as her teeth clacked rhythmically together. Was this what happened before she...?

Lacy sucked air into her aching lungs and stood up taller. She couldn't let Winter kill anyone else.

'Winter,' she said pleadingly. 'This has to sto—'

Winter's teeth chattered together violently, and Lacy stepped backwards, bumping into Chan.

'I think I've finally found it,' Winter said, her smile juddering and twisting over her snapping teeth.

'Found what?' Although Lacy wasn't sure she wanted to know.

'My *calling*,' Winter hissed. 'I'm ridding the world of bad people. And I'm getting more powerful, learning how to have control over myself and how to become more...attached, more solid.'

Lacy suspected that Winter was overestimating how much control she had, given the way her fingers were twisting in the air like claws and her jaw seemed to have a mind of its own.

'I'm like –' Winter paused for dramatic effect, her snarl

turning upwards at the corners '– an angel of vengeance.'

Lacy had seen this before, this fervent excitement that possessed Winter whenever she started a new phase, a new obsession. She would become an expert on whatever it was within days, shunning her previous interests in an instant and becoming completely invested in the new thing.

She wished Winter would regain her enthusiasm for Paris. That obsession had a significantly lower body count.

The twitching was taking control of Winter's body and her neck snapped suddenly to the side, cracking loudly. Winter continued to smile.

Lacy raised her hands but couldn't bring herself to place them on Winter's shoulders. What would she feel like beneath the purple dress? Was there even any flesh left on her skeleton?

'Winter, please—'

But it was too late. Winter was lost to the feral drive that had pushed her to strangle Andy and chase Lee towards the cliff edge. There was a savage rumbling coming from her throat, but she managed to choke out three grating words. 'I'm. Not. Finished.'

With that, she hurtled through the group, flickering wildly in and out of focus as she ran back towards the dorm blocks.

'She said Andy wouldn't be the last,' Marc cried. 'Who was she talking about? Who's next?'

Lacy brought a trembling hand to her face, terror surging into her chest. 'Dylan.'

CHAPTER 41

Lacy ran. Heat from the lactic acid in her legs clashed with the icy coldness of her skin, making her cry out in pain. She pushed forwards, narrowing her eyes against the rain, refusing to let it slow her down. She had to get to Dylan. Had to get there before…

She found fresh speed and pumped her arms, taking the pain from the stitch in her ribs and using it to propel her onwards.

The dark outlines of the dorm blocks came into view in the moonlight, their edges sharp and angular against the black sky. Lacy hesitated, then tracked left, towards the abandoned dorm.

Dylan had been keeping watch outside her room earlier, before disappearing. If she knew him, she'd bet her life that he wouldn't have left voluntarily. And if she knew Winter…

Winter thrived off drama, and what would be more dramatic than taking Dylan to the abandoned dorm for one final showdown?

Lacy didn't dither at the entrance this time. She knew the horror that waited for her now, and it wore her sister's face. The yellow police tape had already been torn, verifying Lacy's suspicions. While Winter wouldn't be hindered by things like plastic tape, if Dylan was in here too, he would have had to have broken through.

The emergency exit lights cast the grotty corridor in a pale-green hue, and Lacy continued sprinting towards the room where she knew she would find her sister.

'Winter!' she shouted.

Please, God, don't let it be too late.

The thought of Dylan – sweet, caring Dylan – being caught up in this mess made Lacy want to scream.

She arrived at the door of the room that mirrored hers and flung it open without hesitation.

Her instincts had proven correct. Dylan was there, his back pressed against the wall, his eyes focused on something opposite him. Something horrible.

The bright moon made the room lighter this time, and Lacy took in the walls smothered with black mould, the damp bed she'd woken on and the window she had seen Winter's face reflected in. The stench of the fetid room mingled with her sister's rotting body and the floral scent of her lavender perfume.

'Winter,' Lacy said, amazed that her voice was somehow steady despite feeling as though she were about to disintegrate after her run. 'Leave him alone.'

Winter was looming over Dylan, her lips peeled wide into a smile.

Without thought, Lacy dashed towards Dylan. She slotted herself between him and Winter, her back pressed against his chest as she confronted her sister. She felt Dylan's strong hands grip her shoulders, holding her steady.

'Move!' Winter screamed. Flecks of spit that smelled like sewage landed on Lacy's cheeks.

Lacy felt Dylan trying to shift her aside, refusing to allow her to be his human shield. But she wrapped her fingers through his belt loops and gripped fiercely. 'If you want him, then you have to take me too.'

Lacy braced herself. She had no faith that her sister's drive to protect her would be stronger than her desire to spill Dylan's blood.

But Winter stepped away, pacing back and forth, her hands opening and closing with frustration.

'He's hurting you!' she cried. 'Why can't you see that?'

Lacy shook her head. 'Dylan has never hurt me, ever.'

She could feel his heart beating through her back.

'His *existence* hurts you!' Winter screamed. 'You can't waste your time with people like him, people like them.' She nodded to the doorway, where Chan and Marc had gathered, their faces frozen with shock as they watched the scene unfold.

'Can't you see?' Winter implored, her gaze intense and terrifyingly compelling. 'They're holding you back, stopping you from being who you should really be. They don't matter – none of them matter.'

Lacy studied her sister. But for once, she listened, truly *listened*. Not to the words, which were bullshit – Chan, Marc and Dylan mattered. They were kind, funny, unique and they *mattered*.

No, she listened to the pain in Winter's dark eyes. Pain she'd never acknowledged before, where it sat hidden behind layers of make-up and a permanent fierce expression.

Winter was hurting. She'd been hurting for years.

And Lacy had seen it – Winter curled on the bathroom floor, unable to voice whatever had happened to her at that party that had led her to change her appearance, her personality, her name. But Lacy had been thirteen years old and too young, too scared, to discover the truth.

Hot tears ran down Lacy's cheeks. She wished she could have done more to help Winter, to get her to see that, yes, there were bad, awful things in this world. But there was also good.

'I'm sorry, Winter,' she gasped, her chest heaving. 'I'm sorry about what happened to you.'

Winter flinched as though she'd been slapped, her eyes bright with fear.

'What?' she breathed.

'Someone hurt you,' Lacy said, struggling to keep her voice steady. 'When you were sixteen, someone hurt you, and I'm so, *so* sorry.'

Winter remained frozen, and her image flickered in and out of focus as though her new form couldn't contain the torrent of emotions surging through it.

'I love you,' Lacy whispered. 'But please, please stop this.'

Winter solidified once more, her face flitting from anger to anguish and back again.

'*Please*, Winter,' she sobbed. 'You don't have to do this. You don't have to protect me anymore.'

Winter took a step forwards and Lacy covered as much of Dylan's body with her own as she could.

Her sister was so close that her features blurred and the familiar smell filled Lacy's nostrils. But it didn't repulse her anymore. It just made her desperately sad. Winter had died before she'd had the chance to learn that she could still find happiness, despite everything that had happened to her.

'I love you,' Lacy repeated. 'You're my sister, and I'll always love you.'

With a shaky breath, Lacy clamped her eyes shut and braced herself.

But the air was still, the bedroom silent. Lacy slowly prised her eyes open to see Winter still standing inches away but no longer wrestling with the emotions that had raged through what was left of her fragile body.

The fury was seeping out of Winter like a balloon being deflated. The sharp angles of her body softened, and her fingers slackened, hanging limply at her sides. She looked slumped, defeated. Small.

Was Lacy imagining it, or was Winter's face changing? She was still a deathly grey colour, but the bloodshot rage seemed to have gone from her eyes. Her fingers were no longer curled into claws.

'I just wanted to keep you safe,' she muttered, staring forlornly at the floor. 'So you'd never have to—'

'I know,' Lacy said, not wanting Winter to have to explain her desperation. Not here, in front of the others.

Lacy was seeing her sister properly for the first time in years, she realised. This was the girl hidden beneath the disguises of fake names, fake personas, fake judgements. This was the girl who had lost her sense of identity even more than Lacy had.

Lacy's heart panged. She wished she'd been allowed to see this side of Winter when she was still alive, before it had been too late.

She gently loosened her fingers from Dylan's belt and stepped forwards.

'Lacy,' he whispered urgently, his hands reaching for her.

She turned to him with a gentle smile. 'I'll be OK.'

Then she returned her focus to her sister, or what was left of her, and opened her arms wide.

As Winter stepped towards her, Lacy had no idea if her sister was about to hug her or plunge her broken nails into her chest and rip out her heart.

But as Winter bent to rest her head on Lacy's shoulder, her face crumpled, and the tears she must have held inside for so many years were finally allowed to fall. Her back trembled as she sobbed, and Lacy felt no fear as she wrapped her arms around her.

Winter felt tiny. It was hard to believe that moments ago she had been a demonic force hellbent on revenge. Now…now it felt as though she was barely there.

Just as it should be.

Lacy steeled herself. She knew that, as glad as she had been to be reunited with her sister, it was wrong. Winter being here was *wrong*.

It was time for her to go.

'You *have* kept me safe,' she breathed, realising that Winter no longer smelled of stagnant harbour water, just her lavender perfume. 'But you have to let me go now. You have to let me figure out who I am. I have to live my own life and make my own mistakes.'

Lacy's cheeks were wet with tears as she stroked her sister's tangled hair. Winter had protected her from the day she was born. She couldn't remember a time in her childhood that didn't involve Winter, always watching. But at some point, that sisterly protectiveness had morphed into something cruel and twisted.

Lacy realised now that it was Winter who had needed protecting. She'd seen her sister as fierce and indestructible, not as the lost, lonely girl she really was.

'I wish I could have kept *you* safe, Winter,' she whispered.

She felt Winter nestle closer to her, getting smaller, as though the vengeance that had fuelled her for months after her death was leaving her.

'Will you promise me one thing?' Winter whispered. Her voice was fragile, all trace of the demonic fury that had possessed her on the clifftop gone.

Lacy tensed and prayed Winter wouldn't ask her to continue her reign of terror.

'Will you still go to Paris?'

Lacy smiled as she cried, grief flooding her exhausted body.

'I promise,' she said to the empty space between her arms where her sister had been moments before.

OCTOBER

It was cold.

Lacy shivered and nestled into her thick coat, rubbing the soft fluff against her cheek. It was a good cold. The kind that made her appreciate the toasty feeling of her skin beneath the layers of clothing and greedily inhale the steam that rose from the hot drink on the table in front of her. Her camera sat beside it, the lens cap off, just in case she was inspired to snap a photo of something that caught her eye.

It wasn't like the biting cold on the clifftop, two months earlier. Lacy hoped never to feel cold like it again, although she'd got off lightly – Marc had ended up with hypothermia and a stay in hospital. It turned out that even at the height of summer, Welsh rain could chill someone to the core.

She sighed heavily, acknowledging the memories and exploring the feelings that came with them, just as her therapist had advised. She wrapped her fingers around the huge mug of steaming hot chocolate and breathed in the rich aroma.

She would never drink black coffee again.

The drink was sweet and delicious. But even better was the fact that she was allowing herself to enjoy something she actually *liked*. Sure, she looked nothing like the stylish French girls sitting at the table next to hers, daintily sipping their espressos…

But she was OK with that.

A flutter of wind blew a curl across her face, and she swept it out of the way. She'd left her hair straighteners back in England and was slowly learning to love her unruly tangle of curls. She smiled to herself as she wiped whipped cream off her nose. If Lacy of four months ago could have seen her now, drinking unsophisticated drinks while wearing a duffel coat with her hair flying in every direction, she would have been appalled.

She leaned back and pulled her sleeves lower to cover her exposed wrists. She'd been right about one thing, at least – she loved Paris.

She loved the effortless coolness of the city, the way everyone seemed to know who they were and where they were going – except for the bubbles of confused tourists, of course. She loved the architecture, the Seine, the iconic landmarks. She loved the food and the language, which she was becoming more fluent in by the day.

She loved this café, just below the tiny apartment she rented, a moment's walk from her college. She had a job serving cakes in a gorgeous little patisserie, and she'd already sampled every single item on the menu.

But despite all this, Lacy knew it wasn't, and never would be, home.

She knew she'd love living here for the next three years while she completed her studies. But there was something lacking – an honest bluntness that she'd found in people back in the UK, people like Chan and Marc. She missed it.

She scrolled through their group chat and smiled to herself. They were just the same, and she'd been amazed to find their friendship enduring despite the distance between them. She no longer wondered if they actually liked her or if their attention was because of pity, or protectiveness, or any of the other reasons her paranoid brain had conjured up while at Peril Bay. They were her friends.

They already had plans to meet up over Christmas, when Lacy would return to spend the holiday with her parents. She couldn't wait to join in with all the cheesy traditions she'd previously scoffed at – making decorations with photos of their faces in, wrapping up random household objects as joke presents, wedging a coin into the shop-bought Christmas pudding to make a wish on. It would be bittersweet now that Winter was no longer with them, but Lacy was determined to show her parents just how much she appreciated them, how much she loved them. She couldn't wait to show them around Paris.

And they weren't the only ones.

In two days, Dylan would be visiting. Lacy still couldn't believe he'd wanted to stay in touch after everything that had happened. But he'd told her he would be there if she wanted to talk.

And she had – because she had questions. After weeks of being kept in the dark, of being spoken about and followed and ultimately confronting a horror worse than anything she could have imagined…she'd wanted to know everything.

Dylan had confirmed that her suspicions had been right – he hadn't kept close to her because he didn't know how to take no for an answer. He'd seen Andy sniffing around and suspected something was off and that Lacy might be in danger. Ceri had told him she'd been assaulted but had felt unable to confide who it had been. But Dylan could see past Andy's façade.

When Dylan had finally confronted Andy, just hours before Rachel was killed, Andy had reacted by punching him, leaving the bruise across Dylan's jaw. Dylan had been about to tell Lacy all this just as the train doors slammed shut on Andy's arm.

After everything that had happened, it was a miracle Lacy had made it to Paris, but here she was. And she was learning more than she thought possible, especially since she'd thrown her assumptions about what made a 'good' photographer out of the window. Now, she focused on whatever drew her eye and made her feel something, which was usually people.

Her first project was a self-portrait, and it couldn't have come at a better time. Lacy had meant it when she'd told Winter that she needed to find out who she really was.

Lacy closed her eyes, feeling the grief instead of hiding from it.
Winter.

Officer Singh had made sure the police got an anonymous tip-off to search the water by the pier in Blackpool, and Winter's body had finally been laid to rest. Winter's soul, or whatever part of her had attached itself to Lacy, had also gone. At least, that's what Lacy told herself.

But could she know for sure? She'd been oblivious to it until she'd arrived at Peril Bay, so how could she be certain that she was alone, that Winter wasn't still 'looking out' for her, ready to slaughter the next person who upset her?

Lacy's feeling of contentment faltered as her heart started racing, just as it always did when she thought of Rachel.

Gary had been released – there wasn't enough evidence, or

even *any* evidence, to tie him to the crime. So the case remained unsolved. Lacy had picked up her phone on many occasions, ready to reach out to Rachel's parents and tell them what had really happened.

But the other people who had been with her that night had convinced her otherwise. What good would it do to tell them that the spirit of Lacy's dead sister had murdered their daughter?

Rachel's head still hadn't been found, and Lacy often woke at night, her skin slick with sweat from nightmares full of the possibilities of where it could be.

She stared at her mug and tried to focus on the bubbles of cream as they dissolved into the rich, brown liquid. She needed something real to keep her anchored in the present. Otherwise she would spiral as the guilt overwhelmed her, insisting she didn't deserve to be sitting on a Parisian street, enjoying the late autumn sun and getting on with her life.

But how could she possibly be normal now that she knew death wasn't always the end, and that three people were dead because of her? That last, tender moment between her and Winter had meant so, *so* much. She wanted to believe that Winter could finally let go of the rage that had fuelled her for so long, but the things her sister had done before that moment were impossible to ignore – the things she was *capable* of.

Her camera screen flickered to life without her touching it. She stared at it, dread filling her stomach and curdling the hot chocolate. She remembered the strange messages she'd seen on both her phone and camera. She was sure now that they'd been caused by Winter, trying to contact her before she had grown strong enough to rip a person's head from their shoulders.

Lacy reached out with trembling fingers and picked up the camera. The screen showed nothing abnormal through the lens – just the white iron coffee table in front of her.

But the fear remained, pressing her into the chair.

For months, she'd been watched. Watched by Winter, who hadn't left her side, even in death. And Andy, who had greedily observed her when she was at her most vulnerable. Even Marc, Chan and Dylan had watched her, though their intentions had been pure.

That feeling was still with her, the feeling that she was never truly alone.

A sour, rotten smell filled her nostrils, and Lacy's breath paused in her chest. Just the drains, she thought wildly. Or the river – that was all. But she smelled flowers, too. The heady, distinctive smell of lavender…

Lacy exhaled with relief when she spotted the flower-seller just across the street. The feeling of not being alone was just a feeling. And the smells – just smells.

But she couldn't shake the tension that had tightened her muscles and set her nerves on edge. She needed to make sure. She slowly turned the camera to point at herself and took a photo.

She closed her eyes for a moment, then swivelled the camera to check the image she'd captured. The selfie showed Lacy's face filling most of the screen, her expression pinched and anxious, the breeze fluttering her curls across her forehead.

And there *she* was too, standing right behind her. Her hand was resting on Lacy's shoulder, and she gazed directly down the lens of the camera. As Lacy stared at the image in shock, a wide smile stretched across Winter's lips.

ACKNOWLEDGEMENTS

When I was growing up, I had my very own goth big sister. And although she was the inspiration for this book, she had none of Winter's fierceness – she was (and is) the kindest, sweetest person I know. She still has a wicked fashion sense, though is less likely to be sporting a spiked dog collar nowadays.

Zoe, thank you for all the memories, and all the adventures we're still having!

I started this book with the intention of having a bit of fun – I wanted to play with that close link between horror and comedy. But as always, things ended up getting rather dark once I started thinking about what might drive people to do certain things. But I hope the message of unexpected friendships prevailed – something I think will always be a theme in my books!

Huge thanks to the team at Rock the Boat; my editor, Katie Jennings, for championing the book from the start and making the process so smooth. Also, Kobe Grant and Helen Szirtes for your eagle-eyed editorial skills, Rowan Jackson, Lucy Cooper and Mark Rusher in marketing, Paul Nash and Laura McFarlane in production, Francesca Dawes and Julian Ball in sales, and Ben Summers and Hayley Warnham in design. And thank you to Marta Barrales, who did such a fantastic job designing the unique and fitting cover!

Thank you to my wonderful agent, Saffron Dodd – you were such a breath of fresh air, and I immediately knew I was in safe hands the second I signed with you. And of course, Alice Sutherland-Hawes for your support.

As always, my family are such an important part of my life. Especially my parents – it's been a tough old year or two for you both, but you're always there with an open ear when I need to waffle about the mysterious world of publishing, and I hope you know just how much I love and appreciate you.

Robyn – you've written many more books than me now, and your imagination both amazes and scares me a little! I'm not sure the world is ready for your horror novels yet, but I can't wait to be your beta reader for years to come.

Tom – I forgive you for not managing to get past chapter four once you realised I'd named the love interest after one of your best friends and you couldn't stop giggling at the comparison to Adonis.

And finally, my writing friends – thank you. The process of writing and then navigating the highs and lows of the industry would be impossible without you all. Ravena – for our endless chats; from querying (thank you for linking me up!), plot brainstorming, edit notes, Mount Everest, caving expeditions gone wrong and *Love Island* – we cover all the important subjects. Carolyn – you were one of the very first people to see something in my work, and your friendship and terrifying ideas continue to be a huge boost to my writing! And to my Shrewsbury writers – our meetups have been my therapy sessions for years now and I'd be lost without them. Amy, Sandra, Carys, Jenny, Lou, Annie, Nicola (and Ko!) – you're all exceptional writers and friends.

I can't quite believe I've got another book out there!

© Florence Fox

Tess James-Mackey is an author based in Shrewsbury who loves writing teens into terrifying situations inspired by her lived experiences. Her YA debut *Someone is Watching You* published in 2023. When she's not allowing her mind to wander to dark and twisty places, she pursues more wholesome activities, like growing mediocre vegetables in her garden, camping with her daughter, and the odd bit of horse riding when she's feeling brave enough.